FEEDING THE PIGS

Thomas Richard Brown

1st Edition Published by Second Child Ltd

ISBN: 978-0-9956709-4-5 (Paperback)

Proofread by Julia Gibbs
juliaproofreader@gmail.com

Cover design by Simon Emery
siemery2012@gmail.com

Mary Matthews
Three Shires Publishing

British Library Cataloguing in Publication Data
A CIP catalogue record for this book is available from the British Library.

Books by Thomas Richard Brown

Mary Knighton
Thisbe
A Knock on the Door
Feeding the Pigs

Table of Contents

Chapter One

Spring 1956

There was a knock at the door of the old dining room of Gaynes Hall, a Georgian mansion now used as the offices and Governor's residence of a Borstal institution.

"Enter," a voice came from within. It was the Governor, Martin Doubleday, who was practising golf with a putter down the green carpet to one side of the long table.

"Ah, Abrahams, it's you." A young man entered, dressed in corduroy shorts, a striped shirt and a linen jacket. From under his shorts on one leg a calliper went down and attached to his large black boot.

"Shall I bring the coffee, sir?" he asked. The Governor looked at his watch, shook his wrist and looked again.

"Not yet, Abrahams, wait until Mrs Howells comes, she should be here soon, just keep an eye out for her and then bring it."

"Very good, sir," and he turned to go, the calliper keeping one leg straight as he limped off with a rocking motion.

Audrey Howells, Chair of the Board of Visitors, slowed as she drove through Dillington, up the narrow lane through the main gate and past the sign which read HMP Borstal Gaynes Hall. As she drove in, to the right were a row of barrack huts and to the left was the big house which she turned towards along a concrete driveway.

She pulled up outside the main door, where two boys were digging the soil out of a large decorative urn into a barrow.

"Good morning, boys," she said as she passed them.

"Good mornin', miss," said the taller of the two, adding a smile.

"Don't I know you, boy, did I interview you last week?"

"Yes, miss, it's Bright, miss, Sunny Bright, miss."

"I remember, you come from North London."

"Yeah, Willesden, miss, like Doug 'ere," and he nodded to his companion, who was shorter with curly red hair. Doug Brown did not speak or smile and looked at the ground as Audrey observed him.

"He's not very talkative, is he? Not like you, Bright."

"No, miss," and Doug blushed as she turned and went up the steps to the front door.

The hall was wide with a high ceiling and a dark oak parquet floor. In the distance she saw a face poke from behind a door as she turned towards the old dining room on the right, knocked and went in. As she opened the door there was a loud tap as a golf ball hit the skirting.

"Ah, I'm so sorry, Mrs Howells, I didn't hear you arrive," said Martin Doubleday as he came forward to greet her, picking up the ball and returning the putter to his golf bag.

"Let's sit down here, it's more comfortable and we can keep an eye on the boys planting the urn. Coffee should be on the way." As Audrey sat, she could see the boys outside had been joined by another with a second barrow, escorted by an officer in a dark blue uniform. There was a knock on the door.

"Enter," the Governor shouted and Lionel Abrahams came in carrying a tray with the coffee. He swayed from side to side, concentrating and trying hard not to spill anything as he made his way to the table.

"Thank you, Abrahams, that will be all."

"Very good, sir," and he made his way out.

"How did he get like that?" Audrey asked, after he'd closed the door.

"Polio, we don't get many disabled in here, but he does come from a very poor area of North London."

"He seems to manage."

"Yes, and he'll be leaving in a couple of weeks so I'll have to train up another one to make the coffee."

"Cheap labour, Governor, anyone else would have to pay a maid. Now let's get down to business, you have got a copy of our draft report on the condition of the old barrack huts?"

Outside the three boys had finished emptying the urn and waited for the officer's inspection.

"That looks satisfactory, now you, Garcia, go and get the plants. You know where they are in the greenhouse. You, Bright and Brown, go and collect the new soil and compost, mix it half and half then fill up the urn, you understand?"

"Yes, sir," they replied.

"I'm going to the kitchen garden and will be back shortly so don't get into any mischief."

"Yes, sir, sorry, no, sir," said Sunny, as the officer marched off.

"Look at that car, Sunny, it's a Jag ain't it," said Doug, and they peered in the window as they pushed the wheel barrows past.

"Doug, look, she's left the keys in it, silly bugger. Someone's gonna to steal it, ain't they?"

"Too right they are," Doug agreed. They loaded up the mixture of soil and compost and made their way back to the urn where Marco Garcia waited with the plants.

"Hey, Marco, see that car over there, you'll never guess what?"

"No, I won't, so what about it?"

"It's got the keys in it."

"Yer joking?"

"No, I ain't, you go and look, the Governor can't see the car from where 'e's sitting." Marco looked left and right then crept furtively over and looked in the car window.

"Yer right. We could be back in London in no time in that thing, I bet it don't 'alf go, six-cylinder engine yer know?" They looked at each other.

"What we gonna to do then?" Doug asked.

"We'll go an' see Lionel. We'll need some more soil when we've got this lot in so we can see 'im when we go past the kitchen. 'e'll know what to do," said Sunny.

"Shall I nick the key then?" asked Marco.

"No, let's go an' see Lionel first." They emptied the barrows and went to the back of the big house to collect more soil, leaving Marco to await their return.

Sunny and Doug looked through the kitchen window and could see Lionel doing the washing up so tapped on the glass. Lionel looked round, dried his hands and came over.

"What do you buggers want then?"

"Lionel, there's a woman just driv up in a big Jag, all la-di-da like and she's left the keys in it."

"So what? I've just seen 'er, she's in with the Governor."

"So, we're gonna to nick it. We'll be back in London in no time in a car like that. Are yer comin'?" said Sunny.

"Not likely, what d'you think I am, stupid?"

"You ain't comin' then?" Doug couldn't believe it.

"No, I ain't. I'm out in two weeks, with any luck, so what do I want to steal a car for?"

"It's got the keys in it, so it needs stealing, don't it?" said Sunny.

"You're stupid if yer take it. You'll be out in a month if yer get through the interview." Lionel turned back to his washing up.

"I s'ppose, it were 'er what did the interview. I 'ad it the other day, she said 'ello when she came in just now, din't she, Doug?" Sunny looked thoughtful, then turned to Doug. "I've never stole a Jag before, 'av you, Doug?"

"No, there ain't none where we live."

"S'ppose not," said Sunny, and they wheeled the barrows on to collect the soil.

As they went back past the Jag Doug looked in the window.

"Look, Sunny, the keys 'ave gone."

They arrived back at the urn,

"Marco, the keys 'ave gone out the Jag," said Sunny.

"I know."

"'ow?"

"I've got 'em."

"Are we goin' for a spin then, I really want to 'ave a drive," said Sunny.

"No, we ain't."

"Oh."

"I bet Lionel ain't coming, is 'e?"

"No," said Doug.

"You see 'e's got some sense, not like you silly buggers. If we nick it, we'll get caught. Look, the bloody Governor is looking at us. You'd be stopped before yer got to the A1. So, I've got the key and I've locked the car, so there."

In the Governor's office the discussions were at an end. Audrey got up and looked out of the window as Marco started to plant up the urn.

"They will look good in a month or so."

"Yes, we do them every year now. Not like when I first arrived when they'd not been touched since before the war. I told the old lady who lived here before what we'd done when I saw her in church. She said it was a pity because she had put her husband's ashes in it."

"Well, I never, do you think she was pulling your leg?" They shook hands, as Audrey continued, "Don`t worry, Governor, I can see myself out."

As she came down the steps and walked towards her car Marco came up to her.

"Excuse me, miss."

"Yes, how can I help?"

"Well, miss, 'ere is your car keys. I see you 'ad left 'em in it and I thought with all the villains around 'ere it would get stole, so I took the keys and locked the car. 'ere yer go."

Chapter Two

November 1962

Pete sat on the back door step of Meadow View, Castle Road after lunch. He threaded the laces of his heavy leather boots through the eyes, passed them round the back then tied them at the front. The second one done, he stood up and stamped his feet to let the legs of his overalls fall down over his trousers. There was a click and the back door opened behind him.

"Haven't you left yet? You're going to be late! Tony's been gone for five minutes." Joyce Wilson, his landlady, stood holding a bucket. She looked in her late twenties with light brown curly hair. She had a white short-sleeved blouse on and a flowery apron over a blue skirt. "Come on, get out the way, Pete. I want to get to the dustbin."

She waited impatiently as Pete put on his cap and grabbed his bike which was leaning against the garage. Her cheeks were red and her hands wet from the washing up. "Blimey, you don't half smell, Pete, I don't know how you can stand it, your overalls look revolting."

Pete looked down but said nothing as he pushed the leg of his overalls into his right-hand sock. She put the bucket on the ground and her hands on her hips as she waited. Her figure was slight, her skin clear and her arms and legs pale as if they'd never seen the sun.

"Tony's gone to the phone and I'm not late," said Pete, pointing to his watch.

She half-smiled, her thin lips parting and showing two large front teeth sticking out over her bottom lip a little. "He's always up the phone box." Then she sighed and fanned the air in front of her face with her hand. "Come on then, get going – I can't stand this smell anymore." She looked peeved as she squeezed her mouth shut, narrowing her bright blue eyes.

Pete held the saddle of the bike and pushed it down the path to the road. He turned back after a few steps. "That better then?"

She smiled again, looking pretty, as she slanted her mouth and slightly tipped her head back. "That's better," she said, and picked up the bucket.

It was late in November; the last leaves were falling and the breeze added a chill to the air as Pete cycled down the hill. At the bottom, he turned left and pedalled harder to get the half mile to the farm where he worked. He heard a vehicle coming up behind and a small black Ford Thames van drew level and slowed down, just keeping pace with him. A hand came out from the passenger side window and grabbed the back of his saddle, shaking it so violently, it was nearly enough to throw him off.

"Don't, you bugger!" Pete shouted, as he struggled

to maintain his balance and Tony, who was the passenger, let go.

There was a big grin on David, the driver's, face and he laughed as he called across, "Come on, Pete, you'll be late, you ain't got all day you know."

The van accelerated away then turned left up the drive to the farm.

Pete pedalled on and caught up with another worker, Steve, also returning after lunch. Steve was nearly seventy and had gone on working long after his retirement date. He was a bachelor and had lived with his mother in the village all his life. He had never seen the sea and never been to London. He was obviously having trouble with his bike, as one of his pedals was not going round and he could only push down on the other one and then reverse it up so he could push down on it again to make any progress.

As Pete drew level with him, he turned and grinned. His cap was too big for his head and rested solidly on his ears. His face was lined and weather-beaten and his mouth sunken in, due to badly fitting dentures. He laughed but said nothing as his right leg continued to keep the bike going.

"What's up, Steve?" Pete slowed to accompany him.

"Cotter pin as fell out, I'm got it in me pocket," and he laughed again. "Helmit'll fix it for me." They rolled down the last two hundred yards to the farm passing the offices and coming to a stop outside the workshop where everyone assembled to await instruction on the afternoon work.

"Got trouble with the old grid iron?" David said, as Steve drew up.

The grid iron was Steve's name for his bicycle, an old woman's cycle with high handle bars and a large saddle. Steve's eyes looked round to David but his head did not move. He laughed again, "Cotter pin," he said, as he leant the bike against the wall. "Helmit'll fix it for me, won't you, Helmit?"

Steve addressed the man standing in the doorway of the workshop. Helmit was German. His real name was Helmut and he had been a prisoner of war after being captured from a U-boat in 1943. After the war he decided to stay in England and he married a local girl, Rose, and worked as a mechanic on the farm. He was tall and powerfully built and had short blond hair. He wore a British army tunic, trousers held up by a thick leather belt and a German cap on his head.

He took a packet of cigarettes from his tunic pocket and put one in his lips, spat out a speck of tobacco, then lit it and leaned on the door joist of the workshop.

Gradually the rest of the farm staff gathered outside the workshop door and waited. The foreman, Viv Lewis, trotted down from the office to where they all stood. Viv was short, with a cap that, like Steve's, was too large for his head and a jacket which hung loosely on his shoulders, his hands peeping out from the end of the sleeves. His trouser legs were tucked into

Wellington boots, which he wore year-round and were turned over at the top.

"Right," he said, "Pete. You and Steve, empty that load of bales and then take the feed down to the pigs. Winston, you go down the mixing shed and get the rations ready," and he handed him a clip board with a sheet of paper on it.

"What's the use of that?" piped up Simon, who, other than Steve, was the oldest of the men. "'E can't read."

Viv peered at Winston, who looked embarrassed, but said nothing. "All right, Winston?" he asked, and Winston nodded and sidled towards Pete and Steve.

The mixing shed was where all the rations were prepared to feed to the animals on the farm. Each ration had a recipe sheet and the ingredients were then weighed out before going into the mixer, thus whoever was on duty had to be able to read each sheet.

Viv turned his attention to the other men. "Right, the rest of you come with me. We're going to drench the ewes. Except you, Helmit, you need to mend the plough."

"Gor," groaned Simon, "I ain't got to come, am I? Can't I help Helmit?" and he glared at Viv. "I can't walk far – it's my feet, you know that."

"We need as many as possible to get all the ewes through in the afternoon," said Viv, and he turned away from Simon and looked at the others.

"David, Sean and Tony, you go and fetch them up

12

and the rest of us will get the pen ready," and Viv turned to go.

"Well?" said Simon.

"Well, what?" said Viv, turning back.

"Am I got to come?"

Simon stood with his hands in his pockets and stared intently at the foreman. Viv looked up into the sky and sighed, then without looking at Simon he said in a resigned tone, "Okay then," and turned to walk away.

"That ain't fair," piped up Sean. "That old bugger always gets away with it. There ain't nothing wrong with 'im." Simon grinned as he walked towards the workshop.

"You heard what I said," said Viv, and he walked off as the others grudgingly went about their appointed tasks. Then Viv turned back and shouted across the yard, "Pete and Steve, you stay down the pigs and help Grafton, there's only him there today."

"Come on then, Steve," Pete encouraged the old man, who ambled slowly after him to unload the bales.

Steve had worked on the farm all his life, but had never learned to drive a tractor. He could only handle the most menial of tasks and could no longer pitch bales or lift sacks of feed so Pete had to do all that.

The piggery was a mixture of buildings with Dutch barns full of straw, the long fattening shed and a shorter barn where the farrowing house was; the dry sows and boars had pens with runs at the back. When they arrived there Pete backed the trailer up to the door of the fattening house while Steve lay on the top of the bags piled in it.

"That'll do," said Steve, and Pete got off the tractor and made his way round to unload the sacks.

The pig unit consisted of about one hundred and twenty sows and their progeny, which were taken and fattened to bacon weight. The manager, Grafton, came up to Pete to tell him where to stack the sacks. He looked much smarter than the other men on the farm, with a broad light tweed cap on his head over jet black hair. He had a smart light brown jacket on with leather patches on the elbows and he wore jodhpurs and leather gaiters over dark brown boots. He tapped his pipe out on the corner of the trailer and then turned to Pete.

"Well, young man, you got here at last then?"

"Are we late then?" Pete replied in an offended tone.

"No, no, not really I suppose," said Grafton, who by now had got his pouch out and started to fill his pipe with tobacco.

"Viv said we've got to stop and help, is that right?" asked Pete.

"I hope so, I'm off out in a few minutes," said Grafton, as he lit his pipe.

"I want you to feed up when you've stacked the bags. You know what to do, don't you, Pete?"

"Yes, I know, but where are you off to then, if it's not a rude question?"

Grafton sucked on his pipe three or four times before answering and blew out a small cloud of smoke.

"Going to look at a new boar. Crucial is picking me up in ten minutes."

'Crucial' was the nickname for the manager, Michael Lockheart, although how he'd earned the name was uncertain. He ran the farm for the feed company that owned it and had been in charge and developed the farm over the last twenty years.

Steve dragged the sacks to the back of the trailer for Pete to carry into the shed. Each one had a label bearing a code. Grafton pointed out where to put them.

"Where's the boar then?" Pete asked Grafton as he stood sucking his pipe.

"Just down the M1. I'm not quite sure where. Crucial's got a mate there with a herd," he said, as a car pulled up beside the trailer and the driver wound down his window. It was Robert, the assistant manager who organised all the feeding of the animals on the farm.

"Come on, Grafton, jump in. Crucial has sent me to fetch you as he's on the phone. They'll manage, won't they?" and he nodded at Pete and Steve.

"Yes, they know what to do." Grafton got in the back of the car and it sped off.

Pete and Steve only had to check the sows and their litters, as the sows had already been fed and they only needed to make sure the hopper that fed the small pigs was working. The main operation was for them to feed

15

the fattening house which contained the rest of the pigs on the unit.

"Are you ready then, Steve?" said Pete, as he put his hand on the door handle.

"What am I got to do then?" He looked questioningly at Pete.

"You can do the water. You know how to do that, don't you?" Steve grinned.

"'Spect I do," he said, as Pete pulled the door open and put the light on.

There was a collective, "Woop," from the animals inside.

The shed consisted of fifty pens on each side of a long central corridor. Each pen had a feed trough along the line of the corridor into which the meal was poured and there was a tap above each pen on a pipe running above the feed trough. From the tap there was a down pipe into the trough with a T piece on it which shot the water each way on top of the food.

Pete pushed the large three-wheeled feed barrow into the corridor and stopped it just beyond the first two pens. On the wall of each pen was a small blackboard with two numbers on – one indicated the number of pigs in the pen and the other the number of scoops of food to give them. Pete lifted the bucket onto the feed tub and the pigs started to squeal. He filled the bucket with the required number of scoops of meal and then poured it along the trough.

By now the noise was deafening as all the pigs in the shed joined in, bringing the high-pitched screams to a crescendo. There was no way Pete could talk to Steve so he nodded for him to come in and carry out his part in the process. Steve stood with his fingers in his ears and grimaced each time he leaned in to turn on the water.

As each pen was fed, the pigs started to eat and stopped squealing but the noise did not abate as the squeals from those unfed further down the shed increased, the sound bouncing off the walls. Pete worked as fast as he could, as the only way to stop the incessant noise was to get to the last pen. Looking at the pigs, it was difficult to see where the noise came from as they didn't seem to open their mouths or at least not very wide, but it was intense and ear-splitting. He looked at Steve who mouthed words to himself that Pete could not hear as he went down the shed turning on the taps for each pen.

They neared the end of the corridor and there were only four pens left to do but although the noise had begun to lessen it was not until Pete poured the meal into the last trough that there was silence.

Chapter Three

A New Boar is Purchased

After feeding, Pete and Steve prepared to go back to the farm. They loaded the trailer with used bags which were to be returned to the food mixing plant to be refilled. Pete got on the tractor and Steve sat on the pile of sacks on the trailer.

"Don't you drive too fast, me boy," Steve grumbled to Pete. "Don't forget you've got me on the back," and they set off down the road from the piggery.

After two hundred yards they passed the drive to The Manor, a large Victorian mansion which could be seen off to the left. It was a tall building with rooms on four floors and at the corner was a round tower which had a conical roof, making it look more German than British. There was a pasture in front of the house and an iron fence separating it from the garden. The Manor went with the farm and was divided into flats. Helmit lived in one with his family, but the rest were unoccupied. There was another flat in the stable block where Wally lived – he was the second pig man, who was off sick.

Pete turned right up the drive away from The Manor and towards the road leading to the main farm. As the tractor made its way up the steep hill, smoke poured from the exhaust. Coming the other way was a girl on a bicycle who was struggling to control her descent of the steep hill, her brakes screeching as she approached the tractor. Pete stopped, stepping on the foot brake and pulling the handbrake on as hard as he could. The girl put her foot down to slow herself and hopped two or three times before stepping off the bike to avoid falling, letting it crash to the ground as she stood and shouted at Pete.

"Look what you've done, you stupid bugger," she said and glared at him.

Rita was the daughter of Rose, the wife of Helmit, and his step-daughter. She was now seventeen and worked as a waitress at the service station on the M1. Her father was an American G.I. That was all she knew about him except that he had been based at Chicksands, that and the fact her mother did not seem to know his name. Rita's cheeks were pink from exertion and her dyed blonde hair hung lank around her face, having lost the bounce it had when she'd washed it the weekend before. Rita was tall and well built – if not a little overweight – with a big bust which strained against her waitress's uniform, which could be seen as her raincoat hung open.

"Aren't you gonna pick it up for me?" she demanded of Pete, as she pointed to her bike which had slid down the bank at the side of the drive.

Steve laughed as he regained his seat on the pile of sacks, having been dislodged as the tractor had come to its abrupt halt.

"Well then," Rita shouted again, "pick it up, can't you?"

"I can't," said Pete, sitting tight, "I can't get off. The handbrake won't hold, and the tractor will run back and crash."

"What am I supposed to do then, you useless sod? I'll tell Dad about you."

Pete flushed red with embarrassment.

"Steve!" he turned and shouted. "Can you get her bike?"

"What?" Steve shouted back, but he didn't look, just grinned and cackled to himself.

"Get her bike!" Pete shouted even louder.

"I'll get it." Pete and Rita turned at the new voice to see another girl, younger than Rita, who had real blonde hair, a very pretty pale face and was dressed in school uniform.

"Oh, it's you," said Rita, with disdain as she addressed Karen, her half-sister.

Karen had got off the bus at the top of the drive which returned her from the grammar school in Flitwick that she attended. She edged her way down the bank towards the bike just as Steve slid off the trailer and came down to help her. She grabbed the handle bars and lifted it up, and Steve took them and pulled the bike up onto the drive and held it for Rita to take.

"You dirty old man. You don't half stink of shit,"

she said as she pulled the bike away from him, holding the handle bars and squeezing the brakes tight as she put one foot on a pedal and got on as it rolled down the hill.

"Who's a pretty girl then?" Steve said to Karen as he straightened his cap, took a hanky from his pocket and wiped his watery eyes one at a time and then looked at her again.

"Ain't she pretty, don't you think, Pete?"

Pete's cheeks reddened again but he said nothing.

"She's more polite than her sister, I know that," said Steve, who then blew his nose.

Karen gave a small smile, but didn't look at Pete.

"She's right, you know, Steve, you do smell a bit."

"I don't smell bad; it's only pigs you know – could be worse."

Karen smiled at Steve and quickly glanced at Pete before walking off into the gloom of the winter evening.

"Come on, Steve, get on, it's getting dark and we have no lights." Steve climbed back onto the trailer and arranged himself on the heap of sacks.

Back at the farm they dumped the empty bags back in the mixing shed, then parked the tractor and trailer and went round to the workshop where Viv stood watching Helmit mend the plough.

"Pete, you've got to go and see Robert, he's in the office doing the rota for Christmas."

The office was not in the main building but in a

Portacabin next to the driveway. There were four offices in all; the secretary, Mary, had the first one, then the accountant, then Robert, and the last one was where the manager, Michael Lockheart, otherwise known as Crucial, ran the whole operation from.

"Put those boots outside," Mary shouted at Pete as he came through the door, "smells like you've been down the pigs."

Pete blushed as he pulled up his socks and placed his boots outside.

"And shut that door quickly, Pete, it's freezing," she snapped as she crashed at the typewriter and banged the carriage across as she completed another line.

She looked up at the tall nineteen-year-old boy and smiled sympathetically.

"Well?" she said, and tilted her head to one side, as she turned her swivel chair to face him.

"I've got to see Robert, is he in?" Pete asked, flushing redder under her gaze.

Mary was twenty-five and had worked at the farm since she left secretarial college. Her high-heeled shoes, tight skirts and white blouses were a great contrast to the rest of those who worked on the farm. She stood up and looked through the glass panel and down the corridor to where Robert's door was open.

"Looks as if he's there," she said "Go on then."

Pete grinned and set off down the corridor.

Robert, the assistant manager, sat with his cap and

overcoat on, a cigarette in his mouth and telephone in his hand, with one foot up on his desk. He nodded to the chair, indicating that Pete should sit as he swapped the phone to the other ear then held it between his head and shoulder while he wrote on a pad, then banged the phone down. After writing something further he looked up at Pete.

"What are you here for then?" he asked, as he continued to write.

"Viv said you wanted to see me about Christmas."

"Yes, yes, you're right, he's right. Let's look then." He turned over the heap of paper in front of him until he came to what he wanted.

"Right, let's see then." He ran his finger down the list in front of him.

"Boxing Day alright for you? Just feeding, it won't take all day, just the morning and just the cattle and sheep, all right?" He looked over at Pete.

"That's fine."

"Oh, yes, and Crucial says that everyone can have Christmas Eve afternoon off. You can get home then, I expect."

Pete nodded and made to leave.

"Are you going down the pub tonight, Pete?" Robert asked.

Robert at twenty-two was just a little older than Pete and had only been on the farm for six months longer. They both went to the same Young Farmers Club.

"I expect so. I'll have to see David, but I think he said he was going."

"Right, see you there then," and Pete got up to go but then turned.

"What about that boar, I forgot to ask, did he buy it?"

Robert grinned and pulled the peak of his cap down. The popper between the peak and the rest of the cap came undone and looked uncouth as he leaned back in his chair.

"Well, it's like this. We did buy it, but only just. Crucial didn't like it, cos it had got no test results and he said he wouldn't pay its money. You've never seen anything like it for eleven months, it was bloody huge and as long as the Queen Mary. Grafton fell in love with it and he got real shirty with Crucial when he said it were too much money, real shirty he was. Never seen him like it before. Then Crucial said that they weren't a proper pneumonia-free herd and all that, but they said they were and they had the paperwork."

"So what happened?"

"Grafton and me went out and left Crucial with the bloke and in the end he came out and said he had bought it and I was to pick it up in a week so that was that and Grafton was all smiles."

"When's it coming then?"

"Not till after Christmas now, he's got to get the paperwork right and anyway we've got the turkeys to do next week, then we've got all the pens to take down before the cattle can come in. There'll be no time."

Pete then returned to the workshop where Steve stood watching Helmit mend his bike.

"Bin to see Mary then?" he said, as he stood leaning on the vice and working his mouth as though he were chewing something imaginary as he grinned. "I know where he's bin, don't you, Helmit? He's bin to see Mary. Any excuse and he's up there sniffing around," and he grinned as his false teeth clattered together.

Pete said nothing but looked from Steve to Helmit and then asked, "Can you fix it, Helmit?" as he nodded at Steve's bike.

Helmit looked up. "Give me a chance. It von't take long if you all keep quiet and leave me to it." He'd lived there for many years but still had a thick accent.

Steve assumed his usual slightly vacant but amused expression as his jaw moved up and down and his lips fought each other.

"Hmm," he went, and then, "Hmm," again and even louder, then he stood up straight as if he were about to make a speech. "Wimin will draw you further than gunpowder can blow you," he said, slowly, "Yes, wimin will draw you further than gunpowder will blow you, ain't that right, Helmit?" He turned to Helmit for an answer which did not come and then looked back at Pete and wiped his nose with his fist. He untied the string round his waist that held his overcoat together then tied it again a little tighter. Then he took one bicycle clip from his pocket, wrapped his

25

trouser leg round his ankle and put it on then stood up, looking flushed from the effort. He turned to Pete again.

"What you go to see Mary for then? You've got something goin' there I bet, she's a bit of alright, you know, wasted on Crucial."

"I didn't go and see her, so there. I went to see Robert about the Christmas rota, din't he see you then?"

Steve looked back at him with the same vacant expression. "I don't do Christmas rota, too old, nor do you, Helmit, do you? Mechanics don't do Christmas rota, do they, Helmit?"

Helmit looked up briefly but said nothing. Steve looked from one to the other and then to the roof and grinned.

"Robert, you said, Pete, din't you say you went to see Robert, 'e don't – 'e don't, you know what I mean, with Mary. No 'e don't." He stopped and chewed again "'E's spoke for he is, he mustn't put a foot wrong, I know that, yes I know that and Robert 'e knows that he don't look at Mary, do 'e, Pete, no 'e don't dare," and Steve walked to the door of the workshop and looked out into the gloom.

The office door banged across the yard, as Mary came out to go home. Steve took a step back and turned to the others.

"Eh, she's comin' look it's her – Mary – her car's over there, now's your chance, Pete, go on, you silly bugger."

They could hear the click of Mary's shoes as she walked along the concrete roadway to where her small car was parked across from the workshop. As she passed the door she looked in and smiled in a dismissive fashion then walked away across to her car. She looked tall with her high heels, and her bottom flexed from side to side in her tight skirt as she walked. The three men watched.

"Cor, look at that," whispered Steve. "I wish I were a bit younger like you, Pete."

Mary reached her car and pulled the door open then bent over and put her handbag on the passenger seat. She then pulled her skirt up a little to enable her to get in more easily, as Steve turned to Pete.

"Did you see that, eh?" and he turned to Helmit. "Did you see that?" He sucked his teeth and his hollow cheeks became dimples each side as he looked at the other two.

"Vhy don't you shut up, Steve, vot do you know about vemen?" said Helmit, who carried on working on the bike as Mary drove off in her car.

"What you mean?" challenged Steve, although he looked away awkwardly.

"How old are you?"

Steve's jaws worked fast and his lips sponged in and out. "Nearly seventy."

"How many vemen 'ave you been out vith in nearly seventy years?"

Helmit looked over at Steve who, for a while, remained silent while considering his reply.

"I don't rightly remember," he eventually said, and he walked to the door and looked out into the yard.

"Ve do, don't ve, Pete?" and Helmit looked at Pete and smiled. "And now your bike is done." And he stood it up and rang the bell.

"You mean the old grid iron is mended? Helmit, you are the best mechanic I ever knowed, ain't 'e Pete, the best I ever knowed, I told Scout that," and he also rang the bell.

"Who's Scout, Steve?" asked Pete.

"You don't know who Scout is? Did you hear that, Helmit? He said, who's Scout, well I don't know." He pulled at the handle bar of his bike, aimed the front wheel at the door and pushed it out. "Now, Pete, I'm got no lights on the old grid iron, you know that, so you will have to go and follow in front of me," and he looked seriously at Pete.

"You what?"

"Follow in front of me and just you get going will you, I want me tea."

Chapter Four

Turkeys for Christmas

Pete arrived at Meadow View and went to open the garage door to put his bike away but it was locked, which it had never been before. He went down the path and tried the side door opposite the back door of the house, which did open. He spotted the car as he put the light on and pushed his bike in. Then he took off his boots, jacket and overalls, which were not allowed in the house. He took a longer look at the car and wondered whose it was. The Wilsons were saving for one and although Freddie – that was Mr Wilson – worked at Vauxhall, as far as Pete was aware he had not got enough cash together yet to buy his own. Pete knew he would have already left for the late shift as he travelled with a friend from up the road.

The back door opened as he stared at the parked car and Joyce Wilson stood in the doorway.

"Is that you, Pete?"

"Yes," said Pete, raising his voice to make himself heard. "Have you got a car then?" he asked as he left the garage.

She didn't answer his question, or even appear to hear it.

"Do you know what?" Her voice was raised and

29

Pete wondered what had made her upset as she repeated, "Do you know what?"

Pete shrugged his shoulders as she ran both hands through her curly hair and clenched her teeth in frustration.

"What?"

"I'll tell you what, that sod of a mate of yours has gone out and not eaten his tea. Hadn't got time he said, got a date, he said and out he went, just like that."

She turned and went into the house and Pete followed her into the kitchen. A small girl sat at the table holding a knife straight up in one hand and a fork upright in the other. A plate of mince and potatoes and vegetables was in front of her as Pete went to the sink to wash his hands.

"Did he tell you he was going out then?" Joyce asked, as Patsy, the girl, gave a silly smile. "Did he then?" Joyce's voice increased in volume with each question.

"No, he didn't," Pete replied, as calmly as he could. "He didn't say anything. But then I've not seen him all afternoon," and he sat down at the table.

The little girl smirked at Pete and then looked at her mother.

"Don't you look at me like that, my girl, and don't hold your knife and fork that way either, they're not flags, you know. Just get on and eat your tea," and she turned to the oven. Getting two plates of food out she banged them down on the table and sat down herself.

"Freddie's going to hear of this you know, he can't get away with it. All that food gone to waste!"

Pete and Patsy sat silently eating as Joyce started her meal, and all was quiet for a while until Pete looked up and asked again. "You got a car then?"

"Have I got a car? No, not yet, won't be long though." She ate another mouthful.

"There's a car in the garage."

"Oh, that one, that's not ours, that belongs to the policeman – Bell. He lives in the police house at the top of the road. Freddie's letting him have it for a shilling a week and he brought the car down today for the first time."

She got up and went to the cooker.

"Pete, do you want some more, there's plenty here now Tony's gone?"

"I'll have some," piped up Patsy, looking at her mother.

"No, you won't, my girl, you haven't finished what you've got." She looked at her fiercely.

"Pete hasn't finished what he's got either," Patsy protested.

Joyce did not answer as she put another spoonful of mince on Pete's plate and more on her own, then sat down again and pushed the brown sauce bottle towards him.

"He don't like brown sauce, he likes ketchup, don't you, Pete?" said Patsy, looking at her mother.

"I don't mind what I have, they both taste nice," said Pete, as he banged the bottom of the bottle.

"You out tonight then?" Joyce enquired. "It's *Coronation Street* on the telly."

"It's what?" said Pete.

"*Coronation Street*, don't you know what that is then?' Patsy answered. "Mum loves it, she always watches it, even if Dad wants the other side." She banged her knife and fork down on her empty plate. "I 'spect you're going to Young Farmers though, aren't you, Pete?" she asked, as there was a knock at the door.

"Who's that then, you expecting anyone?" Joyce asked, but as he shook his head she got up and went to the front door. She put the outside light on, unbolted the door and then opened it. A tall man in uniform stood there looking up and down the street before he turned to Joyce.

"Evening, Mrs Wilson – Joyce, I mean – hope you don't mind me calling, but it's about the car," he said, stood back and looked up and down the street again.

Joyce looked puzzled. "Something up then?" she asked, as Constable Bell turned back to her, looking furtive.

"No, no, just checking, you can't be too careful these days. Never know who's about. Don't want to miss anything, you know. I'm not going to let them get away with it."

"Let who?" said Joyce.

"The criminal classes, young thugs, tearaways,

Teddy Boys and the like." He stuck his chin out.

"There ain't none of them around here is there?"

"Well, there ain't at the moment but as I say, you have to be on your guard, vigilant. That's what I am," and he stuck his chin out again and adjusted his tie. "Freddie out then?" he asked rather slyly.

"Yes, he's on nights this month."

"Ah, pity that. I thought I ought to pay the rent. Yes, pay the rent for the car in the garage, I mean. We agreed a price in the pub you know, the other Sunday."

He took out a leather purse from his pocket.

"It's only the first week, why don't you pay Freddie when you see him up the pub?" Joyce looked at her watch.

"I don't like to owe anything, so I thought I would pay in advance, you know, don't want to be in debt, do we, should I step inside?" And he put a large boot over the threshold and stepped onto the doormat as Joyce was forced to step back.

"I'm sure there's no need. Why don't you see Freddie, as I say?" said Joyce, as she glanced at her watch again, and he looked over her shoulder into the kitchen.

"Got visitors then?" he asked rather nonchalantly as he nodded towards the kitchen.

Joyce felt uncomfortable and turned to look in the same direction then back at the policeman.

"What do you want to know who's in there for? I haven't done anything wrong, have I?"

"No, no nothing wrong, I'm sure. Just making sure everything is fine. It's my duty, you know, can't be too careful these days, you never know who's about." He peered over her shoulder again.

"That's my daughter, Patsy, and our lodger, Pete, if you really want to know. The other one's not here – Tony, I mean – he's gone out. What else do you want to know?" Her voice was raised with the stress of the situation and Patsy came and stood at the kitchen door.

"Is that the policeman, Mum? What does he want?"

"Nothing, dear, just go and finish your pudding."

"Ain't she a lovely little girl, lovely," said the constable as he stood a little straighter and pushed his chest out and shoulders back and sighed. "We don't have a family, you know, my wife's in a wheelchair, has been for some years, you don't know her, I suppose?"

"No, I don't. Now I must get on, constable, so if you will excuse me." She took hold of the door indicating he should leave.

"But what about the rent? I really would like to pay."

"You see Freddie about that, I don't know anything so if you don't mind, I must go. Good evening, constable." She pushed the door which hit his boot hard.

"Well, if you're sure."

"I am, thank you," and he turned and stepped out.

"I'll call again," he said, as she closed the door.

She sat down and dug her spoon into the apple

crumble and custard which was now getting cold. "I don't like that man, I don't like him at all, coming here like that with some excuse about paying the rent. It's not right. And him a policeman."

"What's not right?" said Patsy.

"Never you mind, just you finish your pudding."

"I have done!" she protested.

"Half an hour of telly then, and it's your bedtime. It's school tomorrow don't forget. Pete, are you coming to watch the television?"

"No, I'm going to the pub. Then I'm going to have an early night."

"Early night," Joyce frowned.

"Yes, we're starting turkeys in the morning."

"Starting what?"

"Starting killing them, the turkeys."

"Killing them? It's ages to Christmas."

"I know, but that's what we're going to do, they put them in cold store, I think."

"So how do you kill them then?"

"I don't know, wring their necks I suppose, I've not done it before."

"So do you pluck them and gut them too?"

"I think we just pluck them."

"You're putting me right off turkey for Christmas, you really are."

The next day everyone assembled in the workshop at the farm after breakfast.

"Right," said Viv, as he looked round the assembled farm staff. "Simon, Sean, Winston, Steve, Tony and Pete, that's six, ain't it and seven with me. Turkeys, okay."

"Don't Helmit come then?" grumbled Simon.

"No, he's got work here."

"What about the girls on the poultry? Turkeys are poultry, aren't they?"

"They can't kill them so there." Viv looked away.

"I can't kill them," said Steve, as he sucked a barley sugar.

"I know that, Steve, one of us'll do it for you. Now shut up, everyone, it's going to take us all morning to get ready so let's get on with it." Viv sounded peeved.

By mid-afternoon all was prepared and they went to collect the turkeys. They were in the cattle yards. The first pen was open and they were driven slowly into a big old hay barn. This was where they were going to be killed and they would then be taken into a small adjacent barn where they would be plucked.

"Pete, you'll kill one for me, won't you, boy?" Steve said sadly. "I don't like killin' things any more, boy, not now I'm old," and he took his hanky out and blew his nose.

"Have you killed turkeys before, Pete?" Viv asked.

"No, but I've done chickens and rabbits so it must be much the same."

"Just watch me then, it's easy."

Hanging from one of the many beams high in the

roof was a rope with a noose on the end about five feet from the ground.

"Everyone ready," shouted Viv, and he went forward and grabbed a turkey by the legs. He held it upside down by its legs, made a snickle in the noose and put the legs through it and the bird hung upside down. He then took its head, turned it backwards and then weighed down on it and its neck was broken. It flapped its wings two or three times and then was motionless.

"Pete, Tony did you see how I did that?" They both nodded, but looked a little sheepish.

"Come on, Simon, and all you lot get on with it," and everyone caught a turkey and one at a time they were killed. Pete killed one for Steve as he stood sucking a barley sugar.

"It's like them camps in the war, ain't it, Pete, you know, don't you?" He looked keenly at Pete.

"Well not quite."

"It's still killin', ain't it."

"Yes, Steve." Everyone then took their birds into the small barn next door where seats had been prepared around the wall; they all sat to pluck the birds and the feathers began to pile up on the floor and the room was filled with a fine dust.

"Okay, all done so hang them up and go and get the next one," said Viv, and he plodded off to the hay barn. When he arrived, he was greeted with an unexpected scene as all the remaining turkeys had vanished.

"Bloody hell, where have they gone then? You must have left the gate open, Pete, you were the last one in here."

"No, I didn't. You just opened it so I must have shut it."

"Where are they then?"

"I knows where they are," said Steve.

"Where?" demanded Viv, and Steve said nothing but rolled his eyes upward. Everyone followed and they could see the turkeys perched on the beams high up in the roof. They all burst out laughing and Viv threw his cap on the floor.

"What we going to do then, shoot them down?" suggested Simon, and everyone laughed again.

"No, we'll call it a day, they'll be down in the morning and we can start again."

Chapter Five

The Young Farmers Agree to Produce a Play

Having washed and changed, Pete went down the path of Meadow View to make his way up to the pub. The night was cold and there was frost on the grass in the front garden. There was a smell of sulphur in the air and a slight yellow haze from the brick works about six miles away. A cat dashed across the road, followed quickly by a second one, and they screeched as they came to blows briefly on the pavement and then ran off into the shadows.

He turned right for fifty yards and then right again onto Park Road, which led up to the village green. He could hear footsteps behind him and turned to see Rita following.

"Hang on, Pete," she shouted, and tottered quickly towards him, her tight skirt making her steps very short.

The light from the street lamp illuminated her rosy cheeks.

"Hang on, I said, didn't I?" she shouted again, as Pete walked backwards, waiting for her to catch up. "Just stop a minute will you, stupid, I'm got a stone in my shoe." She grabbed his shoulder to steady herself.

"Hold this a minute," she said and handed him her handbag and then she hitched up her skirt, lifted her leg, took her high-heeled shoe off and shook a stone out of it. Her coat hung open showing her polo-neck sweater pulled tight over her substantial chest. Pete looked down as she put her shoe on again and flushed with awkwardness.

"What you looking at then, you've gone all red? I don't know what you've gone like that for," She put her foot on the ground, pulled her skirt down as far as it would go then pulled her coat together and buttoned it up. She pushed up her hair, which was fluffed up into a bouffant style. "I'll take that then," and she took her handbag back, opened it and took a packet of cigarettes out. "You went on then," she said, as she looked at Pete. "Don't look so scared, I ain't gonna hit you." She offered him the packet and he took one and then got his matches and lit hers and then his.

"Where are you off to then?" he asked, as they walked up the road.

"The Du John in Bedford, they have a dance on Wednesdays. You know it then?"

"Yes, I've been there a few times, but it's a long way. How are you going to get there?"

"On the train." She looked at her watch.

"You're not walking all the way to the station are you – it's over two miles?"

"Not on your nelly, I'm meeting Ruth on the green and we're going to hitch. If we get a lift all the way we get lucky, but if not, we'll get the train."

"Rather you than me," Pete replied rather doubtfully.

"Oh, it's easy. We never fail. I bet it don't take us more than five minutes to get a lift, you'll see." She threw her cigarette end in the gutter. "Where're you goin' then?"

"Just to the pub, to see David and some mates."

"Not the Young Farmers then?"

"No, not tonight; you ought to come to that, it's good fun."

"Me, go to Young Farmers? Not on your nelly. Not with all them yokels. They all smell of pig shit or cow shit, it's one or the other. You smell of pigs you know – I can smell it from here." Pete felt his cheeks grow warm.

"They're not all farmers, you know," he said defensively, "they do all sorts of things."

"Like what then?" Rita demanded.

"Some are secretaries, one works at the vet and lots of other things."

"You don't mean that girls actually go to Young Farmers, do you?" she said with disdain.

"Yes, lots of them."

"So that's why you go then, I know what it's all about now, don't I? How old are you anyway, you don't look old enough to go out with girls?"

"I'm nineteen," he said, a defensive edge tingeing his response. "How old are you then?"

"That's none of your business," Rita snapped back as they reached the top of the road, and she walked to the green where Ruth was waiting in the bus shelter.

"Got a new boyfriend?" she asked, as Pete and Rita walked up together.

Rita laughed and looked at Pete. "Him? You talking about him? No, he ain't no good, he ain't got a car and he smells of pigs don't you, Pete?" and she stuck her tongue out at him.

"Don't say that, Rita, look, he's gone all red," Ruth said, but Pete walked on ignoring them.

The Red Lion, its name picked out in letters above the window, was an old half-timber building painted white between the beams on the other side of the green. The sign hanging from the wall above the door squeaked as it swung in the breeze, and Pete peered through the leaded windows to see if David was there. He pressed the latch down on the door handle and it clicked as he bent his head to go into the saloon bar where David stood ordering a drink. The bar was brightly lit with a good coal fire burning in the grate and the publican, known to all as Desperate, a grey-haired man in his sixties, pulled on the handle of the beer pump.

"Come on, Pete," David said. "What are you going to have then?" and he jangled the change in his pockets.

"Just a small brown ale."

"A what?" said David. "Brown ale, what sort of

drink is that?" as the door latch rattled again and Robert came into the bar.

"Can't have nothing more, can you, there's a meeting tonight, didn't they tell you?" Robert looked at the other two with a know-all gaze.

"What meeting's that then?" demanded David.

"No one told us," Pete replied. "Can't we just have one?" He turned to Robert.

"No, Trisha says we've only got the room for an hour and we've got to hurry."

David tutted and emptied his half pint glass. "If we've got to go, we've got to go, I suppose. What's it about then and where is it?"

"I've no idea what it's about, but it's in the school where we always meet."

"We can walk there then, I suppose, but you're going to miss your brown ale, Pete, sorry about that." David put his hand on Pete's shoulder.

"Come on, we'd better go," Pete said, in a resigned tone.

At the school they met in one of the classrooms and when they arrived, there were already about ten people there, all sitting at the back of the room. Behind the teacher's desk stood the chairman – Trisha – and next to her Pat, the secretary.

Trisha was not very tall and had shoulder-length black hair and a pale complexion. She looked very neat in a white blouse, dark jacket and straight skirt.

"Come on, you boys, I thought Robert would be with you?" she asked as they came in.

"He's just gone to fetch Sally, he said he won't be long, but don't wait," and David and Pete turned towards the back to find a seat.

"Don't go back there," complained Trisha. "Everyone move down to the front or you won't hear what I've got to say."

"I like it at the back," David grumbled.

"But I don't like you all being back there, so come and sit at the front."

David looked peeved and then smiled and turned to Pete. "Come on then, follow me." He went to the front row, took a chair, put it immediately in front of the teacher's desk and sat down and stared at Trisha with a stupid grin on his face. There was laughter from the rest in the room as Trisha raised her voice.

"That's not what I meant and you know it, David, just put that chair back and behave for a change."

She pursed her lips as David sat there defiantly, before turning round to the rest of them with a broad grin, his red cheeks contrasting with his white forehead which was protected from weather by his cap.

"Did you hear what I said, David? It's not the sort of behaviour expected by someone of your age, now just—" and she stopped and grimaced. "Go and sit where you should do, we've only got an hour, you know."

David sighed and stood up, then turned and picked

up the chair and sat down behind a desk in the front row.

"Come on, get on with it," complained one of the others. "What's it all about?" as they settled down in their chairs.

"Can I have silence?" Trisha said, as she put her finger to her mouth. "Shhhh!"

No one took much notice and David was in conversation with Pete.

"Can I have silence?" Trisha raised her voice and then banged on the table with her knuckles, sucking them when it hurt and then she shouted as loud as she could, "Silence!" and the room went quiet. "That's better," she said, as she pulled her jacket down, and brushed an imaginary speck from it.

"Now we've called this meeting of the club to discuss something which has been suggested by Pat." There was an audible groan from the assembled company and Trisha looked down at Pat. "What we would like to do—" persevered Trisha, only to be interrupted by the door rattling as Robert could be seen trying to get in.

"Push, don't pull!" someone shouted.

"Push!" was shouted louder and Robert obeyed, opening the door and coming in, followed by a blonde girl. Her hair was short and she had blue eyes set in a pretty face and wore a thick red polo neck sweater and a tight skirt.

One of the boys wolf-whistled and she blushed and

gave a shy smile, showing her large top teeth. Behind her another boy came in and grinned.

"What did you bring him for?" someone shouted, and the boy's grin grew wider.

"John!" David called out to him, "I'm saved a seat for you right at the back, look over there," and he pointed, and John went and sat at the back of the room.

"Shhhh." Trisha tried to start the meeting again and went to bang on the table once more, but thought better of it. "Silence!" she shouted, and everyone started to "Shhh," and hold their fingers to their mouths as the hubbub died down. "Now, I was saying, what we would like to do would be for the club to put on a play."

"You what?" said John, from the back. "Young Farmers don't do plays, do they?" and the rest of the audience mumbled.

"Let Pat tell you what she thinks." Trisha turned to Pat next to her.

"I think that the Young Farmers Club doesn't have a good reputation and everyone thinks that they are made up of thick yokels who wear wellies and chew straw."

"That's true," someone shouted, and everyone laughed.

"No, it's not," protested Pat. "If we did some sort of drama, it would prove that we are intelligent human beings." She scanned the room for support but was greeted with silence. She looked at Trisha.

"I think it's a good idea, what do you think, Robert

– you're a bit older than the others."

Robert looked momentarily confused and then assembled his thoughts and looked round at the rest, before turning back to Trisha.

"I think Pat's right. Our reputation is not good. We only got this place to meet in because Pat's mum works here, and they won't let us use the village hall anymore, will they? So, I say we should do the play. As she says, it will prove something. I don't know quite what, but it will prove that we can do something other than brewery visits and ploughing matches."

He lit a cigarette and sat back in his chair and there was silence for a few moments.

"Who's going to come to the play then?" John piped up, having moved from the back of the room.

Trisha looked at Pat for an answer. "We'll advertise and we can all sell tickets to our friends and families."

"My family wouldn't come, would they, Sal?" John turned to the blonde girl who had come in with Robert and now sat next to him.

Sally was John's sister, and was working on a dairy farm before she went to college after the summer.

"Why not?" she answered quickly. "Just because you don't want to get up on the stage. I don't see why they wouldn't come," and she smiled at Robert and squeezed his hand.

"I'm not going to do no acting and nor's David and nor's Pete, I know they won't." John folded his arms, pursed his lips and frowned at Trisha, who smiled faintly back.

"Now, John, I think David and Pete should speak for themselves, don't you?" She looked at David.

"I don't see why," said John, as he grinned and gave David a dig in the ribs from where he was sitting in the row behind. David, who was about to say something, jumped instead and turned round and threatened John with a clenched fist and then laughed at him.

"John, just let David express an opinion, will you?" Trisha put on a superior accent.

"Why? He's a thick farmer like the rest of us, chews straw all day like Pat said," and John grinned and looked around the group for approval.

"John, will you just shut up." Trisha raised her voice, which was shrill, as she glared at him.

"Yes, miss," John said and sniggered as he looked at David and Pete.

Trisha frowned as she stamped her foot and shouted at him, "Don't you dare call me miss. Don't you dare say that again, I will not tolerate it, do you hear?" She stopped and glared at John, who looked from side to side and then at her, but said nothing. "Did you hear me?" she shouted even louder.

John's eyes focussed on the floor as he mumbled, "Yes…" and was about to add 'miss' but thought better of it.

There was silence and everyone looked at Trisha,

who trembled a little as she calmed down, and once her expression was again composed the colour drained from her cheeks.

"Now, David, you were going to say what you thought," and she fixed her gaze on him, so he dared not turn and look at John. His face coloured a little once again, contrasting against his white forehead.

"I think we should give it a go. I ain't never acted before, but why not? Pat's right, we don't have a good reputation."

"And you, Pete?" Trisha went along the row.

"Yes, I'll give it a go," one after the other, most people agreed.

"So shall we have a vote," said Trisha, "All those in favour, put up your hands."

Everyone but John did.

"All those against?" She looked round but John did not put his hand up. "That's agreed then, we will go ahead and produce the play."

"Hang on, hang on, that ain't right," John complained.

"What's wrong now?" Trisha sighed.

"You didn't have abstentions, that's not democratic you should always have abstentions." He looked straight at her.

"Very well then, any abstentions?" John grinned and put his hand up, looking round for approval as everyone laughed.

"Can we go now?" John stood up and put his hands in his pockets and jangled his change.

"No, not yet." Trisha had a job to make herself heard above the noise of chairs being scraped back as everyone stood, and several lit cigarettes. "Next meeting," she shouted, "next week, same day, same time," but no one was listening.

"Where we going then?" demanded John.

"Motorway café," said David.

"Right," said Robert, "The motorway café then."

"I'll go with them," said John, nodding at Pete and David, "and order me an egg and chips when you get there, dear sister." He winked at Sally.

"You don't mean that, do you, you only just had a big tea?"

"Course I do, I'm a growing lad you know," he said, and they all dispersed.

David, Pete and John walked back to where David's van was parked outside his house. John jumped in the passenger seat and Pete opened the back door.

"Hang on, hang on, hang on," said David. "That's all muck. I've got a sack here," and he leaned in and found an old meal sack which had 'Toddington Manor Research Farm' written on it.

"You've been stealing sacks," said John.

"No I haven't," said David. "It's no good, it's got holes in it. Here you are, Pete, roll it up and sit on that."

The motorway café was on the M1, but there was a

small accommodation road which led into the car park on the northbound side, which was not signposted, but which everyone from the village used.

"Come on, put your foot down, you're still in bottom gear," moaned John.

"No, I'm not and don't complain, it won't go no faster."

"There's someone following," said Pete as he looked out the back window.

"Can't be Robert – he's in front," said John.

They got to the car park and David reversed into a bay. The car that was following raced in and with a screech of brakes and sliding tyres it parked next to them, the bumper hitting the curb as putting the brakes hard on caused the front of the car to dip violently. The car was a large streamline Vauxhall Velox; a girl got out from the driver's seat and went round to the front of the car and gave the bumper a kick and then laughed.

"I've done worse," she said and laughed again as the boys got out of the van.

The girl was tall and well-built; her round face outlined by dark shoulder-length hair. She wore a baggy woollen sweater with a school scarf around her neck. Her long dark pleated skirt swung round as she turned to greet them.

"Alexandra, darling, how are you this evening?" said John as he sidled up to her, pecking her lightly on the cheek and then slipping his arm round her to pinch her bottom.

She reacted immediately and swung her left arm with such force, the back of her hand caught the side of John's face and he tripped and fell to the ground. Everyone laughed, including John, as he got up and brushed himself down.

"You weren't at the meeting," said David, as a boy got gingerly out of the passenger side of Alexandra's car.

"No, Mother had the car, so I had to wait until she got back."

"We're going to do a play, did you hear?" said Pete.

"Yes, I know, it's great, don't you think? I saw Pat and she told me, so did everyone agree?"

"No, they did not," said John, over his shoulder, "I abstained," as they followed him into the café.

It was now nine o'clock and there were only a few people at the tables, including Rita who was having coffee with her friend, Ruth. Pete went over to where they sat.

"I thought you were going to Bedford, dancing?"

"So did we, but it didn't work out, did it?"

"What happened then?"

"Well, we got a lift with this chap and we thought 'e was going to Bedford, but 'e weren't, 'e were going to London, and before we knew where we were, 'e were going down the M1 at ninety."

"Oh."

"So, we got 'im to drop us on the roundabout at Luton and we hitched back and 'ere we are, wanting a lift home. David will take us, won't he, Pete? He's going that way, ain't he? I don't want to walk all that way in these heels, do I?"

"I'll ask him," said Pete, and he went to sit with the others.

"What's she doing here then, Pete?" asked John.

"She's stuck, and she wants a lift home."

"She can ask herself, I ain't a taxi service, am I?" David protested.

"You can't turn her down, David. Helmit wouldn't be pleased and he's a big bloke, ain't he?" said John.

They all got coffees and sat, and John had his egg and chips.

"Who's your friend then, Alexandra?" said John, nodding at the boy that had come with her.

Alexandra gazed at the lad she had brought, who looked self-conscious as she eyed him up and down.

"He's Jack, he's the son of Mother's friends and she says he ought to join the Young Farmers, so that's him."

Jack looked away to where Rita was sitting, to avoid the gaze from the other boys, only to attract the attention of Rita.

"What you lookin' at, boy?" she snapped as they made eye contact. "Ain't you seen a girl before?" and she pouted and chewed the large lump of gum in her mouth, easing it through her teeth, pulling a length of it away, before gobbling it back in like a rabbit. She then turned back to David and forced a smile.

"Well then, are you going to give us a lift then or

ain't you?" She forced the gum through her teeth again and started to pull at it.

"I'll give you a lift," Alexandra piped up. "We can go that way and there's plenty of room."

"Are you sure?" Rita said in surprise.

"Yeah, that's fine, come on then – are we all done?"

Alexandra got up, Jack following without saying a word, and Rita and her friend brought up the rear.

Chapter Six

The Big Freeze Starts

Christmas soon came, and Pete went home and returned on Boxing Day to feed the beef cattle as arranged with Robert. The morning was cold and it was dark as he left Castle Road for the ride to the farm. As he cycled along, snowflakes started falling and David tooted as he went past in his small van.

Feeding and strawing the yard took until about eleven o'clock, but the snow gradually became heavier and heavier, and as the wind got up the snow began to drift and blow into the yards with the cattle. Pete went to fetch his bike to go home, but by this time the driveway to the farm had completely disappeared under the snow. David turned his van round. The temperature had dropped dramatically and the puddles in the yard were now sheets of ice.

"Come on, jump in, you can push if we get stuck." Pete put his bike back in the shed and got in as instructed. "Where's the road then?" David peered into the driving snow.

"No idea, you'll have to go by the trees," and Pete pointed to the avenue of pine trees which lined the drive.

"If you say so." David revved the engine and let the

clutch out, the van sliding from side to side as he tried to manoeuvre it up the slope out of the farm yard.

"It's no good, I'll have to have a run at it." He backed the van twenty yards onto the level concrete before having another go. This time he got a little further but eventually the van came to a halt in the drifting snow.

"We'll have to walk," he said as he backed the van to park it adjacent to the barn.

"Can't we take a tractor?" suggested Pete.

"You're joking, Crucial would blow a gasket if we did that! Come on then, there's nothing else for it, we'll have to walk." The snow was coming down even harder, blown along by the strong east wind, and it stung their faces as the flakes hit them. At that moment, the noise of Robert's Land Rover could be heard and he tooted as he came through the drifts of snow along the drive. The canvas roof sagged under the weight of snow and the front of the vehicle was full of snow where he had driven through the drifts.

"Thank God I caught you," he said as he came up to them. "Got a job for you. Crucial says you've got to clear the snow from the drive, so he can get out. Then clear down to the piggery as well."

"Why can't you do it?" David protested. "I'm going out this afternoon."

"You ain't going nowhere if you don't clear the snow, so come on – get on with it, and Pete, you go and get some shovels. David, you get the loader tractor and I'll get my boots and come and help."

There was nothing to be done, so David and Pete went to the tractor shed, but the door would not open as the runner at the bottom had frozen. After a lot of kicking and lifting with a bar, the door eventually slid back. David started the tractor, drove it out of the shed and began to push the snow from the yard, but as fast as he could move it, the wind blew it back again. Pete shovelled the snow from the doorway of the workshop, helped by Robert, who had now found his boots. The snow continued to fall as they did so, their breath condensing in the freezing air.

The tractor David was driving suddenly spluttered and stopped. He jumped from the seat, took his cap off and banged the snow from the grille at the front.

"What's up?" shouted Robert. "I bet you've run out of diesel."

David glared at him, unscrewed the fuel cap and peered in. "Full."

"Well, what's up with it?"

"How do I know?" He pulled his cap down tight on his head.

"Try the fuel filter then, come on, don't just stand there," and David unclipped the top and took the gauze out to find that the diesel had frozen into a sludge.

"Look! The diesel's froze! What are we going to do now?" He kicked the wheel of the lifeless machine.

"We've got to warm it up somehow. What about a blow lamp?" said Pete.

"No, you stupid bugger, that's too hot, it will set it alight. Let's get some old paper bags and light them under it, that should warm it up enough and, Pete, you go and get some paraffin and put it in the tank, that should thin the diesel down."

A bundle of old paper sacks was found and after striking many matches, they finally got one lit then held the burning sack around the fuel lines and filter until gradually the diesel thawed. The tractor started and the paraffin kept the fuel running, and eventually David got back to clearing the snow.

By the early afternoon, the drive to the farm was clear as well as the one to the piggery – at least enough to let a vehicle along them – the tractor was put away and Pete and David went home.

Pete left his bike at the farm and walked the last fifty yards from where David had dropped him. When he arrived at Meadow View, Freddie was clearing the drive as the snow had now stopped, but the sky was grey and threatening and the wind bitterly cold.

"Where you bin then, boy? Joyce has had your lunch ready two hours ago. I 'spect she's put it in the bin by now." He pushed the last of the snow into the road, where the little traffic there had been had packed it down into a hard rut, which the wind then froze.

Coming towards the pair very slowly was a small police car, and as it got closer, they could see it was driven by PC Nick Bell, who rented the garage from Freddie. The back of the car slid from side to side as he negotiated the frozen ruts. When he drew level with Freddie, he slid to a halt and wound down his window.

"This is a rum 'un," he said, "Ain't seen snow like this for years," and he rubbed his hands together.

"Why ain't you catchin' villains then, Nick? That's your favourite job, ain't it, or have you locked 'em all up?" Freddie leaned on his shovel.

"I'm bin sent out to report on the conditions, my man, and that's what I'm going to do when I get back to the station."

"You ain't got a radio then?"

"Not likely, they won't spend money on us, I'm surprised they don't give us pigeons." He laughed at his own joke.

"What are the conditions then, constable, will I be able to get to work?" Freddie enquired.

"The conditions, Mr Wilson, to put it mildly, are bloody awful. There's blocked roads everywhere, cars in ditches and everything is frozen solid. But you will get to work if you go up the M1." He looked at Pete and then back to Freddie. "You on nights then?"

"Yeah, start tonight," Freddie said and stamped his feet to get the snow off his boots.

The constable looked at Pete again. "You the lodger then, boy?" he said in an accusing tone.

"Yes, what's wrong with that – it's not an offence is it?"

"*Nooooo*… just like to know who's who, got to keep tabs you know – got to keep tabs, that's right,

Freddie, ain't it?"

"If you say so, Nick."

"How long has he lodged with you then?"

"About five months ain't it, Pete? But he always goes home at weekends, don't yer, Pete?"

"Usually."

"You're going home tonight, ain't you?"

"Supposed to be," Pete replied, "If the train's running to Bedford."

"That's running, boy, you'll make it but you'll have to walk to the station." He tapped his fingers on the steering wheel as snow began to fall again. "Ah, I must go and report or they won't be very pleased. I'll call in, Freddie, with the rent for the garage." And he put his hand up as he revved the car and drove gingerly away.

"Are you going home, Pete?" Freddie asked.

"If I can, he said the train was running," and he walked up the drive to the back door.

"Boots and overalls in the garage, Pete, you know the rules, can't have that stink in the house, Joyce goes mad."

When Pete went into the kitchen, Joyce sat at the table and looked up at him enquiringly.

"Was that the bloody policeman talking to Freddie, Pete?" She pursed her lips and stared at him. "Well?"

"Yes, he was on patrol or something, reporting on conditions, he said."

"I don't like that man, he gives me the creeps, urgh."

She shut her eyes, pulled a face and shuddered. "He comes round here with any old excuse and always when Freddie's out. And him a policeman, should be preventing crime not committing it."

She picked up a packet of cigarettes from the table, lit one and blew the smoke into the air then looked at Pete again. "What else did he say then?"

"Not much."

"Not much? I bet he did."

"He said the M1's clear so Freddie can get to work and he said the train's running, so I can get home."

"And what else did he say?"

"I don't know." Pete looked at Joyce with a slightly hurt expression. "He did say he was going to call in with the rent."

"What?" Joyce raised her voice. "The crafty bugger, the crafty bugger." She drew deeply on the cigarette and then stared at Pete again. "Pete, are you sure you're going home?" She looked imploringly at him.

"Yes, if I can get there I will; I was only on for today and Tony is doing the weekend."

There was a knock at the front door.

"Who's that then?" Joyce looked up at Pete. "On Boxing Day, it ain't that policeman, is it?" She looked at Pete as she got up and peered down the passage to the front door. "No it ain't him, but who the bloody hell...?" She unbolted it top and bottom, then undid the Yale lock and pulled the door open. Snow fell from the door into the hall and onto the mat as she greeted the

61

figure in front of her with some relief. "Oh, it's for you, Pete, it's for you – it's what's 'is name?" and she walked back into the kitchen. "It's for you," she repeated, "are you deaf?"

"Sorry. Who is it then?"

"I don't know – what's 'is name from the farm," and Pete hurried to the front door where Robert stood.

He looked a little stupid as he had pulled his cap down so hard that the popper between the peak and the cap had come undone.

"Caught you then, thank goodness." Robert looked relieved. "I thought you were going home."

"I am in a bit."

"You ain't in a bit. Crucial says you've got to go and help Grafton and the pigs, everything is froze up and you've got to help on the poultry as well, only one of the girls has come in."

"What about Tony?"

"Snowed in, he rung Crucial an' told him he can't get back."

"And David?"

"He's coming – I've just seen him. It's a real mess, no water in the cattle and all the sheep are snowed in down Frog Hole. We've got to fetch them in the morning, it's too late now cos it's all drifted against the hedge. I don't know how many are buried. Come on, Pete, you've got to stop," he pleaded.

"Okay then, do you mean now?"

"No, I'll go down the pigs now, but you go straight

there in the morning until Grafton's sorted and then come up to the poultry. Tell you what – I'll see you up the pub for a pint, seven o'clock okay? No make it eight – after *Coronation Street*."

"Fine," said Pete, and Robert left, as Joyce came with a dustpan to collect the snow from the door.

"What's he want then?"

"He wants me to stop and help. Everything is froze apparently."

"You mean you're here tonight?"

"Yes."

"Thank bloody goodness."

She pecked him on the cheek and went back into the kitchen, followed by Pete, red with embarrassment. "I don't get it?"

"Don't get what?"

"Why do you want me to be here?"

"It's that damn policeman. He knows Freddie's gone back on nights and he thinks you're not here, so he'll be round."

"What for?" Pete looked confused.

"What for...? What for...? Pete, how old are you?"

"Nineteen."

She looked at him and burst out laughing.

"Pete, grow up, will you." She ruffled his hair.

"Oh, I see," he said, and blushed again. "But doesn't Freddie... I mean doesn't Freddie... well, say anything?"

"Freddie thinks the light shines out of his backside,

they are big mates up the Cons, Freddie thinks I should be nice to him."

"So, you just want me to be here?"

"Yes."

"But I'm going up the pub."

"No, you're bloody not!"

"I said I would meet Robert."

"Oh no, what time?"

"After *Coronation Street*, he said."

"Oh, that's okay then, he'll come when it's on, I know him, the sod. He knows I like to watch it and that Patsy will be in bed."

"Why don't you lock the door and not let him in?"

"Not let a policeman in, what would the neighbours say? They know I'm here as well as everyone else, they would have a field day." She lit another cigarette. "Anyway, he would tell Freddie I weren't home and that would be worse, him being on nights."

The back door opened, it was Freddie, and he hung on to the door handle as he shook his boots off.

"Come in and shut the door, it's freezing," Joyce complained.

"You don't have to tell me, I've been out in it for the last hour and now I've got to go to work, assuming my lift turns up. Why'd they start us off on Boxing Day? You'd 'ave thought we could 'ave had one more off, don't you think, Pete? You're off, aren't you?"

"No, he ain't," Joyce cut in with a smile. "They're just bin and he's got to stop here – it's all froze up down the pigs."

"I ain't the only one who works around here then," he said as he went up to Joyce as she stood at the sink, put one hand on her shoulder and squeezed her bottom with the other.

"Get off, you filthy bugger," and she wriggled away from him.

"Be like that then," Freddie replied as he went upstairs to get changed, but then stopped.

"Oh, by the way, Nick come back and said he'll bring the rent round for the garage tomorrow night."

"Not tonight?"

"What did I say then – tomorrow! And be nice to him for a change." He went off up the stairs.

She turned to Pete. "See what I mean," and she stamped her foot. "'Be nice to him… be nice to him...' that horrible sod," and as tears welled she pulled her pinny up and wiped them away.

"Now, you going to be here tomorrow evening, Pete? Say you are?" The tears came again. Pete stood up and moved towards her, but then stopped – he didn't know what to do. "Pete?"

"Yeah, I'll be here don't worry – I'll be here all weekend."

Chapter Seven

In The Pub

The snow continued to come down as Pete walked up to the pub. It was no longer heavy, but was still enough to fill up the ruts that had been made during the day. He walked in the road as it was more even than the pavement where the frozen footprints made it feel like walking on a rocky shore. He opened the pub door and as he stepped down into the lobby, "Take your boots off," was shouted through from the bar. "There's some newspaper there – put 'em on that."

Pete did as instructed and walked in over tiles which felt cold in his stocking feet, until he stood on the large rag mat in front of the fire.

"You're not very busy, Desperate," Pete said, as he looked round the empty bar.

"It's the weather, did you notice it or are you walking about with your eyes shut?" He tapped his pipe into a large ashtray. "What do you want then?" he asked, his tone unwelcoming.

"Just a brown ale."

"Just a brown ale," he repeated. "A brown ale? What sort of drink is that?" and he took a glass off the shelf behind the bar, opened the bottle and poured it out. "You never have my bitter, Pete," he said, as he banged the glass down. "You don't ever drink the bitter."

"No," said Pete, as the door opened with a bang.

"Take your boots off," Desperate shouted. "Put them on the newspaper."

The door slammed shut and a head appeared round the curtain that hung in a forlorn attempt to keep the draught out. It was John from the Young Farmers.

"No, I ain't going to do that," he snorted. "Look at the floor, Desperate, it ain't been washed in years and me with clean socks on just a week ago." John grinned at Pete. "Don't you think the floor is filthy, Pete? I don't know why you took your boots off. You need them on in here, I reckon."

"No beer if you don't take them off," said Desperate.

"Well, there's a welcome if you like – no beer if you don't take your boots off – I don't know how you expect to get any trade in here."

Desperate tapped his pipe again as John stood threatening to walk in.

"It's the snow."

"What snow?"

"On your boots, stupid." John looked down.

"Well, I never. Snow – why didn't you say?" and John took his boots off and walked to the bar.

"Pint?" Desperate asked.

"Pint of what?"

"Pint of bitter."

"Is it the same barrel as last week? I bet it is. It made me puke, that did. Look, Pete won't drink it," and John looked at Desperate, then at Pete.

"Yes, or no?"

"Is it the same barrel?"

"No."

"I'll have a pint then." Desperate tugged at the handle, pulled a pint and banged it down on the bar.

"I thought you'd be snowed in, how did you get here?" Desperate enquired.

"I came on the tractor, you must be glad – or there would be no one here except Pete – that's right ain't it, Pete?" and Pete nodded. "And I was lucky to get here as well; the damn diesel froze. What a mess – got it all over me – can you smell it, Desperate?" John ran a small farm for his father, who was a local solicitor.

"I don't know which is worse, the diesel or the cow muck."

"I suppose there is a bit of both – I better not get too near the fire or I might catch alight." He moved and stood with his back to the fire then took off his donkey jacket and hung it over the back of a chair.

"Don't put it there – it stinks! There's pegs over there." Desperate nodded to a row by the door.

"Blimey, I don't know why we come here, do you, Pete?" John took his donkey jacket, which had *Wimpy* written across the back of it and hung it on a peg.

"Hey, Pete, look what I'm just earnt." He took a one-pound note from his pocket. "That'll buy a few pints."

"How did you do that then?"

"Pulled this bloke out of a snowdrift – he was stuck solid. Luckily, I had a chain with me. He was a posh bugger, but he couldn't drive. I got him out and then had to drive the car up to the green for him."

"Who was he then?"

"No idea but he gave me a quid, not bad, don't you think?"

"Suppose not," said Pete, as the door opened again.

"Boots off," Desperate shouted as the curtain pulled back a little, a head appeared then withdrew and there was a stamping of feet before the individual came in.

He was quite short and wore a long black coat and a flat cap, and he stamped his feet again, getting the snow off his black shoes. Desperate looked at him and was about to shout again, when he noticed he had shoes on, not boots.

"It's damn cold out there," said the newcomer as he blew on his hands.

"It's 'im," said John, as he looked him up and down. "I just pulled you out, didn't I?"

"Yes, you did but I slid off the road again – into the ditch this time. You couldn't pull me out again, could you?"

69

He took his cap off and undid the buttons of his coat to reveal a smart pinstriped suit underneath.

"How much is it worth this time?" John winked at Pete. "Where are you then?"

"Not far – just up the road to Luton – not quarter of a mile, but look here, my man, I gave you a quid last time, that should cover it."

"I don't know about that, my tractor's got no cab, you know and it's damn cold out there and it's dark and I've got a pint to drink and my sister's coming with her boyfriend. Anyway, what you doing out in this weather when you can hardly drive?"

John went over to the fire again to warm up, his big toes sticking out of his dirty socks.

"Can hardly drive? Now look here, I certainly *can* drive."

"How come you got stuck twice in half an hour then?"

"That's the weather – the snow and ice, nothing else."

"What are you doing all the way out in the wilds of Bedfordshire anyway?" John said, as he looked him up and down again and took a swig of his pint.

The newcomer jingled his pockets, took out some change and examined it before putting it back and then withdrew a wallet from his jacket and took out a ten-shilling note.

"Large whisky, landlord, and ice – no soda."

"Ice?" said Desperate. "We don't have ice – you

could go outside if you like, there's plenty out there."

"A splash of water then," he said, put the note down on the bar and lit a cigarette.

"You didn't say what you're doing 'ere." John stared at him.

He looked back, took a deep draw from his cigarette and blew it in John's direction.

"If you want to know I'm a journalist and I came to report on the condition of the roads."

"You don't need to come here to do that, they are bloody awful," Pete said.

"Well, you can still get down the M1 and I can see the trains are running. And now I have seen the constable and he says most of the other roads are blocked, so I'm going to find a phone box and report and then get back to Luton the best I can."

"Not if you're in the ditch and it's dark, if you haven't noticed." John forced a stupid grin at the newcomer. "You say you're a reporter – what paper's that for then?" He peered at the stranger in an insolent manner.

"The *Luton Times* if you want to know," he replied. "My name's Henry Babage, haven't you seen me in print before?"

"No never, have we, Pete, not ever."

"I've never read that paper," Pete added.

"No, we have the *Luton News* in our house. Have you ever read this chap before, Desperate?" John turned to the barman to see him filling his pipe.

At this point they heard the door open again and Robert came in with Sally. They saw the other boots on the newspaper and took theirs off without a prompt from Desperate.

"Crikey, it's cold out there," said Robert. "I've never known weather like it, there's a car in the ditch up the road." They both went over to the fire to warm up. Robert looked at the pint that John was holding. "Is that drinkable then?"

"Yup, new barrel – it don't taste too bad, but Pete won't touch it."

"How's my lovely sister then?" John addressed Sally.

"How much have you had to drink?" she snapped back at him. "And no, I can't lend you any money." She folded her arms, saying, "I'll have a Babycham please, Robert," as he went to the bar.

"And I'll have another pint, Robert." John emptied his glass and banged it on the bar. "And Pete'll have another brown ale, won't you, Pete? Come on, Robert, get your money out."

Robert removed his coat, took his wallet out of his jacket and fingered through the notes before taking ten shillings out. John grabbed it and put it on the bar.

"That will do, Robert," and he put his glass on it and shoved it across the bar.

"I really don't know about you, John, why can't you ever behave? I'm ashamed you're my brother." Sally turned and took a seat near the fire. "Can't you control him, Pete? Someone has to."

"No one can keep him in order, Sally, but he means no harm, or at least most of the time, he means no harm."

"That's right, Pete – you stick up for me, even if my sister won't."

"Whose car is it in the ditch?" Robert asked the assembled company.

"We know that, don't we, Pete?"

"Yes."

"The car in the ditch belongs to the honourable," and John turned to the stranger, "What's his name – 'e's standing right here – the famous reporter for the *Luton Times* who no one has ever heard of. That's right, ain't it, Pete?"

"Don't ask me." Pete turned to Henry. "Don't worry about him – he's alright really."

"I'm pulled him out once and then he went and drove straight into the ditch again. I ask you. You've got to pull him out this time, Robert, you're in the Land Rover, ain't you?"

"Yes, but it's way in the ditch, your tractor is needed."

"But I ain't got any cab and it's bloody cold out there."

"What's your name?" Sally asked the stranger.

"My name's Harry Babage and I work for the *Luton Times*."

"I've heard of you and seen your name in the paper, you're a reporter ain't you?"

"Yes, I am."

"Didn't you report on that hanging in Bedford last year?"

"Yes, I was there for weeks."

"Desperate, you've got someone famous in your pub for a change."

"He ain't famous and he's a bloody useless driver if it comes to that," said John.

"Who is going to pull him out then?" Pete asked, and looked from Robert to John.

"You do it if you're so keen," said John. "The tractor's outside the door and the chain is on the back, it won't take five minutes, but charge him a quid."

"I'm not doing it, I'm in my good clothes. Robert, you do it." Robert shook his head.

"Don't you do it, Robert," Sally said firmly. "John – you do it, you've got a tractor and a chain and you've got your work clothes on." John shut his eyes and grunted.

"Sister dear, you are full of good ideas," he said as he turned to the bar and looked at Desperate. "I'll tell you what, I'll go and pull him out after he's bought me another pint, that's fair ain't it, Pete?"

"Yes, that's fair. Another pint please, Desperate, and this honourable whatever his name is will pay."

John grinned and looked from one to the other of the people in the pub and laughed.

"Okay then," said Henry, as he reached into his pocket and took out some change. "Now how much is that, landlord? I need some of this for the phone."

"The phone's broke," John said with a sly smile.

"How do you know?" said Sally. "You never go in the phone box. Don't believe him, Henry, he's pulling your leg."

"No, I ain't, so there."

"How do you know then?" asked Robert.

"I know cos our wonderful PC 49 told me. He said that it's broken as someone has stolen all the cash out of it, so there, it must be right."

"He didn't say anything to me and I asked him about crime only an hour ago," said Henry.

"He must have forgotten, he's got a lot on his mind."

"I saw him today," Pete joined in, "But he didn't say anything then either."

"Well, I don't know, go and look for yourself if you don't believe me, it's only over the green."

"You can't," said Sally. "The snow's piled up against it, you'd never manage to open the door. I noticed when we came past. You'll have to use Desperate's phone – he won't mind."

"What you want to phone for anyway?" asked John.

"I have to report back on the conditions of the roads and the deadline is nine this evening."

"I thought you had to write it all down?"

"Not necessarily, I can dictate it over the phone."

"Ah, we are clever, aren't we?"

"Henry, don't listen to him," said Sally. "He can hardly read, can you, John?"

"Now, sister dear, don't say things about your one and only brother that are clearly not true."

"Well," said Henry, "I would be grateful if I could use your phone, landlord, and the sooner the better if you don't mind." Desperate lifted the flap and Henry followed him into the house.

"What a plonker," said John, as Henry disappeared.

"I thought he was quite nice," said Sally.

"Putting his car off the road twice in half an hour ain't very sharp if you ask me. Well, we've just got time for one more." John winked at Pete as he finished his pint and Desperate returned to the bar. "Come on, Pete, you owe me one. Pint please, Desperate, and Pete'll pay," he grinned.

"I thought you were going to pull Henry's car out – you'll be drunk before long," Sally protested.

"Drunk? Drunk? This is only my fourth – that's very nearly like being a teetotaller, don't you agree, Pete?"

"John, just stop asking me to agree with you all the time, just agree with yourself for once."

"Very good, sir. Agreed." John stood to attention and saluted Pete and then took a long swig of his pint as Henry returned to the bar.

"If I finish my scotch, could you come and pull me out now?" he asked John, who stood to attention again and saluted.

"I'll tell you what Mr Henry Whatsisname, if you get me a tot of scotch to help this pint down, I'll come and pull you out at no extra charge. How's that for a good deal and the scotch will keep the cold out as my tractor has no cab, as I said before?"

"If you insist, a scotch for the man, landlord, if you please."

Chapter Eight

Stuck In the Snow

The next morning Pete got up to start work at seven as usual, but allowed more time as he would have to walk the mile to work. Joyce was already up and had made his sandwiches and filled a flask for him.

"Don't forget you said you'd be in this evening, Pete," she said.

"No, don't worry," he replied, as he went to the garage to get his overalls and boots.

The overalls were frozen solid and so were the boots. He could only half get his feet into them and had to walk on tiptoe for the first five minutes until the warmth of his feet thawed the boots out. The walking was difficult as the ruts made by the traffic had frozen solid. As he turned into the drive down to the farm, David came very slowly along in his van, his lights making the snow sparkle in the darkness.

"Come on, get in," he called out, as he pulled up, "Blimey it's cold," and he rubbed at the windscreen to clear the front enough to see ahead.

They arrived at the farm to find Viv and Crucial in deep discussion as to how to get all the animals fed and watered. Crucial looked up as he did up the top button of his coat.

"Right, Pete, get down the pigs as soon as possible. David, you go with Viv to get the sheep back from Frog Hole and the rest of you go to the cattle."

It was still dark, and there was no way to get to the pigs other than walk. Grafton greeted him in the food store at the end of the fattening house.

"Thank God you've come. Wally hasn't turned up and everything outside is frozen up."

Hearing the voices, the pigs in the fattening house started to squeak.

"You know what to do." Grafton nodded at Peter, who opened the door, put the lights on and pushed the feed barrows into the deafening noise.

It was lunch time before all the pigs were fed and watered, and the temperature was still well below freezing. After a struggle and a lot of digging, the sheep were driven back to the farm and put in a field next to the buildings where they could be fed.

The snow was still falling in showers but the wind had got up and blew it into enormous drifts and the drive to the farm had to be cleared time and again. The temperature dropped to well below freezing and stayed there for days. The diesel in the tractors became viscous in the low temperatures and most would not go without sacks on the radiator. All the cattle troughs froze in the yards and had to be freed with boiling water every morning. The poultry houses were okay for water, as the birds made enough heat to keep the temperature above freezing but the problem was cleaning the eggs. The staff on the poultry unit was much depleted as they were unable to get there in the snow. All those that normally cycled to work, had to walk as the roads were too treacherous. The frozen ruts carved by the traffic made it hard to even walk.

After the initial shock of the snow and freezing temperatures, everyone got into a routine to cope with the situation and the large amount of extra work that had to be done to keep all the animals fed and watered. Some of the cattle were still outside and David – on his way to feed them – buckled the back wheel of his tractor in a frozen rut.

After a few days the temperature dropped even lower and the water mains to the cattle yard froze under the ground. At night time the temperature went down to under zero degrees Fahrenheit. However, even in these temperatures, healthy calves were born outside.

One morning there was a shower of rain which froze on landing, coating all surfaces with a layer of ice, including the walls of the egg-cleaning barn. The worst job of all was cleaning the eggs for the hatchery as the shed this was done in had no heating and little protection from the weather. The only way to clean the eggs was with wire wool, as washing them would destroy the emulsion in the shells and they would not hatch. None of the girls who normally did this work turned up. Either they could not get to work, or they refused to come, so Pete, Steve and anyone who had nothing else to do were sent in.

The freezing rain also left a sheet of ice over all the drifts of snow and now they could be walked over, which made some jobs easier.

At the piggery the fattening shed and the farrowing shed did not freeze due to the heat the animals produced, but those in pens outside such as the boars and dry sows had no water. To supply them a forty-gallon drum of water was pulled round on a small trolley, but each time the water was drawn off, the tap froze and had to be thawed with hot water for the next bucket.

At the Wilson house in Castle Road, there was no central heating and only a coal fire in the sitting room to keep the house warm. It got so cold upstairs that Pete and Tony took the mats from the floor and put them on the beds and did not take their underclothes or pyjamas off for a week at a time. They still had to leave their boots and overalls in the garage too due to the smell, but every morning the overalls were solid boards and the boots were frozen stiff.

The policeman, PC Nick Bell, continued to use the garage, but did not take the car out in the snow. Every few days, he would come down from the police house at the top of the street and start it up to make sure it was not frozen. About three weeks after the snow started, he came down while Pete and Tony were home for lunch. He leaned his bike up inside the garage and took the car out for a run as the two boys left the house to go back to work.

"There the old bugger goes," said Tony. "You know he stopped me the other day for riding on the pavement."

"Were you then?"

"No, I was just crossing it, or crossing it slowly if you see what I mean." He looked up and down the road.

"You know what I'm going to do?"

"What?"

"I'm going to let his tyres down, serve him right that's what I say," and he quickly bent down and undid the valve of each tyre and let the air out.

"You've left your fingerprints at the scene of a crime." Pete wagged his finger at Tony.

"I don't care, he's not going to take fingerprints off a bike, is he, use your brain, Pete." They walked on back to work.

They caught up with Steve, who was pushing his bike.

"Why don't you leave the bike at home, you never ride it?" said Tony.

Steve looked vacant and then smiled and sucked his barley sugar as his lips sunk into his mouth with his badly fitting dentures.

"What am I goin' to hold on to then if I don't use the old grid iron? It keeps me on the old straight an' narrow," and he grimaced at the two boys.

There was a toot of a car horn as they went up the hill towards the farm entrance and a big Ford Zodiac came up behind them. It tooted again as they all moved to the side to let it pass. Its wheels crunched in the ice of the frozen ruts and the driver put his foot down to get up the hill.

"Silly bugger," said Pete. "He'll never get up the hill like that – too much power."

Sure enough, the front wheels got in a rut and the back swung round as the driver accelerated, and as the wheels spun faster and faster the car slid sideways until the back went into the drift and stopped. The driver got out, slammed the door and shouted at the three on their way to work.

"You silly sods, why din't yer get on the side when I tooted? Now look what yer've made me do." Two other men got out of the car. The driver was tall and fair-haired and lit a cigarette as he surveyed the scene.

"Where the bloody 'ell are we, Sunny?" shouted Lionel Abrahams, who remained in the car.

"I fink we're in Toddington."

"Fink…? Don't yer know?" he shouted again, appearing to be Sunny's boss. "Why I let you drive, I don't know?" Lionel turned to the other two, Doug Brown and Mario Garcia, "an' now we're stuck."

They walked to the back of the car and looked at the wheels embedded in the snow.

"Doug, can we get out of this mess?" Lionel addressed the shorter of the two.

83

"Not on our own we can't," and Doug took his cap off, releasing a mass of curly red hair, and scratched his head.

"Hey, you boy! Where are we?" Lionel shouted at Pete.

"Toddington."

"Where's this road go to then?" He took a long draw on his cigarette.

"Milton Bryan in about a mile."

"Milton what? Where the bloody 'ell is that? We want to get t' Luton, don't we?" He turned to the driver, Sunny Bright.

"In the end we do," he replied rather sheepishly.

"So," said Lionel, "You, boy, does it go t' Luton?" and he stared at Pete.

"Eventually, but why don't you go down the M1, that's the quickest way to Luton."

"We've just come up the M1 and wanted a different route. Does it go past Vauxhall?"

"No idea, I'm not from around here," and he turned to Steve still sucking on his barley sugar. "Does it, Steve?" Pete asked, as Steve looked up in the air.

"Does it what?"

"Go past Vauxhall?"

"What?"

"The road to Luton, does it go past Vauxhall?"

Steve looked vacant and then put his finger to his mouth and rolled his eyes.

"Stupid bugger." Sunny threw his cigarette down.

"Come on you lot, 'elp us push," and he pointed to the back of the car as Steve put his hand up.

"Yes, it does."

"Does what?"

"It goes past Vauxhall," he said as he rang the bell of his bike.

"That's something then." Lionel sounded less agitated. "Come on then push us out of this – you help as well, Marco," and as he addressed the fourth man, Pete and Tony joined Doug and Marco at the back of the car.

Sunny got in and with some effort the four managed to push it out of the drift. Without a word of thanks, the strangers got back in the car and drove off.

"Who the bloody hell were they then?" Tony turned to Steve and Pete, who shrugged his shoulders. Steve grinned again.

"I know where they come from, my boys, don't you?" and he looked from one to the other. "They come from London, I know that, or they speak as though they come from London."

"How do you know, Steve, you've never been to London?"

"I know I ain't, but I'm bin to Luton and these people there come from London so there," and he set off pushing his bike on up the hill.

When Pete and Tony arrived back from work Tony's mother was waiting outside Meadow View in her car, a large Jaguar. She got out as they arrived, swinging both legs out at the same time to reveal high-heeled shoes. She put them to the ground and tried to stand but slid on the ice and sat down again.

"Drat it," she said, and tried again with the same result.

"Tony!" she shouted in a higher pitch. "Come round here and help your mother, don't just stand there!" Tony went round, held the door and offered his hand. She looked up and scowled. "On second thoughts there's no need to get out. Now, Tony, you're coming with me, I've seen Mrs What's her name and told her you won't want tea so get those filthy overalls off and jump in. No! Go and change first, you smell so awful, and don't be long about it, understand?" She glared at Tony and he gazed blankly back at her.

"Why have I got to come?" he protested.

"We're going to a ladies night at your father's lodge – you know all about it, I told you at the weekend. Now get a move on, don't just stand there."

"Do I have to?"

"Yes, you do," she shouted as Tony sloped off.

While she waited PC Bell returned in his car to put it in the garage, but his path was blocked by the Jaguar. PC Bell hooted as he waited on the ice. Tony's mother looked up and round to where the constable sat in his car. He hooted again, but she didn't move, so he got out of the car, went over and tapped on the window. She slowly wound it down and stared at the constable.

"Yes?" she said in a disparaging tone.

86

"Madam, I'm trying to get in that garage over there and you're in the way."

"So I am," she said in the same voice.

He looked keenly at her then stood back a little.

"Can you move?" He stood up to his full height and glared at her. "Move!"

"There's no need to take that tone with me, my man, do you know who I am?"

"No, I don't," he pursed his lips. "And I don't care."

She glared back at him. "I'm Audrey Howells. I'm a J.P. and I'm going to dinner with the Chief Constable this evening."

PC Bell once again stood to his full height and after a pause asked, "Could you please move, madam?"

She shrugged and started the car, put it in first gear and released the clutch but the car spun on the ice.

"Don't worry," shouted Pete from the garage. "I'll give you a push," and in no time the car was parked further up the hill, allowing PC Bell to come down the hill and into the drive.

As he did so the back of his car slipped round and spun until he nearly faced back up the hill.

"Don't worry," Pete shouted again and he pushed the car until PC Bell was able to get it up the drive and into the garage.

The constable then locked the car, got his bicycle, pushed it out and shut the door. At the same time as Tony came out to join his mother, PC Bell discovered both tyres on the bike were flat.

"Oi," he growled at Tony. "Is this your work, boy?" He looked down at the flat tyres. "I bet it was you – you were the one I caught the other day cycling on the pavement. I'm sure it were you."

Tony's cheeks flushed. "I only crossed the pavement, I didn't go along it."

There was a silence, then, "This was you then." PC Bell nodded at his tyres, just as Audrey hooted her horn and shouted out the window.

"Come on, boy, we're late already." The constable grunted and Tony ran to his mother's car.

"No, don't get in, you silly boy, you push until I get to the top of the hill," and gradually they moved off.

The constable sighed as he took the pump from the crossbar to pump up his tyres while Pete returned to the garage to take his boots and overalls off then went inside.

"Has he gone?" Joyce demanded.

"Who?"

"The copper – has he gone?"

"Yes, I think so, he was pumping up his tyres."

"Did Tony let them down then?"

"Yes."

"That's a laugh, serve 'im right. I don't like that man, he gives me the shivers he really does," she said, and she put the tea on the table.

Chapter Nine

Collecting The New Boar

"Quiet, everyone!"

Trisha stood behind the teacher's desk in the big classroom in the village school.

"You'll have to shout," said Pat, who sat at the table with a pile of scripts in front of her.

"Quiet, everyone! Can we make a start?" Trisha tried again, and sighed as she surveyed the chattering audience.

"Do you want me to shout?" offered Pete.

"Go on then."

"Silence! We are about to start," shouted Pete, in a much deeper and louder voice, and the hubbub subsided as people gradually sat down.

"Now, it's good that so many have turned up and you all know what it's about, so let's get started."

"Please, miss," came a voice from the back, "What is it about?"

Trisha's cheeks coloured. "I've told you before, John, you don't address me as 'miss', do you hear?" The room went quiet as Trisha trembled. "Understand?" she shouted as she glared at John. "Understand?" she shouted a second time.

"Yes," John replied, and sniggered behind his hand.

"Now the play that has been chosen is *The Queen of Hearts* and it's a romantic thriller. We have the copies here from the library. We now need to do the casting."

"I bags the Queen." Penny stood up.

"And I will be Prince Charming, so there," said John.

"There's no Prince Charming in the play," said Pat.

"No Prince Charming? What sort of play is this then?" and John came forward, took a copy and flicked it open.

"Right, everyone – take a copy," and Trisha and Pat doled the rest out.

"Now we need volunteers, so have a look and see what part you want to play and if you don't want a part, we need people to do the stage."

Gradually all the parts were allocated, a stage manager appointed and a date for the performance was agreed as Easter Monday.

"Can we go now?" complained John, "it's bloody cold in here."

"Okay. It is cold, so everyone read their parts and the first rehearsal is the same time next week," said Trisha, as she closed the meeting.

As they left the building, the moon shone bright, the snow crisp underfoot. The road down to the pub was a sheet of ice where the snow had melted and refrozen; it glistened in the moonlight and David took a run and skated down the road until the bend, which he could not negotiate so fell into the snow on the verge.

"I can do better than that," said Alexandra and launched herself in the same direction.

She waved her arms this way and that in an attempt to stay upright, but in the end, she landed on her bottom in the middle of the road with her legs in opposite directions and her skirt splayed out around her. She burst into laughter with everyone else.

"That's cold on the old backside," she said, as she brushed herself down.

"Come here, I will warm it up with my hands," and John rushed over, but she stepped back and pushed him and he went over on the ice.

The next morning was grey and overcast when they got to work, David and Pete were detailed to get the cattle trailer prepared as the new boar was ready to fetch.

"You know where to go then?" Crucial asked David.

"Yes, Slip End, ain't it?" he said as he put the draw bar pin in. "Down the M1."

"No, no, you can't go down the M1 on a tractor," Crucial tutted. "Can you find your way on the back roads?"

"Suppose so, but it's going to be cold, there's no cab on the tractor and I'm going to get froze," he protested.

"Take Pete with you and take it in turns to drive and

put some more straw in the wagon. And don't forget to go and get the cheque from Mary."

"Right – come on, Pete, get some sacks from the meal stove, we can stop a bit of the draught," and they tied sacks between the rear mud guard on the engine of the tractor which funnelled a little of the warmth from the engine.

"Do you know the way then?" Pete asked.

"Piece of cake, take about an hour." They set off in the gloom.

The temperature was well below freezing and all the side roads were ruts and ice, which made it bumpy.

They got about two miles and the engine started to splutter. They looked at each other and David pulled the throttle fully open, but to no avail. The tractor chugged a few more yards and then stopped and David put it out of gear and pulled the handbrake on.

"The diesel's froze." David looked at Pete. "Come on, boy, find a spanner – we can look in the filter, I bet there's ice in it."

Pete went to the toolbox, found an old adjustable spanner and offered it to David. "Screw hammer. Is that all we've got?"

"All we've got that'll fit."

"Give it 'ere then," and he looked at the spanner and carefully undid the nut on top of the fuel filter. He took the top off and then the filter and it was full of ice. "That's the trouble – water in the diesel." He blew through the filter and then turned the fuel tap backwards and forwards but no fuel came. "Must be some ice in the pipe, we've got to warm it up somehow."

"Look who's coming," said Pete, as they saw John driving towards them then stop as he drew level.

"Are you froze up then?" he said, as he climbed off the back of his tractor – the only way, as sacks were tied all around the engine and radiator. "You should have put a sack in your radiator, David."

"Don't tell me that now," David snapped.

"Don't get shirty, you should have put a sack in the radiator so there."

"Are you going to help then? If not, bugger off." David stared at him.

"What do you want then?"

"'Ave you got a paper bag we can burn?" David pursed his lips.

"Only the one I sit on."

"That'll do then, fetch it, Pete."

"What am I going to sit on, that seat's bloody cold?"

"Everything's bloody cold," David snapped again.

Pete started to tear up the bag into smaller pieces.

"Who's got a light then? Pete – you smoke, let's have it then," and he took a lighter from his pocket and lit the first wad of paper, which David held under the fuel pipe when it got blazing. "Another bit." And Pete handed him another wad. "Is it coming, Pete?" and they looked at the fuel pump.

"It ain't going to come, is it?" John sniggered. "The tap's turned off – you must have done that."

David sighed and turned the tap on, but still no fuel came. He lit another lot of paper and ran the blazing torch backwards and forwards along the fuel line until eventually a small length of ice came into the pump and then the fuel ran freely.

"Thank God for that," said David, "I'm just about frozen myself," and he put the pump back together and jumped up into the seat.

"Aren't we going to have to bleed it?" Pete asked.

"Let's try first." He pressed down the starting lever and the engine turned over.

He kept his hand on the starter and it fired once then stopped, and it turned over slower and slower, nearly fired up again and then stopped. David released the leaver then pressed it down again and it just clicked.

"Sod it." David looked up to the grey sky. "You'll have to tow us then," he said as he turned to John.

"I can't."

"Why not?"

"'Cos you've burnt my seat," John laughed, but he got on his tractor and backed up to David's.

"Don't let your clutch out till I get going," he said, and eased his tractor forwards until the chain became taut. His wheels spun on the ice but he gradually pulled David's tractor forwards and then pulled the throttle back and they were going at a good speed.

"Get on then," he shouted, and David let his clutch

out but the wheels skidded on the ice and did not turn the engine over until they came to a stretch where the sun had melted the ice and the road surface was clear. The engine finally turned over and after a few yards, started to fire and smoke poured from the exhaust.

"Thank God for that, I thought we would never get going. Thank you, old mate," and he shook John's hand. "Have you got another bag to go in the radiator?" David asked.

"You want blood, you do!"

"Go on, I can see another one on the back there – get it, Pete." He grabbed the bag and they arranged it in front of the radiator.

"We've got rehearsal tonight, David."

"I know, we'll be there, but we must go now or Crucial will slaughter us," and with that they drove off.

Pete drove and David pulled his collar up and his cap down and put his hands deep in his pockets to keep warm. The cross wind was strong, and coming at right angles to the road it blew the snow off the fields until it drifted across the road in places.

They came to Houghton Regis and then skirted round the edge of Dunstable and Luton. The roads were clearer in the towns but the pavements were sheets of ice.

"Are we nearly there?" complained Pete. "I'm frozen."

"Come on, not far now – I'll drive the last bit," said David, and they swapped places.

Ten minutes later, they arrived. Winterbourne Manor, the sign said as they turned into the drive.

"Looks a bit posh," said Pete, as they drove up a tree-lined avenue at the end of which was a big Queen Anne house with the farm behind.

They drove into the farm yard and up to an office with a workshop next door. There was no one in the office or the workshop and the wheel marks left behind by the tractors made it clear they were all out.

"What are we going to do then? Look, the pigs are over there," David pointed. They went over to look and found the boar pens. "Look here – I bet this is the bugger for us. Look at him, he's as long as a bus. I bet this is the one." David scratched his back over the wall.

"We'll have to go to the house," said Pete.

"You go then, they're a posh lot, like Tony's parents."

"Why do I have to go?" Pete protested.

"You're posh, ain't you – anyway – you've got the cheque. You have got it?" David looked worried.

"Yes, I've got it and we'll both go, come on." They made their way to the house and round to the back door.

"What's their name?" Pete turned to David.

"Dawingditmus."

"What?"

"Dawingditmus and it's colonel, don't forget." He pulled the knocker up and banged the door. There was silence for a moment and then they heard a shout.

"Winnie?" came a voice in a loud clipped accent.

"Winnie!" they heard again, shouted even louder.

"Yes," a small voice replied.

"Yes, what?"

"Yes, Mrs Dawingditmus."

"That's better. Go and see who's at the door and if it's the baker tell him we don't want any and I will pay him next week." Even coming from somewhere on the other side of the door the voice was loud and clear.

"Yes, Mrs."

"Yes, Mrs Dawingditmus, won't you ever learn!"

Footsteps could be heard coming to the door and it opened to reveal a short lady in her fifties with a grey face, very thick glasses and short hair that stuck out in all directions. She wore a wrap-around floral apron, crepe stockings and brown shoes with a button strap.

"Morning, what can I do for you? And if you're the baker we don't want any and she'll pay you next week."

"No, we're not the baker, we would like to see Colonel Dawingditmus," Pete said.

Winnie looked vacant and turned, pushing the door nearly shut and walked off. Pete and David put their hands to their ears, straining to hear what was said.

"Mrs Dawingditus?"

"*Ditmus*, you stupid woman… Well?"

"There's someone for the Colonel."

"Well, he's not here, is he, go and tell them."

The footsteps could be heard again and the two stepped back.

97

"He ain't here," said Winnie, and she went to close the door.

"We've come to pick up a pig, we have the money."

Winnie peered at them through her glasses as she considered. She then turned, pushed the door to, and the footsteps could be heard again. The two boys listened at the door.

"Who is it then?"

"It's two chaps come for a pig, they say they've got the money."

"Oh, very well, tell them I'm coming." Winnie made her way back to the door and smiled at the two.

"She says she's comin'. Mrs Ditmus that is," and she smiled again and colour came to her cheeks as steps could be heard approaching.

A tall woman came in view, in her late forties and slim. Her hair was dark and her pretty face was thick with makeup. She wore a tweed jacket and skirt and a tight beige polo neck sweater. She took a cigarette from her mouth as her high-heeled brogues clicked on the stone floor.

"Yes, how can I help?" She made a condescending smirk and stuck her nose in the air. "I'm Julia Dawingditmus."

"We'd like to see the Colonel please as we have come to collect a boar. We have been given the cheque in payment which I have here." Pete took the envelope from his pocket and handed it to her.

She looked critically at the envelope and then

ripped it open. She put the cigarette back in her mouth as she read the invoice and looked at the cheque.

"Winnie, go upstairs and tell Mother to hurry up and get ready. Audrey will be here soon and we don't want to be late." Winnie stared at her. "Go!"

"Yes, Mrs Ditmus," said Winnie, and she trotted off.

"Sorry about that," Julia said, and gave another insincere smile. "The Colonel is not here and I don't think there is anyone else – let me see." She stepped past them and shouted, "Goodson?" at the top of her voice and listened. "No. There is no one there."

Pete pursed his lips and looked at David behind him. "We can't have the pig then?"

"No. Certainly not."

"We've come a long way, and we can see the one we want."

"No! Did you hear what I said? Don't you understand plain English?"

"I'll have the cheque back then," Pete said. "That's right, David?" and he looked round.

"Yeah, that's right," David agreed.

At that moment Winnie came back and stood at the door. Julia turned.

"Well?"

"It's your mother."

"What about her."

"She's stuck in the barf."

"She's what?"

"She's stuck in the barf"

99

The two boys sniggered.

"Well go in and help her out then, you stupid fool."

"I can't do that."

"Why not?"

"She's locked the door."

Julia put her hand to her forehead, took a deep drag of her cigarette and threw it half smoked onto the concrete.

"Heaven help us," she said, and turned to go in.

"Don't go away, you two, we may need help."

Julia ran up the stairs two at a time and along the landing to the bathroom door. She grabbed the handle, turned it and rattled the door hard.

"Mother! Are you in there?"

"Yes, dear."

"Why can't you get out the bath?"

"I don't know, I just can't."

"I can't get in, is the window shut?"

"Yes."

"Wait there." Winnie stood behind Julia, grinning.

"Don't just stand there, stupid, go and get one of those boys, the one who does all the talking, okay?"

"Yes, Mrs Ditmus."

"And, Winnie?"

"Yes, Mrs Ditmus."

"Get him to take his boots and overalls off."

Winnie arrived at the door where the boys looked a little guilty, as they had smoked the rest of Julia's cigarette.

"Now," she said, "Mrs Ditmus wants you, boy, upstairs... and... and you've got to take your boots and overalls off."

"Me?" said Pete.

"Yes you, and you wait 'ere," she said, looking at David. Pete took his boots and overalls off.

"Follow me then," and Winnie led the way upstairs to the bathroom where Julia was waiting.

"Now, boy, what's your name?"

"Peter Dunmore."

"Right, Peter, can you open this door?" Pete tried it and pushed.

"Is it a bolt or is it a key?"

"It's a bolt."

"That's easy, I can just put my shoulder to it."

"Now, Winnie, go down and let Audrey in, I just heard a car."

"Go on then, Peter," she said and pointed at the door.

Pete took one step back and launched himself at it shoulder first and the door burst open. He stood back and let Julia go in.

"I'm so glad to see you, dear, I'm really getting a little cold."

"Serves you right," Julia said as she marched in. The bath was a large cast iron one which stuck out into the room from the wall so she could get round both sides. "Look, how am I going to get you out – I'm all dressed up? I'll get soaked – you are so annoying, you

101

really are." She took off her jacket. "Are you listening, Mother?"

"Yes, dear."

"I'll try and lift you under your arms and you push when I do."

"Yes, dear." Julia went to the end of the bath, put her hands under her mother's arms and pulled.

"Not a chance, how much do you weigh, Mother?"

"Don't be like that, dear, I'm not that heavy."

"Look, look what I've done, I've laddered my stocking, I can't go out looking like this – it's the Flower Club AGM. I can't sit on the platform with a laddered stocking."

"What are we going to do then?" said her mother, as a tear came to her eye.

"I've got this boy here – he looks strong, he will have to get you out."

"What? A man?"

"Yes, a man...well nearly a man."

"Well, if you say so, dear... is he from a good home?"

"God give me strength," Julia shouted, and shook her hands in the air, "Peter, come here."

"What? In there?" He stayed on the landing.

"Yes, in here."

"But she's got no clothes on."

"True. But then people don't usually wear clothes in the bath… Come in here now."

Pete entered gingerly, trying not to look at the bath, his face red with embarrassment.

"Now, Peter, this is Geraldine, my mother – look at her... and tell me how you are going to get her out."

"I can't lift her out unless she helps at the same time. My aunt Mary told me how to do it. If she puts her right hand forward and grabs the side of the bath and then puts her left hand backwards as far as she can on the other side and when I lift under her arms, she must pull with her right and push down with her left."

"Did you hear that, Mother?"

"Yes, dear, but don't shout, it's unbecoming."

"It's unbecoming to get stuck in the bath!"

"Yes, dear."

"Are you ready?"

"Yes, I put my right hand here and my left here and you will lift."

"Yes," and Pete got in position behind her and put his hands under her arms.

"Ah, ha," Geraldine screamed, "That tickles!"

"Mother!" shouted Julia, just as they heard the phone ring.

"Answer that, Winnie."

"Yes, Mrs Ditmus," could be heard from downstairs.

"Shall we try again?"

"Very well," and Pete got in position.

"Are you ready? One, two, three…."

Geraldine trembled with the strain, but with Pete's help as she pulled with one arm and pushed with the other, she rose from the bath with relative ease. As he lifted her, Pete could see tattooed high up on her left arm, seven numbers and a Star of David underneath. She stood there grinning and dripping water, her big bust sagging at the front and her bottom sagging at the back.

"You weren't stuck at all, were you?" said Julia as she put a large towel around her and helped her step out of the bath. "All you wanted was to get that boy up here and you with no clothes on," and she rubbed her dry. "Now, Winnie, come up here and help Mother, I've got to go and see Audrey," and she picked up her jacket and dashed from the room. She opened a cupboard on the landing and grabbed a new pair of stockings then went down the stairs two steps at a time as Winnie was coming up.

"Audrey dear, you will never guess what has just happened, never in a million years. My bloody mother has just got stuck in the bath." She slumped down in one of the armchairs.

"You poor darling, but wasn't the Colonel here to help?"

"No, he bloody wasn't. Winnie said it was him on the phone and he's been stuck in a drift and he will be back in an hour. A lot of use that will be and bloody Winnie's like a light gone out." She sat up and looked at her watch. "Now, Audrey, are we late? Is the demonstrator coming? How long have I got? Just look at me, not at the ladder in my stockings."

Audrey Howells sat bolt upright on a straight-back

chair, with a military style trench coat on and a fox fur round her neck.

"Now, darling, don't panic we have five minutes. It's only four miles, that road is nearly clear and the Jag is all warmed up. I won't put the hat on until we get there, it's a bit big, you know."

"Audrey, do you mind if I change my stockings here, it's like an ice box in our bedroom?"

"No, no, dear, don't mind me," and Julia took her jacket off and wiggled and hitched up her tight skirt until her suspenders appeared.

"Bugger," she exclaimed. "Excuse my French, Audrey, but I've got to change both. The new ones are a different colour," and she kicked off her shoes and ran her hands down her leg to remove the laddered stocking.

"You've got good legs, Julia, you could have been a chorus girl."

"Do you think so?" She kicked a leg in the air, revealing her black pants and corset. "Don't encourage me, Audrey, I'll split my skirt," she giggled. "You can't do much with a bum squeezer on, if you know what I mean."

"If you say so, Julia."

"Now I must concentrate, and not ladder these as I put them on."

"Be careful then."

Audrey lit a cigarette as she waited.

"How did you get your mother out then?"

"Well, there was this boy, Peter, and he did it." Julia was carefully getting her foot into the first stocking. "Where is the boy?" she shouted out the door, "Winnie, where's that boy? I want to see him before he goes."

"I'm here," said Pete, and he walked into the room. On seeing her, he went bright red, put his hand to his mouth and made to leave.

"No don't go, just don't look, alright?"

"I know this boy, Julia, he pushed me when I was stuck recently, he works with Tony. I'm sure I'm right."

"Is that correct, Peter?"

"Yes."

"Well, talk to Audrey while I get straight," and she started to put the second stocking on, the details of which Peter could see in a mirror behind Audrey.

"Now, Peter, where did you go to school?"

"Kimbolton, Mrs Howells."

"And where are you going?"

"London, to read agriculture."

"Are we, my word?" She puffed her cigarette and flicked it against the ashtray. "We sent Tony to the local secondary mod. Russell insisted after he failed the Bedford entrance."

"Was that sensible?" Julia asked. "Now, Audrey, tell me whether the seams are straight," and she turned for Audrey to see.

"Like ramrods, dear," and Julia wriggled again as she pulled her skirt down.

"Now I'm nearly ready. Coat. Hat. Money, you got

it?" and she put on her thick fur coat and carried her hat.

"Now, Peter, my dear, I don't know where we would be without you, so, Trevor – Colonel Dawingditmus – will send you a cheque for ten pounds and, Peter, I hope you will be discreet about what happened, if you know what I mean?"

"Yes, I know."

"I can get your address from Audrey. And, Peter? If you wait about an hour, the Colonel will be back and you can have your pig."

"Very good, Mrs Dawingditmus."

Chapter Ten

The First Rehearsal

David and Pete sat in the kitchen at Winterbourne Manor and ate their sandwiches, while Winnie made them a cup of tea.

"Is the old lady alright?" enquired David.

"She will be," Winnie grunted. "She wasn't really stuck, I bet, she just wanted attention."

"Really?" said Pete.

Winnie looked at the two boys, pushed her bottom lip over her top one and thought for a moment.

"That Mrs Ditmus, she ignores ''er, and if she's not ignoring 'er she's shoutin' at 'er. She shouts all the time. And she's mean – you know? Mean as mean. I really don't know why I put up wiv it."

"What about the Colonel then?" asked David.

Winnie looked into her cup of tea, sniffed and wiped her nose with her fist.

"'E ain't too bad," she sniffed again. "No 'e ain't too bad for a nob, or at least 'e thinks 'e's a nob." She went silent and Pete looked at David.

"When's he coming back then?"

"I don't know, should be about now I 'spect."

At that moment the door from the hall clicked and Geraldine came in.

"Here we are then and here is my hero." She put a hand on Pete's shoulder as he stood, blushing as he did so, "I can't thank you enough, dear boy, can you introduce me," she said, as David copied Pete and stood.

"This is David – he works on the farm." She shook his hand and turned to Winnie.

"You've looked after these boys?"

"Yes, Mrs Wiski."

She took Winnie's hand and patted it before turning to the boys.

"My name is Geraldine Pidlewiski. Quite a handful for Winnie so she calls me Mrs Wiski, quite sweet, don't you think?" and she squeezed Winnie's hand again.

There was the toot of a horn and a squeak of brakes.

"That'll be Colonel Ditmus." Winnie peered out of the window. "Yes it's 'im," and she cleared away the tea cups as he came in.

"Here we are then, sorry! Sorry I was not here for you, boys, you've come for the boar I expect? What!"

"Yes, sir," said Pete.

"Got stuck on a lump of ice in the station car park when I took Louise to the train. Our daughter, you know. And, Geraldine, what are you doing here, I thought you were going to the Flower Club?"

"I was and now I'm not. I will tell you all about it later."

"Very well then, I wait to hear. Now, boys, have you

got the cheque?"

"I gave it to Mrs Dawingditmus, Colonel."

"Well done, well done, me boy – hope she hasn't spent it, what!" he laughed. "Let's go and load you up – it won't take a jiffy, follow me," and he led the way and David followed.

"Peter, before you go," said Geraldine and she drew him to one side. "When you lifted me out of the bath, did you notice something on my arm?"

"Yes, some numbers and a Jewish cross."

"I won't explain now, but I would be grateful if you would be discreet about that as well as the whole event and I will reward you when I can."

"No, no, there's no need. I will be discreet and Mrs Dawingditmus said she is going to get the Colonel to send me a cheque."

She took his hand and squeezed it. "You must go."

They loaded up the boar and started for home. As they got about a mile from the village, they came up behind a girl on a bicycle; it was Rita and she got off to let them pass. David stopped.

"Do you want a tow? We're going to the piggery."

"Yeah, I'm about puffed out and it's bloody cold."

"Hang on to the back of the trailer and we'll pull you along and up the hill, but let go if anything goes wrong or we meet someone."

"Okay," and they started. But they had not gone far when she hit some ice and fell off.

"Look – she's fallen," said David "You ride the bike, Pete, and she can come on here."

They swapped places and were soon back at the piggery entrance where Grafton stood waiting. Rita got down and took the bike from Pete to go the last two hundred yards to The Manor where she lived.

"Pete?"

"Yes, Rita?"

"I 'eard you're doin' a play at the Young Farmers."

"Yes."

"I'm good at drama, or I was at school, I was always the leading lady in school productions."

"But you're not in the Young Farmers, are you?"

"I know, but—"

"I think all the parts are taken."

"Shame, I'm good, you know, but there we go," and she cycled off.

Grafton opened the gate and David drove the tractor through and backed the trailer up to the boar pens.

"Have you got the right one?" he asked David.

"I don't know, do I? This is the one he said, so you tell me." David opened the gates of the trailer and let him out.

"Oh, my goodness," said Grafton, as the boar came down the ramp of the trailer. "He's the one alright. Isn't he magnificent – don't you think, David?"

"If you say so, Grafton, I hope Crucial thinks so. Mary said it's the most we've ever paid for a boar."

"Worth his weight in gold, you see – what do you think, Pete?"

"I'm sure he is, Grafton, and look at his tusks. What are you going to call him?"

"I'll tell you in the morning. You're coming down for weighing, I expect?"

"I expect so, as it's Wednesday. Which reminds me, we have a rehearsal tonight."

"Quiet! Quiet! Let's get started," Trisha shouted, as the cast gathered round at the first rehearsal.

She stamped her foot and slowly everyone got a chair and sat in a circle.

"Where's Penny then, Trisha? She's Queen, ain't she?" said John.

"That's what I have to tell you, I don't know what we are going to do, as she has mumps."

"Bloody hell she hasn't?"

"Yes, she has."

"Never! And we were with her the other day and I haven't had mumps – have you, David?"

"Yes."

"Have you, Pete?"

"No."

"Well," said Trisha.

"Well, what? It's a serious illness for an older gentleman, you know that, I suppose?" and John put his hands in his pockets and thrust them about.

"What do you think you are doing?" said Trisha.

"Just checking – you know what I mean? Well, no, you won't know, will you?"

"Stupid boy," snapped Trisha, as she blushed.

"You better check too, Pete," said John.

"Now! Order! What we will do tonight is that I will read her part as well as mine, I don't think they clash at all."

"And what about Doreen?" said Sue. "She broke her leg playing hockey – so we are two down."

"Her part is small, so I think we can easily replace her, but I don't know about Penny."

"I saw Rita today and she said she was good and would like a part," said Pete.

"But she's not a member," said Trisha.

"And she's so common," said Sue.

"But she's very good," said David. "I was at school with her and she always got the top part in school plays."

"What does everyone think?" asked Trisha.

"I think I should play the Queen," said John.

"You'll be one if you get mumps," said David.

Trisha ignored them both, "I think we should speak to Rita, she would have to join, but we have no one else and the small parts can be done by Judy, she wants to join anyway; I know she's only fifteen, but that doesn't matter."

"Very well then, does everyone agree?" asked Pat, and there was a mumble of approval.

"As long as they join," said John.

"Who's going to see Rita?"

"I will," said David.

"And who's going to see Judy?"

"I will," said Pat.

"So that's all fixed then. I will read the Queen's part tonight and Pat will read the other one if we get that far. Let's get on, it's so cold in here."

The next morning brought no improvement in the weather, but the routine of the farm had adjusted to cope. Everyone had a task to keep all the animals supplied with water. All that were inside a building were alright, but those that were outside, such as the beef, sheep and dry sows, needed attention to the water supply each day. Next to each water trough there was a growing heap of ice, as each morning the ice was smashed and thrown out, and the ball cock was unfrozen.

It was now six weeks since the freeze started and the temperature had not risen above zero degrees Celsius in all that time. When Pete went home at the weekend, the village where he lived had no water as the mains had frozen under the ground. Everyone had opened up the long unused wells for water for washing, and drinking water was carted in milk churns. The snow still lay over all the fields but it cleared from roads in the parts the sun reached.

Tony got into trouble with Joyce and Freddie as he was the last one to leave the lodgings one Saturday and had left the tap in the bathroom dripping. Joyce and Freddie were away on the Saturday night and when they returned, the waste pipe from the basin had frozen from the drain on the outside at ground level, all the way up, and the basin was one large block of ice right up to the dripping tap.

As usual, that morning most of the staff on the farm assembled in the workshop at nine o'clock to have their sandwiches. Some sat on the workbench and others on used spray cans.

"Come on in and shut zee door," shouted Helmit. "Zer is a bloody draught."

"Just a mo, there's Mary just gettin' out 'er car. Look at them legs, come on, David, 'av a look," said Steve, and they could all hear the click of Mary's high heels on the concrete.

"Steve!" shouted Simon. "Shut the bloody door."

"Alright, alright I'm coming," and he banged the door and put his bag on the workbench. He took out a bottle of cold tea and his packet of sandwiches and then proceeded to take his false teeth out. His lips receding into his mouth, which was now nothing more than a little pop hole.

"I don't know how you eat your food with no teeth in, Steve."

Steve's jaw was going up and down at a great rate and he gave a stupid grin. Pete opened his packet and looked at David.

"What you got then?"

"Cheese. You?"

"Pickle."

"Swap?"

"Just one," and they exchanged one sandwich.

"What we all doing after breakfast, Viv? I hope we're not outside in the cold?"

"Well, Simon, Crucial wants his septic tank looking at – the overflow is blocked."

"No, not again – it's always blocking – who's goin' to 'elp me then? I can't do that on me own?"

"Sean can help. Winston – he wants you in the mixing shed."

"How can he do that, he can't read, can he?"

"Yes I can," protested Winston, crestfallen.

"Pete and Steve, you go down to the pigs – it's weigh day."

All fattening pigs were weighed every week to see how much weight they had gained on each of the rations that had been formulated.

"Tony – you stop here and help Helmit," and Viv looked round. "Is that everyone?"

"It is, except you," said Simon.

"I'm going down to the pigs, to look at the new boar."

"Did you hear what happened to Pete when they went to fetch it?" said Tony.

"No, go on," said Viv.

"I rang my mother last night and she was there and she said that Pete had to get an old lady out the bath,

116

who had got stuck. Is that right, Pete?"

Pete said nothing, but blushed crimson and continued to eat his sandwich.

"Is that right then?" Simon grinned and looked at Pete. "I bet you would rather it had been Mary," and he laughed along with all the others.

"Was she very heavy, Pete? Could you lift 'er? When my mother got stuck in the bath, I had to get Scout to come and 'elp get 'er out."

"I hope you kept your eyes shut, Pete. Look, he's gone all red – he must have opened them. Did you have a good look, Pete?" Sean joined in.

"He's not going to say nothing. Quite right, you keep your mouth shut," said Viv. "Don't let these silly buggers stir you up." Pete looked uneasy and turned to Steve.

"Are you done? Shall we go?"

"Just a minute, boy, just a minute. I ain't finished me drink," and he sucked at his bottle of cold tea.

"Pete, did I tell you about Scout?"

"Yes, Steve."

"About the marra?"

"Yes, Steve."

"Well, it were like this. Scout grew a marra for the flower show and 'e brought it round our 'ouse and it were so big it took 'im and another bloke to carry it and when it went past the window it were so big I thought it were—"

"A Zeppelin?" said Pete.

117

"Yes, a Zeppelin," said Steve, and he got his false teeth from his bag and put them in again.

"There's a load of food to go down the pigs, Pete, so take that when you go and, Steve – you can help," said Viv.

"I can't lift them bags you know, I'm too old for them."

"You can drag them to the back of the trailer so don't complain."

When they got to the pigs, Grafton was feeding and admiring his new boar as Pete backed the trailer up to the fattening shed.

"What you going to call it, Grafton?" Pete asked.

Grafton took his pipe from his pocket and a pouch from the other pocket and started filling it with tobacco.

"I've been thinking about that overnight."

Steve had got himself off the trailer of bags and picked his way across the icy yard.

"Is this the one?" he said, as his mouth opened, but his teeth did not. He pulled his cap down and pulled at the string that went round his waist holding his long coat together. "I know what I'd call it."

"What's that then, Steve?" asked Grafton.

"I'd call it Zeppelin," and Pete and Grafton burst out laughing.

"Don't tell me, Steve, it's the story about Scout and the marrow." Steve grinned and looked coy as his eyes did a circuit of their sockets.

"You think I'm stupid, don't you?" he said to Grafton, who had found a box of matches and attempted to light his pipe, drawing the flame down into the bowl.

"I don't *think* you're stupid, you *are* stupid." Steve laughed again, sucked his cheeks in and rounded his mouth. "Why do you want him to be called Zeppelin – that's German?"

"Because 'e's so long – look at 'im," and Steve pointed. "Any road, Helmit's German ain't he, and Rita, she's part American an', Pete, I bet you've got some on your farm?"

"Yes, we've got two Italians and one Latvian."

"There we go then; every farm's got 'em."

"What's that got to do with our pig, he's a Large White and that's British?"

"Pete, where's Latvia?" said Steve.

"I don't know."

"You should know, you've bin to a posh school."

"So did Grafton."

"Where's Latvia, Grafton?"

"It's a Baltic state and now part of Russia. And it's time we did something, so unload the meal and then we'll get on with the weighing."

Steve got onto the trailer and dragged the bags to the back so Pete could carry them into the fattening shed and stack them up, being very careful not to make a noise so the pigs did not start squealing for food.

That evening was a rehearsal for the play and the cast assembled in a classroom at the school again.

"It's bloody cold in here," moaned John.

"Well, let's start. We'll have one more read through and next time we'll set out the stage," and Trisha ran her finger down the list of the cast. "We're not all here, are we?"

"David's gone to fetch Rita, and Tony went home, but will be here soon."

"Thank you, Pete."

At that moment Rita and David arrived. Everyone looked up as Rita's high heels clicked on the wooden floor. She looked round and then took her thick coat off while she chewed a large piece of gum, which she rolled around her teeth. She handed her coat to David and patted her dyed blonde hair.

"Hello – my name's Rita."

Trisha stared at her, "Pleased to meet you," she said in a dismissive tone. Rita wore a tight skirt and a V-necked sweater, showing her cleavage. She had a thick black patent leather belt tight round her waist and she lightly brushed her skirt for imaginary hairs. There was silence and she found a chair and sat down, crossing her legs and pulling on her skirt which was well above her knees. Trisha handed her a copy of the play and then cleared her throat.

"We have another new actress – Judy," and Trisha smiled in her direction as Judy blushed.

The door banged and Tony came in.

"Sorry, sorry. My mother, you know, she shouts and one has to jump."

An hour and a half later, the rehearsal was over and everyone was in the pub.

"She shouldn't be in here," said John, pointing at Judy. "She's only fifteen."

"Shut up, you great oaf, she's okay if she doesn't drink alcohol and anyway, she looks a lot older than fifteen," said David.

John looked away and then moved over to where Rita sat.

"Now, my dear, has anyone got you a drink, and if not, what would you like?" John smiled.

Rita looked at him with a blank expression and chewed her gum then pushed it forward with her tongue and waited for a moment or two.

"My name ain't my dear, it's Rita, and if you insist I will have a Babycham and ice," she said, staring intently at him as he stepped back.

"They don't have ice, but I can go and get some if you like – there's plenty outside."

She rolled her eyes up and said nothing as John stared at her cleavage.

"Oi, Pete," Rita called, "Come and sit here," and she nodded to the chair next to her. As he sat she said, "Is that bloke thick or something?"

"No, he's alright."

"I think all farmers are thick."

"Oh, do you."

"I didn't mean you, Pete, I thought he were going to fall over looking at my tits."

Pete went red and glanced at Rita, then looked at the ceiling.

"You're doing the same," and she grabbed his knee as he tried to look anywhere but at her. "Pete, you've gone red – you always go red. Dad told us about you getting an old lady out the bath. I bet you went red then – what with 'er with no clothes on – did you, Pete?" She grabbed his knee again as John came with the drinks.

"Come on, Pete, out of there – that's my seat," and he put the drinks down, sat and put his hand on Rita's knee. She then put her hand on his, and lifted it onto the table.

"Never know where it's been," and she grimaced at John.

"Pete, can I have a word?" It was Tony, who was pushing his way through the crowded bar. "It's my mother again. Pete, do you have a DJ?" he asked in an embarrassed tone.

"Yes."

"Great, now it's like this," and he took a swig of his beer. "My mother always organises a party for the Hunt Ball and invites the Dawingditmuses, you know them, that's where you fetched the boar from. Well, they have a daughter who has no partner and Mother says I am to ask you. Can you dance, Pete?"

"Yes. Well, sort of. I went to classes, but that

doesn't mean much."

"Don't worry, you'll be fine and you went to public school."

"No, I didn't, my school was a Direct Grant Grammar and there were lots of scholarship boys."

"Don't worry, not important, I only went to the local Secondary Mod."

"When is this ball?"

"Saturday."

"But my DJ is thirty miles away and I only have a push bike."

"Oh well, we must think of something, do you want to come?"

"Maybe, what's this girl like?"

"Mother says she's very nice."

"And…?"

"Well, she wears glasses."

"What's her name?"

"Louise."

"Is she pretty?"

"Not sure, but she's going to university. London, I think."

"Who are you going with then?"

"Mother says I have to take Nancy."

"Oh."

"Well?"

"Well, what?"

"Will you come?"

"Yes, but as long as I can get my DJ."

"Great. I'll go and phone Mother, she likes you, Pete." And Tony downed his beer and went out to the phone box.

Chapter Eleven

Cleaning Eggs

"Pete? Penny for them?"

Pete looked blankly at Joyce.

"What?" He came round from being deep in thought.

"Penny for them? You're away with the fairies," and she smiled at him.

"Oh, it's nothing. Just trying to sort something out."

"Like what?"

"I was just trying to work out how to get my DJ from home."

"Your what?"

"My DJ – dinner jacket, I mean."

"Oh, my word, we are going posh. DJ. Whatever will happen next? And what do you need a DJ for, may I ask, or is it a secret?"

"No, no, it's just that I have been asked to a dance."

"Come on then, Pete, tell me what dance and where and who. Come on, I never go to dances," she said, and ruffled his hair.

"It's the Hunt Ball and Tony's mother has asked me to go with the daughter of a friend of theirs who has no partner and that's all I know. Except that it's on Saturday."

"That's going to cost you a pretty penny, Pete."

His eyes narrowed with concern. "I hadn't thought about that. They will pay, I think, I hope."

"I wish someone would ask me to a dance like that. The Hunt Ball, eh? I bet it's posh. All the nobs will go to that."

"Doesn't Freddie take you dancing?"

"Pull the other one, he can't dance to save his life. Useless, I would call him."

"I bet PC Bell can dance," Pete grinned, as Joyce's lips pressed tight together and she scowled.

"Don't you mention his name, Peter Dunmore, or I'll knock your block off. Anyway, you're not going if you can't get your DJ, are you?"

"You have a point," and he took some change from his pocket and counted it out slowly. "I'm going to ring my mother and see if she will get it to Bedford station one evening and then I will go on the train and meet her."

"Do you think she will, I thought you said they had no water where your mum lives?"

"Yes, I mean no, they have no water at the moment. The mains are frozen underground, but she may do – I can only ask."

Two days later, he cycled to Harlington station and took the train at 18:10 to Bedford where he waited for his mother in the freezing cold. After fifteen minutes, she arrived and took a small suitcase from the car.

"Here we are, boy, it's all there and the shirt, cufflinks and tie. I don't know whether it's clean. I had no time to check," and she passed him the case. "Now, let me have a look at your hands. I've put some cream in the case for them."

He held them out and showed her that all his fingers had split across the ends, his thumbs as well.

"What's done that then?" she demanded.

"Cleaning eggs."

"What?"

He explained that since they were short-staffed on the poultry, he and Steve had been set cleaning eggs for the hatchery. To keep the eggs in best condition they had to do this with wire wool in the egg store, which had no heating or draught prevention, and after two or three days his fingers split.

"Don't you complain, boy? You ought to go on strike – do you want your father to ring up the manager?"

"No, no, don't do that – it must thaw soon, don't you think?"

"I suppose it must, but make sure you use the cream – it will sort them out."

He got the next train south but when he got to Harlington his bike was missing and he had to walk the two and a half miles to Toddington. When he arrived, he found his bicycle in the garage. He went into the house and found Joyce sitting in the kitchen and voices coming from the sitting room.

"It's you then," she said, looking up at Pete. "You've got it?" and she nodded at the suitcase.

"Yes, but where is that sod Tony? He took my bike from the station and I've had to walk. I'll kill him."

"He's gone up the pub."

"I'll kill him," Pete repeated to himself.

"You won't be going to the Hunt Ball then."

"What do you mean?" Pete snapped.

"Ain't it Tony's mum who's paying for your ticket?"

Pete thought for a moment. "What if she is? It's no reason for him to pinch my bike," and he banged his fist down on the table. Taking a breath he changed tack. "Who's in the sitting room with Freddie then?"

"You guess, it's your favourite policeman, PC Bell. He's been here for an hour and they've just got the whisky out so he'll be here another hour," she scowled.

She stood, took her apron off and hung it on the door then went to the small mirror on the cupboard door and looked at her face, turning her head from side to side and pushing up her hair with the palm of her hand. Then she turned away and brushed down her blouse and skirt quickly.

"Are you going to show me then?"

"Show you what?"

"Your DJ."

"I suppose so," and he put the suitcase on the table and clicked it open.

Joyce peered in and lifted out the shirt. "This needs a wash, and an iron."

128

"Yes, Mother said she had no time to do it."

"And look at this jacket, it's full of moth holes." She held it up by the shoulders and turned it round.

"It is a bit old, it was my uncle's."

"Don't he want it then?"

"Not really. He's dead. Killed in the war."

"Look here, there's a label – *Harry Hills, Bedford* – I know that shop. And there's a date – 1938. It's twenty-five years old, no wonder there's moth holes."

"Mother puts black shoe polish on them, no one will notice."

"Peter Dunmore! Come on, give it all to me and I will sort it out and you can go up the pub and give Tony a rocket," and she folded everything and put it in a pile on top of the washing machine.

At the pub, Pete found Tony deep in conversation with Henry Babage, the journalist from the *Luton Times*.

"Ah, Pete, you remember this chap? Henry – this is Pete," and Pete nodded and turned to Tony.

"What about my bike then?"

"Your bike, yes your bike." He fumbled for his cigarettes. "Yes, well I found it down at the station and I thought I ought to ride it back for you."

"I can see that, but what about me?" Pete stared fiercely at Tony.

"Want a fag?" Tony offered the packet to Pete, who took one.

Henry took a silver lighter from his waistcoat pocket.

"Light?" He flicked the lighter and offered to light Pete's cigarette.

"Gas, you know," and he looked at the lighter in his hand before he put it back in his pocket "Much better than the old petrol – they stink in your pocket. Awful smell."

"Well?" said Pete, looking Tony.

"Yes," said Tony.

"I had to walk all the way back from the bloody station in the freezing cold. Two and a half miles that is – do you know that, Tony?"

There was silence for a few moments.

"Drink, Pete? Brown ale isn't it... Brown ale, Desperate."

The drink came and Pete raised his glass.

"Cheers, Tony." He took a stool and sat down with the other two.

"You didn't get stuck this time then?" Pete looked at Henry.

"No, fortunately," he said, and took a sip from a pint of beer and then another sip from a glass of whisky by its side.

"John pulled you out okay the last time?"

"Yes, and handsomely he got paid for it as well. Mind you," he whispered, "Thick as two short planks," and he took two more sips and put his finger to his mouth again, "like most of the farmers I know."

"Oh, you're sure of that, are you?"

"Certain. Sure. All the sharp ones in the family leave the land, leaving the thick ones to carry on. Seen it times, seen it times."

"So how do you know Tony?"

"School."

"But Tony went to the Secondary Mod."

"I went to Bedford, with his brothers."

"Okay."

"Where did you go?"

"Kimbolton."

"Oh God," and Henry got out his cigarettes in a silver monogrammed case and offered them around.

"Pete, Henry's going to the Hunt Ball."

"So?"

"So, we'll see him there, won't we, Henry?"

"If you say so, Tony. With all those farmers too, half of them will be farmers I bet. What a bloody bore."

"Why are you going if you think it's a bore?" asked Pete.

"Because, dear boy, I am employed to go. I write for the *Bedfordshire Life* sometimes and they want a piece on the Hunt Ball, so I go along with a photographer and he takes pictures of Lord and Lady this and that and the Honourable Miss etc etc and I write the bit underneath. Get the picture – if you will forgive the pun?" He stubbed his cigarette out and looked at his watch. "Time for one more, landlord, if you please. Fill them up again, Tony, and sorry I've forgotten…" and he looked enquiringly at Pete.

"Pete – yes, thank you, a brown ale."

"That's an old lady's drink."

"So, if you don't like reporting on the Hunt Ball, what *do* you like?" Pete asked, ignoring the put-down.

"A juicy murder, bank robbery, plane crash… You know, awful things – they're the best, that's what interests people."

"You'll have to come and report on our play – that's got a murder in it." Tony smiled and then thought better of what he had said.

"Play? Who's doing a play?"

"The Young Farmers."

"Whatever will happen next? The Young Farmers producing a play? Half of them can't read and write and the other half can't act, I'm sure of that," and he banged his beer mug on the bar. "Landlord! Can we have some service here?"

By now the long freeze had gone on for nearly two months and the fields were still covered in snow. The soil was frozen to a depth of several feet so no work on the land was possible. The potato store was left unopened in the hope that the frost would not get into them under the covering of straw bales. The beef cows still spent most of the time outside and calves were born in the field in the freezing temperatures with no apparent ill effects. On sunny days the surface of the snow melted and then froze again at night, making it possible to walk over even the deepest drifts which only gave way when jumped on. Where hedge cutting was done by hand it was at the level of the snow, not at six inches above ground as usual.

The cleaning of eggs was still the worst job as it remained freezing in the egg store. It was left to Steve and Pete to do this when the staff on the poultry section couldn't cope.

"Come on, Steve, we'd better go and make a start," Pete said, as they finished their sandwiches.

Steve faced Pete but looked sideways, making himself look completely stupid as he still had his teeth out and his lips had receded into the little pop hole of his mouth. He burst out laughing and put his teeth back in as they made their way across the yard to the egg store.

"Look at 'er, boy – Mary's coming, she must be late, cor, look at her, boy, look at 'er." Pete smiled at Mary and waved but Steve pretended not to look.

"Wimin will draw you further than gunpowder will blow you." Steve looked at Pete and nodded.

"Who said that, Steve? Was it Scout?" Steve looked vacant and munched his jaw up and down and then he said slowly again.

"Wimin will draw you further than gunpowder will blow you...did you know that, Pete?" and he started munching again. "It were me that said that," he laughed.

When they got to the store, the eggs to be cleaned

had been stacked up in trays on the bench with a roll of wire wool by the side. No sooner had they started than Viv came in.

"Come on, Pete, we need you. There's a load of soya coming and you will have to help unload it."

"What about Simon?"

"Bad back."

"And Winston?"

"Bad back."

"Skivers," said Steve.

"There's no one else, so you will have to come."

"Who's goin' to 'elp me then?" Steve complained, but no one answered.

The soya was stored in twelve-stone sacks on the first floor of the feed shed and arrived up on the elevator through a window from the lorry parked at ground level. The sacks were then lifted onto the backs of Viv and Pete and carried across the building and stacked against the wall. The sacks came up the elevator tied end first, and the trick was to grab the tied end and push up facing the sack and then as it went up, turn and it would fall across the shoulders. Twelve stone was quite easy to manage, but bigger railway sacks could contain up to twenty stone of beans.

When the load was empty the elevator was pushed away and the window shut.

"Pete, before you go, fill up the hopper with soya and turn on the hammer mill. If you come back in an hour, you can fill the hopper again."

The hopper was in the corner and would hold about a tonne and was directly above the hammer mill which ground the grain, which was blown into one of four holding bins, ready for mixing up the rations for the animals. When the hopper was full, which did not take long, Pete went back to join Steve.

"Where you bin then?" he demanded and pulled his cap down and tied the string round his waist once again.

"You know where I've been."

"You called in to see Mary, I know," and he tapped his nose. "Any excuse will do an' you walk straight past her door. I notice what goes on. I 'spect you invited her out this even', eh?" He winked at Pete.

"We've got a rehearsal this evening."

Steve didn't answer, but continued to slowly rub an egg with wire wool.

"Are you coming to the play, Steve?"

Again, Steve did not reply but after a few minutes he burst out laughing. "Coming to the play?" he laughed again.

"Well?" said Pete. "Are you coming?"

"I go to bed at eight o'clock so I can't come. I watch *Coronation Street* an' go to bed." He held an egg up and turned it round.

"You know, Pete, if they put more litter in these hen houses, the eggs would be a lot cleaner. What do you think?"

"I'm sure you're right, Steve. How many trays are there left?"

"Seven. Pete?"

"Yes, Steve."

"I'm just thought you should take Mary to the 'unt Ball. What d'you say to that idea then? She's got a car, so what about it, Pete?" He grinned and his eyes went left then right, making him look completely stupid.

"How did you know about the Hunt Ball?"

"Scout, he goes 'untin' you know. He follows on his bike. Yer, he knew all about it. You didn't say nuthin' about Mary, Pete."

"There's nothing to say."

"You din't ask her then?"

"No, I didn't."

"Why?"

"I'm going with someone else."

Steve dropped the egg he was cleaning.

Chapter Twelve

A Director is Appointed

"Quiet, everyone." Trisha looked over the assembled cast. "Who's not here?"

"Tony. That's all I think," said Pat.

"Well, folks, I don't know whether we're going to be able to continue rehearsing here as the boiler has broken. It looks as though they're going to close the school until it is mended so we're looking for somewhere else. Does anyone have any ideas?"

"What about the fattening house at The Manor; it's lovely and warm in there an' there's an audience – two hundred and fifty pigs." John looked round the faces as they all groaned. Then he had another go. "There's a room at the back of the Sow and Pigs, we could use that. And it's in a pub. Couldn't be better."

"There's only a fire to heat it though and a room charge, we couldn't afford it," said Pat.

"What about our front room, it's huge? I could ask Mum and Dad. I'm sure they wouldn't mind," said Gill.

"Are you sure?" said Trisha.

"If we all go down there now, they can hardly refuse, come on, let's give it a try."

They quickly left the classroom and made their way

to "Chez Nous" in Mander Close, where Gill's parents immediately agreed to host the rehearsal. The front room was large, and when the furniture was moved to the sides there was enough room for a stage.

"Right, let's start," shouted Trisha, over the top of everyone talking, "and can I thank Mr and Mrs Cotton for so kindly letting us use their front room."

"It's a pleasure, my dear, a real pleasure and call me George and this is Thelma."

"Thank you, George and Thelma."

"Can we watch then? I don't want to miss anything." George sat in one of the armchairs pushed against the wall, clutching a large glass of whisky.

"Who's the director?" he asked.

Trisha looked confused. "We hadn't thought of having one. I thought we could manage without."

"What's the director do?" John asked.

"He tells you what to do, where to stand, how to speak and all that."

"Oh. Anyone have any suggestions?"

"My brother could do it," came a quiet voice from the back of the room.

"Who said that?"

"I did," said Judy. "My brother's an actor. He's been on the stage in London."

"I've seen him," said Alexandra. "He was brilliant."

"He's out of work at the moment. I'm sure he'd do it."

"And he wouldn't charge?"

"No, he wouldn't."

"Sounds like he's the man for the job," said George. "What's his name?"

"He calls himself Crispin Vandyke."

"What?" John looked incredulous.

"Crispin Vandyke – that's his stage name, but he was born on the farm like me, so he knows what to expect."

It was all agreed that he was to be asked.

"Let's go, let's go," said Alexandra, once the rehearsal had finished. "Does anyone want a lift?"

"Can you go up Castle Road?" enquired Pete.

"No trouble. Anyone else? No? Right, onward we go."

Alexandra had her father's big Vauxhall again. The gears were on the steering column and she always had trouble finding reverse and ground it into gear and then tried the clutch several times before she found it. In the front was one large bench seat and they had to wait for the window to defrost.

"Shall I get out and scrape it?" Pete offered.

"No, don't worry. It won't take long and there's nothing to scrape with."

She opened and shut the glove compartment, which only contained hand cream.

"Pete. A question?"

"Yes, Alexandra, I'm all ears."

"Are you going to the Hunt Ball?"

"Yes."

"Thought so."

"That means you're going?"

"Yes, but I didn't want to ask you when all the others were about, makes it look a bit...you know what I mean?"

"Snobbish?"

"Yes, but Tony is going, isn't he?"

"Yes, and that weird reporter. What's his name? Henry something."

"Yes, he's an old public school twit. He went to Bedford, like my brother. Got to go to the right school, you know. Where did you go, Pete?"

"Kimbolton."

"Oh dear, not a proper one like mine."

"Where did you go then?"

"It was a farm school, my father didn't think I was good for anything else, so we ran the farm along with lessons."

The screen had now cleared and she put the car into reverse and tooted the horn. The wheels spun on the ice as she revved the engine and it suddenly jumped backwards as the tyres gripped the gravel on the drive. She stood hard on the brake just before she ran into David's van.

"That was close," she said, as she looked round to see what she had nearly hit and burst into peals of laughter.

"Forwards now." She fiddled with the switches,

until she found the lights. "That's better, now I can see where we're going."

She edged the big car out of the gate and turned up the hill towards the village. She stopped at the junction and looked each way, but as she tried to move out and turn right, the car spun round as she put her foot on the accelerator, turning the steering wheel from side to side as the car slid sideways and came to rest with a bump against the curb on the opposite side of the road. There was a loud clatter as her hub cap fell off. Alexandra burst out laughing and banged the steering wheel with the palms of her hands, tooting the horn.

"This is bloody good fun, don't you think, Pete?"

"Yes, but wait while I find your hub cap." He jumped out and fell over on the icy pavement.

"Have you found it?"

"Yes and I'm about to put it on so don't move."

Alexandra waited, occasionally putting her foot on the accelerator and revving the engine. Lights appeared behind them as David drove up with Rita. She wound down the passenger window of the van.

"D'you need any 'elp?"

"No, we're fine, just lost a hub cap. You didn't slide as much as I did," replied Alexandra.

"That's because we've got John in the back for extra weight," said David, and John poked his head out from behind Rita.

"What we need is you in the back, Alexandra, for a bit of extra weight."

"Shut up you, cheeky sod, I'll come and show you what a bit of extra weight can do if you're not careful," and she stuck her tongue out at him.

"Come on, David, let's see yer do a bit of real skidding." Rita wound the window up as they pulled off down the road.

Under the trees where the sun didn't reach there was still ice, and David got to about twenty-five miles per hour and then put his foot on the clutch, pulled the handbrake hard and the van spun round until it was facing Alexandra and Pete. David drew level. "Go on, you have a go." Alexandra looked at Pete and laughed.

"Shall I?"

"No!"

"How did he do that?"

"With the handbrake."

"So why can't I?" She looked at Pete.

"You can't alright, this isn't your car, is it?"

"I suppose not, but you'll have to teach me, David?" and they waved and drove off.

When Pete got in, Joyce was still up ironing. "Just the man I want to see."

He sat at the kitchen table.

"Look, Pete." She held up his dress shirt and put it on a hanger. "And here's the rest of it," She pointed to the dinner jacket hanging from the door handle. "Now, I want you to put it all on so I can see there's nothing wrong."

142

"Do I have to? It's very late and it's cold up in the bedroom."

"You can change down here, there's a bit of the fire left."

"I'm sure it will be fine, Joyce, but look, there's no braces; the trousers won't stay up without braces."

"Just do what I say and I will go and get a pair of Freddie's braces. He won't mind, go on, get on with it before I lose my temper."

Pete had put on the shirt and the trousers before Joyce returned.

"Here we are," and she buttoned up the braces and adjusted the tension.

"Is that alright – do you want them any higher? Might do you a mischief," she laughed. "You've gone red, Peter Dunmore. Don't worry you're safe with me. Put this on." She handed him the cummerbund.

"Now where's the tie? Tie, Pete?"

"In the jacket pocket usually," and she found it.

"Here we go. Just stand still while I do it." She made him face her then turned up his collar and tied the tie and turned the collar back down again.

"Now, Pete, be careful of the jacket because I did what you said your mother did and put black boot polish on the moth holes."

Once he had the jacket on, she stood and looked for more moth holes.

"Turn round then. Yes, there's another one." She dabbed it with black polish on a cloth and then stood back.

"Very smart." She put her hands on his shoulders, pulled him to her and gave him a kiss. "Ask me to dance then."

"What? Not in here?"

"Yes, we can push the table back." She gave the table a shove to the side.

"What about Freddie?"

"Don't worry about him, he's dead to the world already," and she looked at Pete. "Well?"

"Well, what?"

"Dance, you moron, you can dance, can't you? You said your mother sent you to classes?"

"Yes, but—"

"No buts, get on with it."

"There's no music."

"I'll hum, it's a waltz," and she put one hand on his shoulder and grabbed his hand with the other. "Alright?"

"Okay."

"Forward – side – together – remember what you were taught."

"Yes," she said as Pete started to sashay round the small kitchen.

"And what did your teacher tell you to do?"

"Hold her closer."

"Go on then." Pete did as instructed, as Joyce

hummed the tune.

"Stop!" Joyce pushed Pete away. "Look at me, I've still got my pinny on, can't dance in a pinny," and she undid it and grabbed him again.

"Closer!" she demanded, and Pete could feel her small bust against his chest.

"You ain't a very good dancer, Pete."

"It's not like the real thing, is it?"

"No, but you could try a bit harder."

"What if Freddie comes in?"

"Him? Never mind about him." She stood back and looked at Pete at arm's length.

"We're not getting anywhere are we, so take it all off before you mess it up," she said as she took the jacket from him as he shrugged it off. "Who are you going with?"

"Tony's mum and dad."

"No, not them, didn't you say that you had a partner or something?"

Pete coughed and looked awkward.

"Go on then tell me, it's a blind date, isn't it?" She grabbed his waist and tickled him. "Go on then."

Pete's skin flushed. "I'm told that I have to escort someone called Louise and she's the daughter of the people we got the boar from the other day and that's all I know."

"What's she like then?" Joyce pressed on.

"I don't know. I've never met her."

"And that's all you know?"

"Tony said she had glasses and she's going to London University."

"You're going there, ain't you?"

"Yes, but it won't be the same place, I'm sure."

"Why?"

"I'm only doing agriculture. I'm sure she's not doing that."

"Agriculture. I suppose that's the posh name for farming." Joyce winked at Peter, but he said nothing.

"So where is this Hunt Ball going to be held?" she asked.

"I think it's Melchbourne Park."

"That's miles away. Nearly back where you live, ain't it?"

"I suppose it is."

Chapter Thirteen

The Hunt Ball

There was a toot as Pete sat on a seat on the village green. It was just before seven in the evening and the frost sparkled on the heaps of snow pushed up onto the green. The toot came from a Thames van which skidded to a halt then reversed to where Pete was sitting.

"What you doing sitting there then?" David demanded as he wound his window down.

"I'm waiting for Tony."

"Oh, what you got on then? You look a bit posh, don't you think, John?" he addressed his passenger.

"He's got a dickie-bow on, David, you look – that's what he's got on under that scarf."

"Well, I never," said David, "a dog's dinner I'd call him. Where you going then?"

"Just out for the evening with Tony and his parents," said Peter defensively.

"I know, David. I know where the bugger's going, can't you guess? Come on, work it out," and John clapped his hands.

"I've got it, I've got it!" They looked at one another and shouted together.

"The Hunt Ball!" They burst out laughing.

"That's right, ain't it, Pete, we've got it haven't we?"
Pete looked sheepish.

"Yes," he answered, just as there was another toot.

It was Tony's father, Russell Howells, who had just
driven up in his Jaguar with Audrey, his wife, and
Tony and Nancy in the back. Tony wound the window
down.

"Come on, Pete, we're late as usual. Hello, David,
John." Tony nodded at them.

"Have a good time," David said, as Pete got in the
back, pushing Nancy into the middle.

"Mind my dress, you stupid boy," she squealed, as
Pete got in, "And what's that smell?" David and John
laughed.

"Well, Dunmore, that's right, isn't it? You are
Dunmore?" As Russell drove away he looked in the
mirror at Pete in the back.

"Yes, sir," said Pete.

"You well then?"

"Yes, sir."

"You were Bedford, were you?"

"No, sir, I was Kimbolton."

"Oh."

"Did you get a scholarship then?"

"No, sir."

"Tony didn't get one either, did you, boy?"

"No, Dad."

"Thick as two short planks, eh?"

"Mr Howells, please!" said Audrey. "What a thing

148

to say, he is your son you know."

"Hmm." A silence followed.

"We should have sent him to Rushmore, I suppose."

Silence fell again as all those in the back of the car looked straight ahead.

Forty minutes later they arrived at Melchbourne Park and drove up to the big house. Most of the snow had now gone, but it remained a frosty night as they went gingerly up the steps to the entrance. As they entered the band could be heard playing in the background. Coats and hats were taken away and they walked into the ballroom where a toast-master waited to announce them.

"Howells," Russell barked, then he turned to indicate to Tony first, "he's Howells and Nancy is Miss Finch and he's... what's his name?"

"Dunmore," said Pete.

"He's Dunmore."

The room was enormous, with a stage at one end and tables around the outside of the dance floor. Huge portraits hung on the walls. Pete could see Henry Babage, who was catching people for group photographs as they walked in. Henry smiled at Audrey.

"Shall we?" he said and smiled again.

"Oh, do we have to? Not now, find us later," she said as she spied someone across the room and went off.

"You made it then," Henry addressed Tony, "and who is this you have with you?"

"Oh, this is Nancy." Henry grabbed her hand and pecked it.

"Photo?"

"Why not," said Tony, and he stood next to Nancy.

"Put your arm round her," Henry demanded. "Make her look a bit special."

Nancy smiled as Tony coyly put his arm round her waist as the photographer clicked, and then they crossed the room after Audrey.

"You're here too then." Henry looked at Pete. "Can't take one of you on your own so we'll wait," and he took out a packet of cigarettes and offered one to Pete. "Been here before?"

"Yes, I came to a fête here last year."

"You live nearby?"

"Yes, just up the road."

"You'll know a lot of this hunting lot then?"

"No, I don't go hunting."

Henry turned to Pete and put his hand to his mouth.

"'The unspeakable in pursuit of the uneatable' old Oscar Wilde said." He stood back and grinned. "But don't tell anyone I said that," and he went off to deal with the next couple.

Audrey had found her way to the table where the Dawingditmuses were already seated.

"Julia darling!" said Audrey. "You made it! And here we are and I've got this boy – what's his name –

to partner Louise. Well, he's here somewhere." And she looked round.

"Tony? Go and fetch what's his name – look he's over there – talking to Henry," and she gave him a little push.

Louise sat at the other end of the table with her grandmother, Geraldine.

Tony returned with Pete two moments later.

"Come on – Peter, isn't it? My head's like a sieve when it comes to names. Come and let me introduce you." Audrey took his hand and dragged him towards the other end of the table.

Meanwhile, knowing what was coming, Louise looked sideways and then turned to her grandmother.

"Granny, is this the boy with Audrey?"

"Yes, dear, that's him."

"Do you know him then?"

"Yes, dear."

"You didn't tell me what he's like. Do I have to? It's like a cattle market with people looking you up and down, I hate it, I really hate it."

"I know, dear, but it can't be as bad as all that."

"It can." She pursed her lips and clenched her fists in her lap.

"Louise dear, how lovely to see you and you as well, Geraldine," they heard as Audrey pulled Peter out from behind her.

"Can I introduce Peter. Peter…" and she paused.

"Dunmore, Mrs Howells."

"Yes, Peter Dunmore. This is Louise."

Louise grimaced and then forced an insincere smile as Peter held his hand out at the same time as he spotted Geraldine. His mouth fell open and he blinked as a red flush spread across his cheeks.

"And I think you know Geraldine already? Peter? You look as though you've seen a ghost, boy. Say something then."

"Yes, Mrs Howells. Hello, Louise and Mrs..." and his voice faded.

"Audrey, let the boy sit down and tell us about himself." Geraldine winked.

"What a good idea."

Peter sat and Louise looked from Peter to her grandmother and then back to Peter again.

"You already know each other?" Louise looked from one to the other again. "Granny?"

"Yes, dear."

"You know Peter?"

"Yes."

"Tell me how, or Peter, you tell me—"

"Well, you know that I got stuck in the bath about two weeks ago, your mother told you, I'm sure?"

"Yes, what about it?"

"Well, Peter was the one who got me out."

Louise shrieked and put her hands over her face in dismay. "How awful! I don't know what to do or say..." She looked at Geraldine again. "Tell me it's not true, Granny, tell me it's not, it's so embarrassing."

"Darling, just calm down a moment."

"Calm down?"

"Yes, dear, calm down. I was stuck. Your mother couldn't lift me but with the help of Peter she could, so that's all. Peter is very discreet, aren't you, Peter?"

"Yes." Pete tried not to look at either of them.

"You can forget about it, Louise. Why don't you go and have a dance?"

"Dance? Do I have to?"

"That is the general idea at a Hunt Ball, my dear."

Louise took her glasses off and polished them with a small hankie, then put them on again and sat tight-lipped. Geraldine turned her attention to Peter.

"Now, Peter, tell us about yourself. I know you're working on a farm."

"Yes, I am working on the same farm as Tony for a year, before I go to university."

"And where are you going to university?"

"London."

Louise looked surprised and then frowned. "Which college?" she asked quickly.

"Wye," Peter answered, and silence fell between them for a few moments.

"You're going to London in the autumn too, aren't you, my dear?"

"Yes, Granny."

"And which college, dear?"

"Royal Holloway."

Geraldine looked from one to the other and tutted.

"This is like getting blood out of a stone. I'm going to get a drink." And she got up and walked away.

Pete cleared his throat and fiddled with his bow tie. "What are you going to read?" he asked as she took her glasses off again, huffed on the lenses, polished them and put them on before answering.

"Biological science. What are you doing?"

"Agriculture," Pete replied.

"Farming, you mean?" Louise smirked.

"I suppose," said Pete. "What's wrong with that?"

"Nothing," and the conversation ground to a halt again.

"Can you dance, Peter?"

"Not very well."

"Shall we have a go? I'm no good. I'm really clumsy. I went to classes but never really got it."

"I went to classes too. My mother insisted. But I only know the basics."

"Here we go then." Louise smiled for the first time and stood.

She was tall and so slim her cream ball gown hung limp on her featureless figure. Her hair was rolled up in a bun on the back of her head, the blonde of childhood disappearing to become a darker shade of brown. Her face was pale, as were her arms that showed below the three-quarter length sleeves of the dress. She wore only a little makeup and her fingernails were varnished, showing off her elegant hands. Her only jewellery was a gold necklace holding a mount with a large sapphire in the middle surrounded by small diamonds. The stones stood out against the pale cream skin of her neck and the sapphire matched the blue of the eyes behind her glasses.

Peter took her hand, to lead her to the dance floor when he heard, "Blimey, it's you. I thought it was," shouted from the other end of a table by Alexandra, "Hang on, you're not going dancing, are you?"

"That was the general idea," said Pete.

"Wait a mo, I just want to say hello to Louise. I haven't seen her for ages." She put the pint of beer she was drinking down on the table and pressed her cheek to Louise's. "Darling, how are you, my dear?" she asked, imitating Audrey and Julia perfectly.

"Darling, I'm absolutely wonderful," Louise replied in the same tone.

"You look absolutely divine, darling," gushed Alexandra, standing back and admiring Louise.

"Shut up, Alex, and don't talk such rubbish. This dress is hanging off me, it was a hand-me-down from my sister."

"Well, I can hardly get into mine," and she burst out laughing. Alexandra's dress was bright red and her ample figure was only just contained. Her jet-black hair was full and down to her shoulders, her complexion still maintaining last year's tan. "Look," she said, and pulled down her wide waist band, "We had to cut the seam to get me in it," and she laughed again. "Cheers, dears." She lifted her pint and had a swig. "Haven't you got a drink?"

"Not so far," said Louise.

"What a state of affairs! Pete, go and get Louise a drink and have one yourself and put it on Colonel Dawingditmus's slate."

"How do you know him, Alex? He seems to know everyone."

"Young Farmers."

"I thought all farmers were thick as two short planks."

"Most of them are, but what's wrong with that? They're still good fun."

Pete came back.

"I forgot to ask you what you want, Louise?"

"Just a tonic water. I don't really drink."

"Go on with you. Put a gin in it, Pete, you can't enjoy yourself without a little alcohol. And we all need something to liven this event up." She shooed Peter off. "And get me another pint."

Alexandra and Louise sat again, while Pete fetched the drinks and Geraldine joined them.

"You know Alex, don't you, Granny?"

"Of course, I do, dear, since she was a child. Alex, what on earth are you drinking?"

"I'm drinking a pint of beer. All the boys do, so why can't I?"

"Well, it's not very ladylike, is it?" Geraldine frowned.

"But, I'm not very ladylike, am I?" and they all laughed.

Pete came back with the drinks.

"Now what's this I hear about you getting stuck in the bath, Geraldine?" Alexandra looked from one to the other and grinned.

"And what did you hear, Alex?"

"I heard a certain young gentleman had to come and rescue you. Isn't that right, Pete?" They all laughed as Pete went redder and redder.

"Would you come and rescue me if I got stuck in the bath, Pete?"

"No. I couldn't lift you!"

"He's got his own back on you, Alex," said Louise. "Come on, Peter, the dance floor."

The evening wore on, the meal was served and Pete was sent to the bar again, where Henry was standing.

"You still here then?" Pete asked. "I thought you would have gone by now."

"I would have, but the photographer just took a whole lot of pictures with no film in the camera so we had to start all over again."

He took a packet of cigarettes from his pocket and offered one to Pete.

"No thanks, I've got to carry all these drinks and I'll drop them."

"Is that the Dawingditmuses you're with?"

"Yes, them and the Howells."

"You know the old lady?"

157

"Yes."

"She's a Jew, you know."

"No, I didn't, but does it matter?"

"It does to some and not to others."

"And to you?"

"Yes and no. She was in the camps you know, but they don't talk about it. Did you know that?"

"No, I didn't, but does it matter?"

"Not really, but this area has no end of Italians, a lot of Germans as well. Every farm has two or three. The Italians work the brickworks and the Germans are all about. They couldn't go back to East Germany, could they?"

"I suppose not," and Pete, who then returned to the table with the drinks.

As the evening proceeded, the usual format was followed and traditional country dances replaced the ballroom favourites. As the Gay Gordons was announced, there was a chorus of shouts and hunting horns were blown.

"Come on, you lot, let's have you," shouted Alexandra, and all the youngsters got up to dance, leaving their elders behind.

"Come on, Pete, Louise, you're with Tony and Nancy with him." Alexandra pointed to a young man nearby. "We need another couple to make eight." Two more volunteered. The caller shouted as the music played and the dancing got faster.

"Come on, Pete," Alexandra shouted. "Swing me

round," and they got faster and faster until Alexandra clashed with Tony.

"Bugger," she exclaimed. "Pete! Pete, come here and help," and she got on her knees and started crawling around the floor amongst the dancers.

"What is it? What are we looking for?"

"My teeth!" she shouted, and she clenched her teeth, parted her lips and grinned, revealing the gap where her top middle teeth should be.

"There they are!" she shouted, but then they were gone – kicked across the floor by one of the dancers.

They finally came to rest under a chair and Alexandra retrieved them.

"Give me a hand, Pete," she said, and he hauled her up. "I thought you said you couldn't lift me!"

She looked at the teeth, which were all dusty from the floor, and dipped them in Henry's beer, who was sitting at the next table, swished them about and then put them back in.

"Knocked them out playing netball," she explained, as they carried on dancing.

"My feet are killing me," said Julia, as she lifted one leg and then the other and took her shoes off.

"I don't know why we come to these events year after year, they're always the same – what do you think, Audrey?"

"I don't know, my dear, I quite like dressing up now and again, but it's not quite what it was, is it? There're

159

so many farmers coming now."

"We are farmers," Julia said defensively.

"I know you are, dear, but you know what I mean."

"I don't know if I do! You'll be pointing out I'm half Jewish next."

The conversation stopped. Julia flipped open her cigarette case, offered one to Audrey, who refused, then took one herself.

"What about Louise? It's a good place to marry her off at a Hunt Ball."

"I suppose so, but she's not interested in boys. She's always got her nose in some book or other and keeps on about going to university."

"What about that boy we brought?" Julia puffed on her cigarette.

"I don't know. He looks alright, but is there any money there? He lives up this way, didn't you say?"

"Tony said he went to Kimbolton."

"Oh."

"He's going to London, Tony said."

"Oh."

"Reading agriculture."

"That's farming, Audrey."

"You're farmers, Julia."

"No need to tell me. I don't smell of pigshit do I?"

"Don't be so vulgar, Julia, it's all very well you complaining about what you are, but pigs are what Trevor earns his money from."

The band had started playing ballroom dances again.

"Where are all the men?" asked Audrey.

"Standing at the bar, as if you couldn't guess," said Julia. "Anyway, I've done enough dancing for this year, we can drag around when the last waltz comes." She looked at her watch.

At the other end of the table sat Geraldine and Louise waiting for Pete, who had been sent for more drinks.

"Granny?"

"Yes, dear."

"In the war, were you in Germany?"

"No, dear, I was in Europe, shall we say, and you know I don't like to talk about it."

"I know, but that journalist, the one who was writing the details for the photographer…"

"What about him?"

"I overheard him talking about the Howells and he said that Audrey was part German and he said it in a very nasty way."

"Did he?" Geraldine frowned.

"But you're Jewish, aren't you, Granny? So how are you friendly with Audrey?"

"Now, my dear, this is not the time or the place to go on about such issues – suffice to say that after the war there were millions of displaced people and many of them had nowhere to go, as their homes had been occupied by the Russians, so they came here and the

161

only way to survive is to get on. Got it?" She smiled at Louise. "And here is Peter, with the drinks, what a lovely boy."

"If you say so, Granny."

"Don't say it like that, dear. It's not very friendly. And what did I just say? Everyone has got to get on."

Pete held the three drinks in his two hands, with his pint in the middle and each index finger round the stems of the two wine glasses.

"Made it!"

"Cheers, Peter, that's very kind of you," Geraldine smiled at him as she took her glass of wine.

"Oh, I didn't pay."

"Who did then?" asked Louise.

"I've no idea, but he seemed to know everyone so I didn't argue."

Louise turned to Pete, took his hand and patted it.

"Now, Peter, you must now dance with Granny, she hasn't been on the floor for ages, have you, Granny?"

"Don't worry about me, dear, the poor boy doesn't want to dance with me."

Peter stood and bowed as the band started up again and Geraldine looked up at him and winked.

"He's not very good at it, Granny, so watch your feet."

"Louise, don't be so rude." She got up, took Pete's hand and followed him onto the dance floor.

"Is it a waltz?" Pete asked.

"Yes, my dear, can't you tell?"

"No, I have no idea, but I can just about do a waltz: forward, side, together, I think we were taught." Pete held her right arm up and put his right arm round her waist and set off.

"Now, Peter. You have had dancing lessons then?"

"Oh yes, Mother insisted, but I didn't learn much I'm afraid. I still can't do a foxtrot."

"And what was the main thing your dancing teacher always said to you?"

"I don't know. She said a lot of things."

"Did you dance with her, Peter?"

"I had to, I'm afraid."

"And she always said…?"

"Ah, yes, she always said 'hold me closer'." Peter blushed again.

"Well?" said Geraldine, and with his right hand he pulled her closer and as he felt the roll of her torso over the top of her corset, her ample bosom pressed against his chest. "That's better, it's so much easier to dance if the partners are closer, don't you think?"

"I suppose so," said Pete. As he looked down at her, his eyes momentarily glancing at her cleavage.

"You needn't look down there, boy, you've seen it all before, haven't you?" she laughed. "I shouldn't tease you, should I? I'm making you embarrassed." Pete looked away.

The dance finished after a while and they made their way back to the table, where Alexandra had joined Louise.

"Thank you, young man," Geraldine smiled as she sat down.

"Oh, Pete, was that your pint I've just finished? Sorry!" said Alexandra, giggling.

"Don't worry, I've got to work in the morning so I can't get too squiffy."

"You'll be fine. You can go in your DJ." Alexandra laughed. "Now, Pete, what's the name of the chap that runs your place?"

"Mr Lockheart."

She turned to Louise. "There, I said it was. Pete, Louise is coming to your place as part of a pre-university what's it called?"

"Yes, we have to do a presentation on a practical application of biological science and it said it was a research farm, so I wrote to Mr Lockheart and asked if I could come and make a report."

"It's not quite research."

"What is it then, as it sounds like it might be a waste of my time?"

"No, it's not, but you'll see when you come."

Chapter Fourteen

Zeppelin Escapes

The dance dragged on for another hour before the last waltz was played followed by the National Anthem. It was over an hour, and nearly three thirty in the morning before Peter was dropped on the green at Toddington. He set off down Park Road to walk the quarter mile to Meadow View. Most of the snow had gone from the pavements and the road was now completely clear, but it was still very cold and the thin soles of his shoes were no protection from the icy pavement. In the distance, he could hear a car coming and as it approached Peter recognised the Ford Zodiac they had pushed out of the snow some weeks back. It passed him at speed then the driver put his brakes on, skidded to a halt then backed up as the he wound the window down. The man in the passenger seat leaned over the driver and shouted out the window, "Oi! Boy! M1?"

Peter stopped. "Up there, turn left and it's about a mile."

"What did I tell you?" He turned to the two passengers in the back. "I was bloody right I knew I was," and he turned to the front and tapped the dashboard in front of him. He looked back at Pete.

"Thanks for that, boy." He looked at Pete again. "Where you bin, boy, dressed up like a dog's dinner? Look at 'im, Sunny, looks like 'e should be walkin' up Piccadilly," and he laughed. "Right, you 'eard what he said." He tapped the dash again. "Up 'ere and turn left."

The window went up and as the car sped off Pete noticed that the right-hand side of the back bumper was missing.

When Pete got back to Meadow View the back door was unlocked. He took his shoes off and tiptoed towards the stairs meeting, Joyce who was coming down. Her hair was sticking up in all directions, and she pulled her dressing gown around her and tied it.

"Come in here and shut the door," she whispered, as she went into the kitchen. "Do you want a cup of tea?" She smiled and picked up the kettle. "I'm going to have one, I can't sleep," and she held the kettle under the tap and filled it.

"I've got to be at work at seven," Pete looked at his watch, "and it's nearly four now."

"Don't worry about that, you can do it at your age. I was young once," she said as she looked in the mirror. "Good God! Look at my hair, what do I look like?" She held her hands to her face. "Well then?" she said, and looked at Peter.

"Well, what?"

"Do you want a cup of tea?"

"Alright then, but aren't we going to wake Freddie up?"

"No, not 'im. He were up the pub with PC 49 again, he won't wake till the alarm goes. Anyway, it's Sunday so the alarm *won't* go." She filled the teapot and waited for it to brew. "Tell me about the dance then, Pete, was it very posh?"

"I suppose it was."

"Was there lots of lords and ladies and all the nobs then?" She grabbed his hand and patted it. "Come on, Pete."

"Well, I suppose there were some lords and ladies but I don't know who they were. The ones I knew were farmers and horsey people. I knew some of them from home."

"And what was this girl like you had to escort, come on, tell me?"

"She was very nice, but she didn't like dances."

"I know," Joyce grinned, "her mother was trying to marry her off. I bet that's what it was and she – the girl, I mean – didn't like it. Am I right, Pete?"

"She said it was like a cattle market."

"There, I told you so. Were you married off to her then?"

"No, nothing like that; she's going to university, so she's a bit serious."

"And was she pretty? What did she wear, was she a blonde?"

"Well, she was just a nice person."

"But what did she wear?"

"A dress, but I don't remember much about it."

"Typical, just typical – you're nearly as bad as Freddie."

Pete drank his tea and went to bed.

In the morning, Pete was on time despite the late night, and cycled straight down to the pigs. He was the only one on duty and had to feed everything. The fattening house was first, and then the sows and the dry sows in the yard and then the three boars. All went well, until he got to the boars, where he found that the new prize one, the one they called Zeppelin, was missing. He searched all around the buildings but there was no sign of him. The phone at the piggery was in the locked office so Pete got on his bike and cycled to the main farm. David was there feeding the cattle.

"What's up with you then, you look a bit hot and bothered."

"It's Zeppelin."

"What about him?"

"He's got out."

"Bloody hell, how did that happen then?"

"No idea, I went to feed him and he's gone."

"Go and see if Robert is in the office. I'll just finish off here and then I'll come."

Pete went to the door of the office and called out. There was no answer but he could hear Robert on the phone so he called again. After a while he could hear movement.

"Alright, alright, keep your hair on. I'm coming," he heard as footsteps banged along the corridor.

"Pete, what do you want? Have you finished the pigs? I was just coming down."

"It's Zeppelin."

"What about him?"

"He's gone."

"Bloody hell, how did he get out?"

"No idea, but he's not there. David's coming."

"Right. You cycle back and I'll bring David. Is Grafton about?"

"No, he's away, I think."

"Crucial's away as well."

Pete got on his bike but halfway down the drive to the road, he saw Zeppelin across the field heading for the poultry sheds. He turned to meet Robert and David in the Land Rover.

"I've seen him, he's over there," and he pointed to where Zeppelin was trotting along over the frozen ground.

"We haven't got any boards up here, have we? No one's to go near him without one. I know his tusks are short but he'll still do you a lot of damage. I'll go and get some from the piggery, you go and shoo him into a corner or even a barn if you can."

Robert sped off and the other two climbed the fence and walked cautiously over to where Zeppelin was

169

now ambling along. With his big ears covering his eyes he could only see straight in front of himself. He got nearer and nearer to the first of four sheds which supplied the eggs for the hatchery. Each shed had ten deep litter pens with one hundred hens in each and six to eight cockerels.

"We could get him in one of them, Pete. Go and hold the door, open it if he comes that way, we can catch him in the food store at the end."

Pete did as instructed and David walked behind shooing the animal along. Robert returned with three boards and gave one each to David and Pete and kept one for himself.

"Pete. Open the door when he comes along and we've got him. Stand behind it, mind."

David and Robert came up close, holding the boards between themselves and the boar.

"Right, Pete, open the door."

Zeppelin moved slowly forward, sniffing the air as he made his way to the doorway. The warmth of the chickens inside and the smell of the meal wafted out.

"Right, keep behind that door, Pete, I think we've got him." Zeppelin slowly walked through the doorway.

The first part of the building was where the food was kept and the eggs were stored before cleaning and going to the hatchery. Behind that, were the chickens and an alleyway down the middle gave access to the pens.

"Right, David, get on the tractor and fetch the cattle trailer then we can load him up and take him back. Pete, you stay here and we will try and stop him eating the chicken food."

Robert gingerly opened the door as Zeppelin knocked over the table with all the eggs on it with a crash.

"Bloody hell, he's going to smash the place up." Robert shut the door again.

"Right, Pete, let's see if we can get him in the corridor. Get your board and just watch them tusks of his, they're razor sharp. Right, are you ready?"

Pete nodded and held his board by the handle cut into it. The boards were made of plywood and were about one metre square with a hand hole on one edge. Across the middle was written *PROVIMI* the name of the fish meal produced by the feed company that owned the farm. Robert opened the door and they both rushed in and shut the door behind themselves.

"Where has the bugger gone?" said Robert. "I can't see him."

The lights were on but were not bright.

"There he is, look, he's eating the eggs." They could see his back over the top of the upturned table.

Zeppelin lifted his head and turned to look at them, chomping the eggs with froth coming from his mouth. He bent down and took another mouthful and they could hear the cracking of the shells. He turned and looked again and they could see his little eyes behind the big ears that pointed forward. The chomping stopped for a moment, started again, then stopped. Suddenly he put his head down and charged at them. The table was turned completely over as he dashed forwards. He reached Pete who parried his head with the board, but Zeppelin tipped his head sideways and lifted it, at the same time digging his tusk into the board and throwing Pete on his back as Zeppelin then turned on him and put his head down.

Robert threw down his board as the boar rushed past and grabbed his tail with both hands as he swung round.

"I've got him, Pete, get out the way." Pete turned over and leapt in one jump up onto the stack of feed sacks where he was safe.

"I can't hold him," yelled Robert, and he let go and jumped onto the sacks with Pete. "Did he get you?"

"No, but he got my welly," and Pete pulled open the leg of his boot, showing it was ripped from the ankle to the top.

"Where's the bugger going?" They watched as he ambled towards the corridor down the shed.

He then woofed, threw his head up and charged.

"Come on, Pete, let's get the table across the end."

They scrambled down, grabbed the table and blocked the end of the corridor as Zeppelin charged back at them. He crashed into the table as Pete and Robert pushed from the other side. He then went back a little and jumped his front feet up onto the edge of the tipped-up table. His mouth still frothed and his tusks stuck out menacingly.

"Hold it, Pete, he can't get over, I'll grab some bags of food, he won't push it over then."

They put bags against the table so they now had him contained. He woofed again and turned and raced down the corridor once more.

"Go and see where David is and tell him to hurry."

Pete rushed off and found David outside the workshop.

"What's up?"

"Got a puncture, it's going to take some time, ice has got inside the tyre. You better go and tell Robert."

Pete returned to the chicken shed. He opened the door to pandemonium and chickens flying everywhere.

"What's happened?" Pete shouted to Robert.

"The bloody animal's got in one of the pens. Look at him!"

Zeppelin was in the middle of the first pen on the left, rootling in the deep litter with a cockerel on his back. There were chickens on top of the nest boxes and in the corridor and the feed store where Robert was standing.

"Look, Pete, I've never seen anything like it," and he pointed to where the boar was digging up the litter; every time he brought his nose up mice scattered in all directions. Zeppelin was obviously eating some as he chomped the litter.

"There's a plague of mice. Can you see them? I

couldn't work out why this shed was getting through so much food, much more than the other three. Now I know the reason."

"What are we going to do then?"

"Nothing," said Robert. "Zeppelin's happy. Where's David?"

"Puncture. And he's going to be a while, there's ice in the tyre."

"Right. You go and help him. I'll wait here."

Pete gazed back at Zeppelin, "How did he get in there?"

"Just put his nose in the gate, lifted and the whole thing come off. How did he get out in the first place is the main question?"

"I've no idea, but I haven't looked yet, I just came to find you and David."

"Well, it's a question we can't answer now."

Chapter Fifteen

The Great Freeze Ends

"Quiet! Quiet everyone." Trisha shouted to make herself heard as she stood in front of the fireplace in the front room of the Cottons in Mander Close.

Everyone carried on talking as latecomers entered the room. Trisha clapped her hands to no avail but then John saw a gong hanging on the wall, took the padded drum stick from the hooks underneath and gave it a hard whack. Everyone looked round and the chatter stopped instantly.

"Haha," said John, and he gave the gong a rolling series of strikes.

Everyone laughed and Trisha started again. "Thank you, John." John bashed the gong. "Thank you!" and he did it again until David grabbed the stick from him. "Thank you, John," she turned to him and smiled, "And I would also like to thank George and Thelma for the use of this magnificent room." Everyone clapped.

"Now at our last rehearsal, we decided we needed a director and I would like to introduce Judy's brother Crispin who has agreed to do the job. Crispin!"

She held her hand up as he walked into the middle of the room and took a bow. He wore a long fur coat and a silk scarf around his neck. His hair was blond and he smoked a Black Russian cigarette. His patent leather black shoes shone against the white carpet. He turned and smiled to Trisha, who for a moment did not know what to say.

"You're the professional actor, Crispin, so I will leave it to you to take it from here," she said as she shrank away looking embarrassed.

"Darling," he said, "how kind, and can I say what a pleasure it is, and, my dears, what a splendid play – *The Queen of Hearts* – one of my favourites." He tottered to the fireplace and flicked in the ash from his cigarette.

John stood leaning on the mantelpiece and smirked at Crispin, who stared straight into his eyes and held his gaze until John looked uncomfortable.

"You're a nice big boy," Crispin said in a gravelly voice smirking back at him, "and what part are you playing, darling?" He kept his gaze on John who became more and more uncomfortable but could not look away from him.

"I'm a policeman," he stuttered.

"You're not? How wonderful," and Crispin did a little clap. "And your name is?" He made a stupid smile.

"John."

"What a nice name – so easy to spell. Now, my dears, you have all read the play I'm told and have discovered that the queen of hearts is a playing card, not a person. Yes?" He looked round and they all nodded but no one spoke as he took off his fur coat.

"Can I take that?" said Thelma.

"So kind, my dear, my mother's you know, just the ticket for this weather." Underneath he wore a tight-fitting white polo neck sweater and black trousers. "Now, who has the other parts?" Crispin clapped his hands. "Who is Lois?"

"I am, I am!" shouted Rita, and she leapt up to greet him. He put his hands out to grab her arms and give her a hug as she blew her bubble gum into a small balloon.

"How vulgar," he said, and turned his nose up as his cheeks met hers in turn and then he backed off. "But I do like vulgar, don't you?" he tittered. "And, darling, at least you don't smell of pigs." He went round the room finding out who was playing which character. "You've done a read through, I understand, and another rehearsal. Who has done some acting before?"

They all shook their heads, except Rita, who put her hand up and grinned.

"Let's have one more read through this evening and then next time, we can lay out the stage here if we can't be at the hall."

The next day, Pete was at work littering the yards of cattle. Steve was throwing the bales down from the stack on top of the silage clamp and Pete was cutting the strings and spreading them when Viv appeared.

"Pete. Crucial wants to see you up in his office."

"Now?"

"Yup, I'll help do the last few bales."

Pete got to the offices, took his boots off and looked into Mary's office.

"Pete, do stand back, you really smell."

"Is Crucial in his office?"

"Yes, he's expecting you," she said, so Pete made his way down the corridor and tapped on the door.

"Enter," Crucial shouted, and Pete went in to find Robert in there already.

"Two things, Pete," Crucial said, tapping his desk with the end of a pencil. "The escape of the boar. Robert says you found where it got out."

"Yes, the fence was knocked down along the drive down to The Manor. By the tyre marks it looks as though someone had come down the drive, then decided not to go any further and backed round, knocking the fence over in the process. A bit of the bumper was pulled off and still lay there."

"Robert says that the fence is mended."

"Yes, we did it that morning."

"Do we need a gate at the top of the drive to stop this happening again, Robert?"

"There is a gate, but it's not been moved for years and it would be an awful bind to have to open it every time someone went through it. Also, there would have to be a padlock and who would have the key?"

Robert looked at Crucial, who, deep in thought, continued to tap on his desk.

"I think I know who did it," Pete said, as he looked from one to the other.

"Who then?" Crucial asked.

"I was walking down Park Road the other night, Saturday night that is, or rather it was Sunday morning and some blokes in a Ford Zodiac stopped and asked the way to the M1. I noticed they had a bit missing from their bumper."

"What time was this?"

"About a quarter to four, I suppose."

"What were you doing walking down Park Road at that time of the morning?" Crucial asked, and looked at Robert, whose face suddenly lit up.

"I know. You went to the Hunt Ball, didn't you? It's alright for those who move in those circles, you were with all the nobs I bet," and he grinned as Pete looked embarrassed.

"Be that as it may," said Crucial. "We have to decide about the gate and it looks as though we do nothing for now," and he continued to tap with his pencil. "That's all then," Crucial looked at Pete. "Actually, no, it's not. I've got a letter from this girl who wants to come as she has to do a presentation or some such on the practical application of biological science. She wants to see what we do and she's going to London and I think you are too, aren't you, Pete?" Pete nodded. "And her name is… pass me the letter,

179

Robert. Her name is Louise and she's the daughter of Trevor Dawingditmus, who the boar came from and who you've met."

"Yes," said Pete, "I've met her."

"Oh, you've met her too, I didn't know that."

"I met her—" and Pete stopped, looking embarrassed again.

"You met her at the Hunt Ball?" Robert clapped his hands. "That's where all the mothers get their daughters married off." He laughed and winked at Crucial.

"Just shut up about the Hunt Ball, Robert, you're becoming a bore. She says she's reading biological science at Holloway so I doubt she's getting married off. I'm a scientist too you know, so keep your views to yourself," and he tapped the table again. "She's coming on the sixteenth of March, so, Robert, you can show her your office and explain our feeding and weighing research and, Pete, you can show her round the farm. Let's hope it's thawed by then."

"Ah, and…" Crucial tapped on his desk, "one more thing. I forgot to say that I have let the top flat in The Manor too," and he stopped and turned over some papers on his desk, "to a Henry Babage. He's a reporter on the *Luton Times*."

"I know him," Pete grinned.

"Don't tell me, he was at the Hunt Ball too?" Robert pointed at Pete and laughed. "I know him as

180

well, met him in the pub didn't we, Pete. He got stuck in the snow."

"Be that as it may, he's paid a month in advance and he moves in on the sixteenth of March and said he would appreciate a hand with his furniture. Also, he's apparently a keen snooker player and wants to use the table."

"Does Helmit know?" Robert asked.

"Not yet, but I'll see him this morning."

"And Wally?"

"It doesn't affect him as he lives in the stable block, but anyway, he may not be here much longer."

Crucial looked at Robert, then at Pete.

"Are you going to sack him then?" Robert asked.

"I didn't say that, did I, and you didn't hear this conversation, Pete."

The thaw started on the sixth of March. The remainder of the snow melted away and the ground became soft, exposing burst pipes all around the farm. The potato store was opened to find that the crop close to the ventilation channels had been frozen and turned into a stinking mushy mess when moved.

The chicken shed, where Zeppelin was caught, was emptied when the mice were discovered. The pens were dismantled and all the litter cleared out. There were mice everywhere and each bucket full of the litter contained hundreds as it was loaded into the spreader. The litter was taken to an adjacent grass field and spread and the crows came down to pick up and eat the mice as they ran about the field. By the end of the week, the big freeze had all but been forgotten and everything was back to normal.

The sixteenth of March arrived and Robert came to find Pete, who was in the mixing shed.

"This girl, Pete, what's her name?"

"Louise Dawingditmus."

"You don't mean that! Where did she get a name like that?"

"Louise is alright."

"I know, but Dawingditmus, what sort of a name is that?"

"I'm not sure but it's where Zeppelin came from."

At that moment, Steve walked in.

"What do you want?" Robert demanded.

"That's not a very nice way to speak to an old chap," Steve said, as his mouth chewed an imaginary sweet.

"Well then," said Robert, sighing.

"I ain't gonna tell yer."

"Come on, Steve. Alright, I'm sorry I was sharp, but what do you want?"

"Viv sent me," and his eyes looked sideways, not at Robert.

"And…?"

Steve burst out laughing.

"And…?" Robert tried again.

"I'm got to 'elp Pete finish off this ration and

then 'elp him get it down the pigs."

"Well why didn't you say that the first time?"

Steve went cross-eyed then laughed again.

"And..." he said. "Crucial says you've got to go to the office, there's a girl come. And..." Steve looked sideways again and laughed, "And Crucial says that the man who's comin' into the top flat in The Manor will be there at two o'clock. So there, that's what I come to tell you so there." He pulled his cap down and untied and tied the twine around his waist.

"Right, I'd better go, I'll take her round the poultry and then I'll bring her down the pigs and by that time you'll be there, so you can show her round, Pete, and we'll go from there, okay?"

Pete nodded and put another bag on the chute and pulled the slide to fill it. Steve got the sack barrow and stood behind Pete who tied the bag and lifted it onto the sack barrow.

"Grafton don't like your knots, Pete. 'e says he can't undo 'em," Steve said, as he wheeled the sack away and onto the trailer.

When Pete and Steve arrived at the pigs, Grafton was castrating and sat on a chair as Wally brought the piglets to him. Wally went into each of the pens, the sow was shut out. then he'd catch the boars and bring them to Grafton. Wally held the piglets up by the back legs and Grafton pinched each testicle between his thumb and forefinger. Then with a scalpel he made an incision about an inch long in the scrotum and going into the testicle. He then squeezed and the testicle popped out of the scrotum; he cut through the blood vessels and ducts and the testicle came away and he threw it over his shoulder, where his collie dog would eat it up. Each one took less than a minute and when each piglet had been dosed with antiseptic spray it was put back in the pen.

Pete and Steve were unloading bags into the feed store when Robert arrived.

"You know Louise, don't you, Pete?"

Pete smiled at her and nodded.

"Can you show her round when you've done the unloading and I'll come and fetch her in an hour or so? Steve, you come with me."

Steve touched his cap and chewed the imaginary sweet again.

"We meet again." Louise looked quizzically at Pete through her horn-rimmed glasses.

"Shall I help empty the last few bags?" She climbed up and pulled a bag to the back of the trailer, where Pete took it on his back and into the food store of the farrowing shed.

"You didn't think I could do that, did you?" she said to Pete, as she pulled the last bag to the back of the trailer.

Pete smiled but didn't respond to her question, raising one of his own instead.

"What shall we look at first?"

Distracted, she nodded to where Grafton sat.

184

"What's that man doing?"

"He's..." Pete stopped.

"He's what?" Louise looked enquiringly at Pete.

"He's castrating the boars."

"Oh."

"Do you want to look?"

"Yes, of course I do, I've got to see what goes on, haven't I?"

"I suppose so."

She followed Pete up the central walkway of the farrowing shed to where Grafton was sitting. He was on the last pen and the sow could be heard squeaking in the dunging passage.

"Grafton, this is Louise, she's come to, well, I'm not quite sure what she's come for."

Grafton stood and took his pipe from his mouth, put it in his top pocket then took his cap off.

"Very pleased to meet you, miss," and he offered to shake hands but then quickly pulled his hand back. "Perhaps not," he said as they both looked at the spots of blood on his fingers. "You're studying, miss?" he enquired instead.

"Yes, I'm doing a study on the practical applications of biological science for my degree course."

"Ah ha, very interesting, so do you want to watch this? It's a bit bloodthirsty, you know," Grafton grinned.

"Of course I do. I'm not going to faint, if that's what

you are thinking."

"Very well then, let's carry on," and Grafton replaced his cap, sat and put his pipe back in his mouth.

"Right, Wally, the last litter, let's have one," said Wally and went and grabbed a piglet.

"Where's the sow?" Louise asked.

"She's in the dunging passage," Grafton replied.

Louise turned to Pete. "In the where?"

"The dunging passage, through that hole," and he pointed. "Pigs always do their business in the same place."

Louise looked embarrassed. "I suppose I should have known that, my father keeps pigs."

Wally held the piglet by the back legs and Grafton quickly castrated it and sprayed the antiseptic on and he went back for the next one.

"Don't you give them an injection first – surely it must hurt?"

Grafton looked up as the dog behind him gulped down the second testicle.

"No, we don't inject them and I don't know whether they feel much. I suspect not. They don't give boys an injection before they circumcise them, do they, and it's the same sort of thing."

Grafton glanced at Louise as she put her hand to her mouth and said nothing. She stroked the dog as it nuzzled up to her.

"And the dog?" Louise turned to Grafton.

"He loves them," he smiled. "A lot of people save

them and fry them up, but it's not to my taste."

"No."

"Pete, have you had them?" Grafton asked.

"No, never," he said, and the subject was dropped.

"Where would you like to look next?" Pete enquired.

"Well, everywhere."

"Okay, so let's go to the fattening house."

"I ain't cleaned that out yet," said Wally. "You can do it, Pete, show 'er 'ow it works."

"You idle bugger," Grafton snapped. "You said you were all done."

"I was, 'cept for cleaning out the fattening 'ouse."

"Wally, I don't know what you get paid for sometimes." Grafton picked up his chair and went back to his office shouting over his shoulder, "And, Wally, you can go and clean out the fatteners."

Wally grumbled and trudged off to the fattening house, followed by Pete and Louise. The building had a large open area at the front where all the food was stacked in bags and then there were three doors. The middle one was the feeding passage and Pete opened the door to show Louise. On each side of the passage were pens of pigs contained by metal rails with the feeding troughs below. Each pen had a water pipe into the feeding trough with a tap level with the top of the rails. The pigs woofed as they opened the door and squeaked a little but then they were distracted by the banging of other doors.

Wally had gone into one of the dunging passages, which ran each side of the shed and one by one he shut the doors and drove the pigs into their pen. When he got to the end, he opened the last door, which led to the muck heap. Along the ceiling of the dunging passage was a wire rope which was attached to a pulley over the muck heap. The wire rope was in a big loop and at the other end was a scraper and when the button was pressed, the scraper was pulled along the passage taking all the dung and urine with it out onto the dung heap. When this had been done, the scraper was pulled back ready for the next day. The doors were opened again and he then did the same on the other side of the shed.

"When do you feed them?" Louise asked.

"First thing in the morning and last thing in the afternoon. I can show you later."

"Where does the research happen? It says 'Toddington Manor Research Farm' on the gate, but I can't see any research being done."

"We weigh them, that's the research."

"Why?" Louise still looked puzzled.

"We weigh them to see how much weight they've gained for a particular quantity of food and we test out various rations to see how much weight they gain on each ration."

"Is that all?"

"Yes," said Pete. "I told you it wasn't quite research, it's just feed them and weigh them, that's all."

"What am I going to put in my report then?" She looked disappointed.

"I don't know, do I? What about the castration of pigs, you've just seen that?"

She stuck her tongue out at Pete, grimaced and stamped her foot. There was silence.

"Did Robert show you where the rations were made up?"

"No."

"You need to start there; I'll show you when you've seen around here."

"Haven't we finished?"

"No, we've hardly started and we're doing it all back to front. We should start with the boars. Don't forget, the best one came from your father."

"Go on then, show me." Louise looked fed up.

"Follow me then." Pete led the way to where the boars were housed. "This is Zeppelin, he came from your dad."

"What? Why did you call him that?"

"It was Steve's idea, and it's a long story, but he's the best boar so he serves most of the sows."

"Serves?"

"Mates with them."

"Yes, I know, I know, don't look at me like that." She took out a notebook. "I'd better write something down. So how do you, I mean, who decides which sows he serves?"

"Grafton does it. He selects the sows that he wants

189

to put to Zeppelin and when they come into season, he brings them to the crate and then Zeppelin is brought to the sow."

"Where's the crate then?" She followed Pete.

"This is it, the sow goes in and the boar follows."

"Just like that?"

"Yes, just like that and look, Grafton's coming with a sow now."

She looked up and could see Grafton holding a board and guiding a sow down the passage.

"Out the way, Pete," Grafton shouted and they stood back, as he manoeuvred the sow into the crate.

"Get a few nuts, Pete, that'll keep her quiet until we get Zeppelin."

Grafton looked at Louise and touched his cap, "Do you want to watch?"

"It happens, doesn't it, and if it happens, I must watch."

"Very well then," and he went to fetch Zeppelin as Pete returned with the nuts.

He put them on the concrete in front of the sow and she immediately started munching them.

"Stand well back, miss," Grafton shouted. "It won't take too long."

Zeppelin waddled forward to the back end of the sow, sniffed, lifted his head up in the air and sniffed again.

"Come on, old boy," Grafton encouraged him and Zeppelin took a small step back and launched himself onto the top of the sow.

Louise started as she could see Zeppelin's penis emerge with the end shaped like a corkscrew. At that moment there was a shout.

"Anyone about?"

"Who's that?" Grafton sounded peeved.

"Anyone there?" the voice said again.

"Go and see who it is, Pete," Grafton said, without taking his eyes off the procedure.

As Pete went down the passage, he could see a well-dressed figure coming the other way.

"Come on, get it in," Grafton complained. "Go on then."

Zeppelin struggled to mate, and eventually Grafton put his hand under and guided the penis into the sow's vagina.

"Won't take long now, miss," Grafton looked at Louise, as the well-dressed newcomer arrived at the scene.

As Pete had, Louise immediately recognised Henry Babage, who wore a long black coat over a pinstriped suit and black shoes.

"What have we got here then, eh?" He looked at Pete, then Louise. "Fornication by the look of it to me, the Bible says it's a sin, doesn't it?" And he looked from one to the other again.

"Who's this joker?" Grafton asked, as Zeppelin slid backwards off the sow and sat down on his back legs.

"My, my, what a performance, don't you think?"

Henry said, as Zeppelin got up, looking a bit dazed.

"Who is he, Pete?" Grafton demanded, as he guided Zeppelin round with the aid of the board to face him back towards his pen.

"Grafton, this is Henry Babage, he's a reporter and he's going to live in the top flat of The Manor."

"A reporter for what?" Grafton growled.

"The *Luton Times*."

"That's where you are wrong, Mr Farm Worker. I am no longer employed by the *Luton Times*, as I am now freelance."

"You may be freelance, but I have to work for a living, so, Pete, you take Zeppelin back and I will deal with the sow."

Henry looked over to Louise. "Well, Miss Dawingditmus, you're the last person I'd expect to find watching fornicating animals; a bit voyeuristic, don't you think?"

Louise looked at him with disdain. "I'll ignore that comment. Can't you think of anything more sensible to say?"

"I'm a reporter, I report and put down what I see with my own eyes, that's what it's all about, the public has to know, wouldn't you agree?"

"Do you think the public has to know about the mating of pigs and has someone sent you out here to report on it? I don't think so. What are you doing here?"

He pursed his lips and looked at her. "You're right, I've been sent here to find Pete. He's going to help me move into the top flat in The Manor, or that's what they told me."

"Why don't you live in Luton? That's where the action is."

"I told you, I'm now freelance. I sell my stories to whoever pays the most, or I do assignments, and here comes Pete, so I have to go."

Pete came back, having got Zeppelin back into his pen.

"Are you ready?" Henry demanded.

"Ready for what?"

"Ready to help me move into the top flat in The Manor, that's what Robert said."

"He told me to show Louise around the pig unit, so that's what I'm doing and I'll be another half an hour, so you'll have to wait or do it all yourself." Pete grimaced at him.

Chapter Sixteen

The Motorway Café

An hour later, Pete drove up to The Manor with the tractor and trailer, which was empty apart from Steve who sat on a pile of used sacks. Outside the main door was a heap of cases and pieces of furniture, which had been delivered by a carrier that morning. Henry sat in one of the chairs smoking a cigarette and reading a paper.

"I thought you were never coming, have you got the key?" He held his hand out.

"No, haven't you?" Pete said indignantly.

"No, I haven't, so who has?"

"I'm got it," said Steve. "Robert give it to me and said I was to give it to Pete, but I forgot," and he stood up on the trailer and searched his pockets.

"Here we are," and he threw it to Henry, who dropped it. "Butter fingers," Steve giggled.

Henry picked up the key and they followed him through the main door and then to the staircase, which led to the flat. The stairs were spiral and went up the round turret which gave the building its Teutonic look. Halfway up, there was a landing and a door, which was the entrance to the flat where Helmit and Rose lived with Rita and Karen.

They climbed on until they reached the top landing and there was the door to Henry's flat. Opposite was a window, which looked out on the garden and the drive up to the road with the piggery on the right. Henry put the key in the lock and opened the door.

"Cor, it smells a bit," said Steve. "But it ain't bin used for a year or two, you'll 'ave to open a window, young man."

"Why do you want to live here then?" Pete asked.

"I told you, I'm a freelance journalist and this is a good place for my investigations and it's close to the M1, so communication is good."

"What are you investigating?" Pete asked.

"I concentrate on the London gangs. They're moving out of the city because it's easier to commit crimes here than in London, where everyone knows them."

"What they goin' to do 'ere then, 'old up the stage coach?" Steve cackled.

"No, I think they are planning a raid on Vauxhall."

"What? Stealin' cars?" Steve giggled again.

"No, stupid, I reckon they're going to snatch the wages when they come from the bank. Must be hundreds of thousands every week."

"How do you know that then, and why are you telling us?" Pete said, as he rubbed the window to see out.

"I get tips and I'm telling you as you may have seen something. I think they use the service station as a meeting place. It's the first one out of London and it's not far to the Vauxhall plant, either down the M1, or cross country from here."

"Rita works at the service station, don't she, Pete?"

"Yes, and I did see something strange the other day," said Pete.

"Did you?"

"It was the night of the Hunt Ball, I was walking home down Park Road and this carload of blokes stopped me. It was after three in the morning and they asked me where the M1 was."

"And, Pete, din't you reckon they were the ones who let Zeppelin out?"

"Yes, they lost a bit of their bumper, caught by the fence."

"That's why I told you, in case you see anything, and I must have a word with this Rita if she works at the service station. Do I know her, Pete?"

"I don't think so, but you are going to pass her door every day from now on."

"Come on, let's get everything up here then," Henry demanded. "Oh, I just remembered, Pete, Robert said there was a snooker table I can use, is that right?"

"Yes, it's on the ground floor at the side of the house."

When they had finished, Steve got back on the trailer and they went back to the mixing shed to return the bags. When they arrived, Robert was there with

Louise showing her how the rations were mixed.

"Did you get Henry into the flat, Pete?"

"Yes, it's a long way up those stairs."

"That bloke talks a lot of rubbish," said Steve. "I don't believe any of it, d'you, Pete?"

"What don't you believe?" asked Robert, as he and Louise smiled.

"'e says that someone from London's goin' to rob the Vauxhall wages money, 'ave you ever 'eard such rubbish?"

"Why doesn't he go and live near Vauxhall then, it's nowhere near here, and much closer to where I live?" commented Louise.

"I don't know," said Robert. "But we have to get on if you want to see everything."

"I'll be an expert on farming by the end," she said, and followed Robert towards the cattle sheds.

"Come on, Steve, let's get those bags off," said Pete. "Then we'll go and see what Helmit's up to."

When they got to the workshop, Helmit was working on the tracks of the crawler, which lay in two lines on the floor of the workshop.

"Pete, Steve," Helmit nodded to them. "Vhat're you doing?"

"We're skivin'," Steve grinned. "Yeah, we're skivin', ain't we, Pete?"

"Have you seen Viv, Helmit? We've finished what we were doing and there's still half an hour to go."

"No," said Helmit, as he lifted his hammer to knock out a pin from the track.

"You've got a new neighbour, Helmit, did yer know?" said Steve. "'e's a reporter, 'e says, talks a lot of rubbish, so 'e must write rubbish, that's right ain't it, Pete?"

"If you say so, Steve," and there was a loud bang as Helmit hit another pin out of the tracks.

"Vhy don't you ask Robert vhat to do, he's somevhere about."

"'e's got his girlfriend with him, ain't he, Pete, he ain't bothered about us. Wimin will draw you further than gunpowder will blow you. That's right, ain't it, Pete?" and he looked sideways again and laughed at his own joke, as Robert came through the door with Louise.

"And last of all, this is the workshop and this is Helmit, I mean Helmut, our mechanic."

Helmit put his hand out to Louise but then looked at the black grease it was embedded with and withdrew it. Instead, he touched his cap.

"Pleased to meet you, miss."

Louise smiled and noted his German accent. "What are you doing?" she asked.

"I'm replacing the pins and brushes on these tracks because the stupid driver insists on throwing vater on them to stop them squeaking, vich turns the dust to grinding paste, vich vears out the pins and brushes." They all looked at each other as Helmit was clearly angry. "Do you understand?" he said, staring at Louise.

"I think so," she said. "Who throws the water on them?"

"Simon."

"Why doesn't he mend them?"

"Because he's a bully and he doesn't like Germans, or Italians, or any foreigners come to that and I have to clear up his mess because I am an inferior prisoner of war."

There was silence as Helmit, red in the face, breathed heavily. No one said anything until Steve spoke up. "You're alright. Helmit, you mended the old grid iron." Helmit's face relaxed.

"My mother's half Polish," said Louise. "The other half's Jewish."

Helmit looked up, his jaw clenched.

"And my grandmother is Jewish and she lives with us. Pete, you know her, don't you?" Pete said nothing, and they stood in an awkward silence.

"Well, we all know where we stand then," said Robert. "Helmit."

"Yes, Robert, I know vhere I stand, I'm sorry if I have caused any offence," he said, addressing Louise.

"No, it's not easy for anyone. I didn't expect to hear all this from a question about tracks, so we perhaps better stop now," she said as she put her notebook in her bag.

"How are you getting home?" Robert enquired.

"I have my own car; it's parked just over there."

"Oh," said Robert.

"Does anyone want a lift?"

No one answered.

"Are you goin' to join the Young Farmers then?" Steve asked. "They're doin' a play, yer know," and he went cross-eyed.

Louise burst out laughing. "How does he do that? He looks so stupid when he does it."

"He is stupid," the others said in unison.

"I must go and thank Mr Lockheart before I leave."

"I'll come with you," said Robert, and they walked out of the workshop.

"Well," said Steve, and he looked from Pete to Helmit.

"There ain't many Jews around 'ere, are there, Helmit?"

There was silence.

"Steve."

"Yes, Helmit?"

"Leave it alone."

"Yes, Helmit, I'll get the old grid iron; it's five, you know, Pete, and your bike's got a puncture."

"Oh no, I'll have to walk, the puncture kit is at home."

"You can get a lift with what's her name, Pete, she's got a car, that's what you need, a car not a bike."

Steve rode off and Pete started to walk down the drive. Halfway home Louise caught him up.

"Do you want a lift?" she said, as she wound the window down.

"That's alright, I smell of pigs and it will stink your car out."

"I smell of pigs after two hours with them anyway, so that won't matter."

"Okay then," and Pete jumped in.

"Where do you live?"

"Not far along the road, and on the right, but you can drop me on the junction and I can walk from there."

"Okay," and she drove on and tooted as she overtook Steve.

She pulled up at the junction of Castle Road.

"I would say we could go for a coffee at the motorway café, but then I would have to drive all the way to Luton to get you back."

"There's no need to do that, we can get at the northbound café from this side."

"How on earth do you do that against the traffic?"

"There's an accommodation road into the car park, it was done when they built it and it's never been closed, all the workers use it."

"Very well then, shall we go, if you're free?"

"Yes, I'll go and tell Joyce I'll be late for tea, it won't take a minute."

Pete dashed the fifty yards to Meadow View, told Joyce, stripped off his overalls and then ran back. As he arrived, a car pulled up as it passed Louise's car.

The driver wound his window down and shouted at Pete.

"M1?"

"Straight up, turn left at the junction and it's about a mile."

The driver nodded and drove on.

"Who was he then?" Louise asked. "Not from around here, he had a London accent."

"I think I've seen him before," Pete said, as he got in the car.

Louise drove off and Pete showed her the way to go down the accommodation road just before the M1 and into the car park of the café on the northbound carriageway. In the café, Rita was behind the bar, serving hot drinks.

"Pete, what are you doing here at this time of day?"

"We're just having a coffee? What you want then?" Pete looked enquiringly at Louise.

"An espresso."

"And I'll have the same," Pete smiled at Rita.

"You can't, the machine's broke. It's either black or just milk."

"Just with milk then," said Louise.

"I'll have the same."

"Anything to eat?" and Louise shook her head.

"No, that's all thanks," Pete said, and put his hand in his pocket for the money.

"One and eight pence," Rita said, as Pete banged the pockets of his trousers and then his jacket.

"Damn, I've got no money." He turned to Louise.

"Don't worry, I've got it," she said, and handed it to Rita.

"Sit down then and I'll bring it over."

The café was not busy and they easily found a seat. Quarter of an hour later two men came in, the same two that had asked for directions to the M1. As they walked past the shorter one recognised Pete and stopped.

"'ow d'you get 'ere then?" he demanded, looking at his friend, "din't we just see 'im less than twenty minutes ago, Marco? You can't 'ave bin to Luton an' back an' got 'ere before us." He looked at Pete quizzically.

"I didn't."

"So 'ow d'you get 'ere then?" he demanded menacingly, leaning in closer to Pete.

Pete stood to his full height.

"I drove," said Pete.

The two men looked astounded and then seeing two others in the far corner went over and sat with them.

"What was all that about, Pete?" Rita said, as she came over to chat, "I'm seen 'em before, but I don't like the look of 'em."

"So have I, they were the ones that I saw on the night of the Hunt Ball and also the ones we pushed out of a snowdrift."

"Hunt Ball?" Rita said. "Alright for some, eh?" and she looked at Louise. "Don't tell me, you went as well?"

"Yes, I did," said Louise, and looked embarrassed.

Rita smiled. "Don't take it to heart, darlin', I'm only pulling your leg. Pete, knows what I'm like don't you, Pete?" and she nudged him suggestively with her elbow. "He'll go red in a minute... There we go what did I say?" and she laughed.

"Who's your friend then, Pete, you didn't introduce me." Rita grinned at Pete.

"Oh, sorry, this is Louise."

"Is she in the Young Farmers then? I 'aven't seen her there."

"No, I'm not, but perhaps I should be."

"Yes, you should be. I am, ain't I, Pete?"

"You are now, Rita. Rita has got the lead in the play we're producing."

"So, what play is that?"

"*The Queen of Hearts*, ain't it, Pete?"

"And are you the Queen?"

"No, it ain't like that, the queen of hearts is a playing card... Oh sorry, I've got to go – it's them blokes over there," and Rita went over to the four men in the corner.

"Perhaps I should join, Pete, but I'm no good at acting."

"We have a rehearsal tomorrow night, if you want to come along."

"I could come with Alex, she's in it, isn't she, and we live quite close to her?"

"Okay then."

"What's the play about?"

"It's set in a casino and Lois, who's played by Rita, is the croupier and there's this gang who come in who... well it's all a bit complicated, but it all relies on Rita dealing the queen of hearts."

"Will I get a part?"

"I don't think so, but there's plenty to do with the set and costumes and all that."

"Sounds good," said Louise, as Rita came back.

"You see them men over there," and she nodded to them in the corner. "They want to know how you got 'ere so quick. I'm seen 'em in 'ere before, they're Londoners, you can tell it a mile off. I didn't tell 'em anything. I better go and get their drinks," and she headed towards the counter as another customer arrived.

It was Henry Babage. Rita shouted the order for the drinks and then turned to Henry. "Fancy seeing you 'ere, and you a famous reporter for the *Luton Times*."

Henry looked at her vacantly. "Do I know you?" he asked sharply.

"You should know who your neighbours are. I was taught that when I was a kid." She pulled a face at him and then stared blankly waiting for him to catch on.

"Neighbours?" Henry looked quizzically.

"Yes, neighbours. I live in the flat below you in The Manor," Rita replied forcefully.

"But I thought a German family lived in that flat?" Henry now sounded defensive.

"There is one German in the flat and one English and one half German and half English, and one half American and half English and that one is me," and she pulled a face again.

"I'm sorry if I caused offence," Henry said meekly, "But I don't recall seeing you, it all sounds very complicated."

"Not really," said Rita. "It's just one of 'em things, it's the war, you know."

"Quite right," said Henry. "But now I want something to eat. I'm starving."

"Here's the menu then, find a seat and I'll come over."

He looked round, spied Pete and Louise and went over to their table. "Fancy seeing you here, do you mind?" he said, and he sat.

"No, help yourself, we'll soon be going."

"Young Farmers meeting then?" Henry looked from one to the other.

"No," said Pete.

"You're both from farming families, so it must be," he said as he scanned the menu.

"You catching bank robbers then?" Louise challenged him.

"I don't catch bank robbers, that's the job for the

police, but I am investigating them, or rather criminals, not bank robbers as such. Now where is that waitress," and he clicked his fingers.

Rita stood by the counter, but didn't move and Henry clicked his fingers again. She took her elbow from the counter and sauntered over.

"You forgotten something then?" she asked, as Henry looked up at her.

"What?" he said.

"You forgotten something, clicking like that?" and Rita clicked her fingers.

"No, I haven't forgotten anything" Henry replied tersely.

"Yes, you 'ave," and Rita bent forward and looked Henry in the eye. "Yes, you 'ave, you've forgotten your manners, ain't he, Pete, and what's your name?" She looked at them for agreement.

Henry sighed. "Very well then, I want something to eat."

"What?" Rita snapped.

"Please."

"That's better. Now what can I get you?"

"Do you do a Full House?"

"Yes. Sausage, egg, bacon, chips, beans, mushrooms, tomatoes and a cup of tea; seven and six."

"Just the job. I'm starving and I can't cook." He turned to Pete and Louise. "You're not going to join me?"

"No, we have to go. I've got to get Pete back for his

tea, his landlady would not forgive him if he didn't turn up."

They got up and went to the door. As they did so, one of the four men in the corner, who Rita had just served drinks to, got up and came over.

"Oi, mate," he addressed Pete. "Now look 'ere, just tell me 'ow you got 'ere, on this side of the motorway, so quick. I get confused with all the roads around 'ere, I really do."

"What do you want to know for?"

"I just do. I'm interested, know what I mean."

Pete did not respond.

"Well then," he said, this time with no threat.

"If you really want to know."

"Yes?" he said expectantly.

"There's an accommodation road that goes out of this car park to the village, it's not marked, but comes out just short of the main junction."

He looked confused. "Say again?"

"I just told you," said Pete. "Now we've got to go," and he took Louise's hand and went out of the door.

"That was odd." Louise turned and glanced back. "He didn't seem very sharp."

"No, he seemed lost, didn't he?"

Chapter Seventeen

Planning the Raid

The four men sat facing each other.

"You 'eard what I said, Sunny, go an' follow 'im and find out where 'e goes." Lionel pointed to the door staring at Sunny until he got up, knocking his chair over in the process, and headed for the door. "Typical."

Lionel was about forty, with black hair greased tight to his head with a parting down the middle. He was slightly built and wore a dark pinstriped suit. On his left foot was a large boot, and the metal rod on each side of his leg showed he wore a calliper. Two sticks hung on the back of his chair.

"Marco... fag," he addressed the chap who sat opposite.

Marco stood and walked round the table, taking out a packet which he opened and pulled one cigarette out of before offering it.

"Here, Lionel," and he took a lighter from his other pocket and lit it for him.

Marco then returned to his seat. His black hair protruded from under the flat cap he wore; he took hold of the peak and wriggled it with one hand while he pushed down with the other as he sat again.

"Are we goin' to 'ave any food?" Doug said, as he looked at Lionel, "I'm starvin'."

"How can you be hungry, you've just eaten a whole bag of chocolate?"

At that moment, Sunny returned. "'e's right, I see 'em go over there, look, you can see through the window; the access road is in the corner of the car park," he said as he pointed through the window. "See, Lionel?"

Lionel eased himself round, holding the table, and turned to look where Sunny was pointing.

"See?" said Sunny again.

"Hmm." Lionel looked thoughtfully at the car disappearing up the accommodation road. "Why did it take you so long to get 'ere?"

"It was Doug's fault, he thought there were a bridge across the motorway so there we were in the caff the other side thinkin' we were going to walk over, but there weren't one, so we 'ad to go to Luton and back to get 'ere."

"Stupid sod," Lionel grimaced, "But that's given me an idea," and he looked at each of the others in turn. "A very good idea."

"I'm 'ungry."

"Shut up, Doug, just let me think. That road is going to solve a big problem for us."

"Oh, yes?" said Sunny. "I'm 'ungry too, Lionel, can't we 'ave some grub?"

"Yes, can't we?" said Doug.

Doug was short and fat with a round face, curly red hair and chubby hands with a small tattoo on each finger. His grubby short-sleeved pullover had a hole in the front and his woollen trousers shone with ingrained dirt.

Sunny picked up the chair he had knocked over, sat, and tipped over a half full mug of coffee.

"Now look what you've done, you filthy bugger, I don't know why we bring you, I really don't. You're like a light gone out," Lionel complained.

"But I'm the driver, ain't I?"

"Only just," Lionel moaned. "You don't even know yer left from yer right."

"And he's lost his licence," chipped in Marco.

"I don't need a licence if we're robbin', do I?" Sunny stuck his tongue out at Marco.

"So, are we gonna 'ave anythin' to eat?" Doug started again.

"Okay, okay, just keep yer voices down. Go and get the waitress, Sunny, and get 'er to bring a cloth to wipe this mess up."

Sunny got up, knocking his chair over again. Lionel looked and tutted as Sunny made his way to where Rita stood against the serving hatch. Henry looked up as he passed and nodded at Sunny, then went back to eating his Full House and reading the headline in the paper:

'Robbers move up the M1'

Sunny smiled at Rita. "Can we have some food then?"

Rita blew a bubble with her gum and sucked it back into her mouth. "S'pose you can. What d'you want then?"

Sunny frowned and looked back at the gang.

"I'll come and take the order if you like?"

Sunny smiled again. "And we need a cloth for the table. Coffee got spilt." Rita tutted and gave him a hard stare until he turned and walked back to the gang.

Moments later Rita sauntered over and without a word wiped the table.

"What d'you want then?" she enquired once she'd finished, taking her pencil from behind her ear and blowing another bubble.

"What's 'e got?" said Marco, and he nodded to where Henry was sitting.

"He's got a Full House."

"What's that then?"

"Sausage, egg, bacon, chips, beans, mushrooms and tomatoes and a cup of tea."

"I'll 'ave that then."

"Same for me," said Sunny.

"And me," said Doug.

Rita wrote the order down and then looked at Lionel with a questioning gaze.

"Yes?" she said, "another one? Full House, I mean?"

"No, dear, just a black coffee."

She made a note. "I don't like being called dear," she said, and crossed her arms under her big bosom and stared at Lionel.

"If you say so, dear," and he looked away, opened his paper and read the headline:

'Robbers move up the M1'

Once Rita had retreated to her counter to put the order in, Lionel turned to the others. "While that's comin', 'ere's the plan. This is the third time we've bin up here and it's come to me."

"Who we gonna rob then, Vauxhall or Electrolux?" Sunny asked.

"Neither."

"Why not, there must be thousands and bloody thousands they get from the bank every week."

"Keep yer voice down, someone will 'ear you, you silly bugger," said Lionel. "Those are too big for us, they have guards and there's only four of us."

"Only three really. You ain't much cop, Lionel, with yer leg I mean."

"I'm the brains alright," he said, and put his finger to his mouth. "Now we ain't doin' Vauxhall or any of them. We want somethin' at night an' small, so we're gonna do The Honey Pot."

"What's that then?"

"It's a dance hall."

"And?"

"And, you stupid bugger, on a Saturday night they take the takings for the week to the safe in Barclays

Bank in Dunstable and that's what we're gonna take – it'll be a doddle." He looked at the others. "Well? What d'you think?"

"How much then?" asked Doug.

"Could be ten grand, could be twenty. It's a big place, it's full every night and it's got the pub next door."

"Where is it then?"

"Just at the edge of town, on the main road next to the old cinema – that's now a bingo 'all." Lionel stopped and looked at the other three. "What d'you think?"

There was silence.

"So, we grab the bags and drive back to London?" asked Marco.

"No, my friends, that's where we're gonna be clever. We're gonna drive north and dump the car to put 'em off the scent."

"Put who off the scent?"

"The police, who d'you think!"

There was silence again.

"Where do we dump the car?" asked Sunny.

"Here."

"Then?" said Doug.

"Then, my dear friends, we'll get in our second car and make our way 'ome."

"Down the M1?"

"No, we'll be cleverer than that. We'll go up that accommodation road and across country. A piece of cake. What d'you think?" He sat back in his chair and looked at the others. "Eh? A good plan?"

There was silence for a few minutes this time.

"Did you just think that up, Lionel?" Sunny asked.

"When that bloke said about that road, it all fell into place – it's such a good plan, we'll never get caught."

"I bet there's snags, there always is a snag," said Marco.

"We'll do a dummy run, won't we. That'll show us the snags."

"If you say so, Lionel, you're the brains after all."

"Why aren't we doing somethin' a bit bigger like Vauxhall, that's what I want to know?" Doug said, looking disappointed. "We keep comin' up 'ere and we don't do nuffin'!"

"No, my boy, we're startin' small. If it works, we'll move on to bigger things."

No one had anything left to say so Lionel continued to lay out his plan.

"Next Saturday, we come again. We'll start in the car park at the back of The Honey Pot an' will go from there and run through the plan as agreed."

This was met with silence again.

"Agreed?" said Lionel, and the other three nodded.

"Three Full Houses," Rita said, as she arrived with a tray, "and one black coffee."

"'Ave you got any ketchup?" Sunny asked.

"On the table, look," and she pointed at the small condiments tray. "You need specs, you do."

Lionel opened his paper on the table and started to read as the others tucked into their food.

'Robbers move up the M1'

That was the headline and he ran his finger along the line as he read.

Across the room, Henry had finished and he waved to Rita who came over with the bill, which he settled, and she returned moments later with the change.

"You ain't goin' back to The Manor, are you?" she said, as she picked up his tip. "Oh, thanks for that." She looked at the coins and put them into the pocket of her apron. "You ain't goin' back to The Manor?" she repeated.

"Yes, I am, why?"

"You couldn't give me a lift, could you? Your car's much better than my push bike and I can get Helmit to drop me in the morning."

"Who's Helmit?"

"He's my stepdad, he's the German – I told you."

"Yes, yes, I remember."

"He ain't bad really, although I say it myself, for a German I mean. So do I 'ave a lift?"

"My pleasure," said Henry unconvincingly.

"I'll just be a couple of minutes; I 'ave to get my things."

"Okay. I'll be in the car park," and he got up and moved slowly to the door.

As he did so he could see Lionel reading the article and he went over and pointed to the headline.

"Look at that," he said. "It's just waiting to happen."

Lionel looked up at Henry as he held his finger on the paper.

"What's waiting to happen?"

"A big robbery, that's what it says."

Lionel stared at Henry, took his finger off the paper and sat up in his chair.

"And 'ow do you know that, clever clogs?" Lionel replied, in a slow, slightly threatening manner. "You seem to be very sure."

"I'm sure because I wrote that article. Look, it's got my name, Henry Babage, under the headline there," and he pointed.

"Yer don't say," said Lionel. "And where did the great Henry Babage come by all this knowledge of the criminal world?"

"I've got my contacts, yes, plenty of contacts in the Met you know, yes, it's all about who you know."

"Hmm, and 'ow many criminals d'you know? They've told yer too, 'ave they?"

"Well, I actually—" Henry stopped and looked a little thoughtful.

"So, how many criminals?" Lionel asked again.

"Well, I don't actually know any real criminals."

"So 'ow d'you know they're gonna come up the M1?"

"It stands to reason, doesn't it?"

"What?"

"It stands to reason as the M1 is an excellent getaway for criminals."

Rita now stood by Henry with her coat on and her bag slung over her shoulder.

"I'm ready," she said.

"We must go then." Henry made a small bow towards Rita, and she led the way out of the door and into the car park.

"Who was that then?" Sunny enquired of Lionel.

"If 'e was who 'e said 'e was, 'e was…" Lionel picked up the paper and looked at the article, "'e was Henry Babage, a reporter or journalist if yer like."

"What's he know then?"

"Nothing," said Lionel. "'e's just guessing. 'e's making it up to sell his article, so don't worry about it, although I don't s'ppose you ever would."

"What's that mean?"

"It means that not much goes on in that brain of yours."

"I'm the driver ain't I?"

"But yer ain't got a licence, 'ave yer?"

"I don't need one, do I, not if I'm a villain."

"And yer don't know yer left from yer right."

"Who said that then?"

"I said it, so eat up an' let's make a move."

Chapter Eighteen

Rehearsals Continue

The main hall of the Toddington Secondary School was large and utilitarian, with chairs for four hundred and a stage at one end. Footsteps echoed on the wooden floor as the Young Farmers assembled for the first rehearsal on the stage.

"Is everyone here?" shouted Crispin, and he clapped his hands.

"Act one, scene one – let's have you all on the stage please – the rest of you down here. Lois? Lois, are you here?"

"Yes," shouted Rita, and Crispin went round counting heads and mouthing the number of people present.

"We've got more, haven't we?" He turned to Trisha. "We've got more than we need."

"It's Louise, she's with me," shouted Alexandra, "she can do something else, like costumes."

"Which one is Louise?" Crispin raised his voice.

"Me," said Louise, and she tentatively raised her hand and blinked through her thick glasses.

"Okay, darling, what can you do? I know! You can be the prompter, we'll need one, of that I'm sure. You can read can't you, darling?" Crispin, momentarily distracted, turned to those on the stage. "Let's have you," and then he looked back at Louise. "Yes," he said. "You look like a reader."

Louise blushed.

"Script! Script? Who's got a spare one? The prompter needs a script. The rate we're going you might have to read the whole thing," Crispin said to Louise then stamped his foot.

Gradually there was silence. Crispin had cowboy boots on, with blue jeans and a checked shirt and he clicked his heels.

"I like your trousers and the boots," shouted John.

"Darling, how sweet of you to say so," he said and pointed at John. "But they are jeans not trousers, my boy, haven't you ever seen jeans before? Come on then, where are you all, we must make a start. Act one, scene one," and he stamped his foot again. "Lois, are you ready?"

"Course I am, but I'm the only one who is."

"Come on, where are the hostesses? Who's a hostess? And, John, you get up there."

"I'm a hostess," called out Alexandra.

Crispin looked at her. "You're a hostess? Who gave you that part?"

"I volunteered, why don't you think it suits me?" She giggled as she went up onto the stage, where she put her hands on her hips and wiggled.

Crispin put his hands in front of his face. "Oh my God!" he moaned, as he took his hands away and

Alexandra wiggled again. "No, no, don't do it again, it's too painful. The policemen, who are the policemen? Come on, quickly!"

"I am," said John.

"And me," said Robert.

"Come on then, on the stage, we must make a start."

The rehearsal began, but no one except Rita knew their lines or had any idea how to act, and after two hours, they had only got halfway through the play.

"That was truly awful," said Crispin. "Truly awful. I have never seen so many useless people on a stage. You told me you wanted to show everyone that you are not a bunch of thick farmers. But you are well on the way to proving that very fact." He marched up onto the stage. "What we want is more effort. Learn the damn lines and try to act your parts. If you're no better next time, I'm going to pack it in." He looked round the cast and shouted, "Understand?" so loudly that several jumped. "I'm not wasting my time trying to force you idle lot into performing this play. If you want to do it, you're going to have to put in a lot more effort. Understand?" He shouted the last word and this time was greeted with a murmur of responses.

"Yes, I understand and agree," said John. "He's right, we are rubbish, so let's go down the pub and sort it out, don't you agree, Crispin?"

"All you think about is drink, Farmer John."

"No that's not true, but what about it then, the pub?"

"Why not, it's time we got out of here."

As they walked the short distance from the school to the pub, they met PC Bell coming the other way, pushing his bicycle. He looked them up and down as they walked past.

"Evening, constable," said John, as they passed, "still on duty?"

"That you then, young John? The answer to your question, John my boy, is that I'm always on duty. Yes, always on duty catching criminals, they are everywhere, especially in Toddington."

"That so?" John paused while the others walked on towards the pub.

"Yes, they're everywhere." He tapped his nose as he got a little nearer John and in a whisper said, "We've bin told to keep a special eye out for criminals coming from London."

"Why's that?" John asked.

"Them in the know reckon that they're coming up here as there are rich pickings and they reckon that they are planning a big wages snatch on one of the factories in Luton."

"Which one then?"

"I don't know that, do I, no one knows except the criminal class, but just look at it." He counted on his fingers. "Vauxhall, Skefco, Electrolux, the list goes on, all doling out hundreds of thousands each week," and he took his helmet off and with his hanky he wiped the leather rim and then put it back on his head.

"So have you seen a suspect?" John asked.

"No, but I keep looking. It's easy for them. Get in a big car up the M1, snatch the wages and then they're back down the M1 and in London in twenty-five minutes. So, Master John, you let me know if you see anything."

"Very good," said John. "But I've got to go before the pub closes," and he followed the others.

In the pub, Crispin was at the bar. "Now, I'm not buying everyone a drink, just my dear sister, are you here, sister dear?" he said, as he looked at the change in his hand. "I'll have a gin and it please, landlord, and Judy will have a golden lemonade."

"Can't I have a Babycham?" Judy said, as she looked over her shoulder.

"No, you certainly can't! What would your mother say? You're underage and I would be arrested."

"Spoilsport, everyone else has got a drink. I'll get Pete to buy me one."

"No, you won't and he won't anyway."

"Pete, are you going to buy me a Babycham?"

"Watch out, Pete, the policeman's just outside the door. I'm just been talking to him," said John as he pushed his way through to the bar.

"Didn't he arrest you then?" Judy quipped, as she was handed a golden lemonade.

"What he did say was that them above him reckon there's going to be a wages snatch at one of the factories in Luton. London gangs are going to do it."

"Funny you should say that," said Pete. "Henry said the same thing the other day. He said that he's investigating the gangs, that's why he has gone freelance."

"You don't believe that, do you?" said John. "I bet he was sacked from the *Luton Times*, he's a useless driver as well. Where did you see him, Pete?"

"He's moved into the top flat in The Manor."

"Who are we talking about, am I allowed to know?" Crispin joined in.

"He's Henry Babage, a reporter. He was with the *Luton Times* and he's moved into Toddington," said Pete.

"I know him, yes, I know him. He reviewed a show I was in. Gave me a bloody awful write-up, didn't know what he was talking about, got all our names wrong, it was a disgrace."

"I bet he's been thrown out and that's why he's moved to Toddington," John added. "Talk of the devil, look who's just walked in."

They all turned to see Henry, who pushed his way past Judy to get to the bar, making her spill her drink.

"Don't mind me then," she snapped, as she wiped her hands and brushed down her skirt, where the golden lemonade had spilt. "Look what you've done, I'll never get that stain out," and she looked at her skirt and then at Henry, who glanced at where she was indicating and then turned without saying anything, going towards the bar to order a drink. "Crispin, did you see that, did you see what he did? Pete, did you see?"

Pete didn't react but Crispin put his hand up.

"Sister dear, you deal with him. I'm sure you're more than capable of sorting him out."

She pursed her lips and then went and tapped Henry on the shoulder. "Look here, whatever your name is, what about my skirt? Look at it, it's ruined. I'll never get the stain out."

He looked at her and said nothing, but took out his cigarettes and his gas lighter. He opened the packet and offered her one.

"I don't smoke."

He still said nothing, but took a cigarette and lit it.

"Drink?" he said, and then drew on his cigarette and gazed at her, as she thought through her next move. "Drink?" he repeated but again she did not reply.

He shrugged his shoulders and then she smiled to herself. "Babycham."

"Babycham, landlord," he said, and then took a sip of his pint then a sip of the whisky beside it.

"She's underage," said John, without much conviction.

"She's not buying the drink is she, I am?"

"The policeman is outside, I just saw him."

"I've just seen him as well and he's gone home to look after his poor wife."

"Poor wife, I didn't know he had one. No one would marry him, would they?"

225

"His wife has a condition and he looks after her and he has gone home to put her to bed, so we will not see him this evening."

"What about my skirt then?" Judy started again.

"Do you want this?" Henry held out the Babycham.

"Yes."

"Well shut up then."

"Sister dear, is this man being nasty to you?" Crispin pushed his way to the bar. "Look, he's got you a Babycham and I told you that you were underage."

"Yes, I know but..."

"What would Mother say if she knew?"

"But she won't know unless you tell her, will she?"

"I don't know. Young people these days. What about the nasty Mr Henry Babage pushing people about as if he owns Toddington, eh?" Crispin looked Henry up and down. "Newspaper hack, all gas and no gaiters," and he pointed at Henry, whose brow was furrowed in thought but who remained quiet until he clicked his fingers.

"I never forget a face, never forget a face. I know who you are, you're an actor, I did a review of a show you were in."

"And a bloody awful review it was as well."

"It was a bloody awful review because it was a bloody awful show. Everyone said so, not only me and it was taken off after a week, you know that."

"You're right, it was awful, but there are ways you can say that."

"Don't shoot the messenger, that's what they say."

"Why not? That's what *I* say," and the argument came to a halt.

"What are you doing in Toddington anyway, shouldn't you be treading the boards in London?"

"I should and I will be soon but at the moment I am directing a play for these young people." Crispin turned and swept his arm towards the assembled troop.

"This lot – the Young Farmers? I had heard they were trying but come on – thick as two short planks most of them. I'm surprised they can read the script."

"Hang on, who pulled you out of the snow?" John shouted across the crowd. "Twice I had to do it."

"And why do you live on a farm then, if you think everyone's so thick?" Robert joined in.

"And who carried all your furniture up those stairs then?" Pete looked angry as Louise put her finger to her mouth.

"Shh, everyone, let's find out a little more about our friend Mr Babage." She took a step forwards. "Now, Henry, I'm going to London University, so's he," she pointed at Pete. "So, which university have you been to?"

"I haven't."

"So she's going to college." Louise pointed at Sally then Robert. "He's been to college and got distinctions, so which college did you go to?"

"I didn't."

"So, this one and this one," she pointed at Sue and

Gill, "Are doing A Levels, so how many A Levels have you got."

"None."

"Even John here has four O Levels, how many do you have?"

"Three," he replied miserably.

"I rest my case," she said and everyone clapped.

Henry put his hands up in defeat.

"Where did you go to school?" Trisha asked.

"Bedford, but I was expelled for smoking." Henry turned to address the crowd. "So, folks, I apologise for what I said, but I got what I wanted, which was a response. I didn't mean what I said however, but now I know a lot more about you all, so, a drink, everyone?" he finished just as Alexandra came into the bar.

"What's all this then, you buying a round, Henry? In that case, mine's a pint," and she gave him a peck on the cheek and looked round at the others. "What's this then? No, don't tell me. I can guess. Henry, you've been giving one of your speeches about thick farmers, haven't you. I can tell, because that's why you're buying the drinks?" She pulled the stool away that Henry was leaning on and sat herself at the bar, grimacing at Henry.

"Pint!"

"Yes, yes sorry. A pint, landlord, and one for the rest of them."

"So, Henry, have you caught all these robbers then? You're going on about thick farmers but you're doing no better."

"I don't catch robbers, I investigate and report on them and the police catch them."

"Nick Bell says they're going to do a wages snatch on one of the big factories. Have you found out which one?" asked John.

"No, I haven't, and I wouldn't tell you if I had."

"He's going to start again," Robert grinned.

"No, I'm not, so shut up, you lot."

"Temper, temper." Alexandra put her hand on Henry's arm. "Come on, have another swig of your beer and you'll feel better."

"I don't feel bad," Henry snapped back at her.

"Cheers then." Alexandra raised her pint glass and took a big swig.

"Cheers," said Henry half-heartedly.

"Come on, Henry, what's up?" and she put her hand on his arm again. He looked at her and then blew his nose and leaned on the bar. "Henry, come on, there's something up, I've known you for years, you were at school with my brother."

The others had got their drinks and stood round the fire chatting as Desperate said, "One pound ten shillings please, Henry."

"Bloody hell, that's half a week's wage for a lot of people."

"One pound, ten shillings," Desperate repeated and Henry took out his wallet and handed over a white five-pound note.

Desperate unfolded it and held it up to the light. "Looks alright I s'pose," and he took it to the till and brought the change back.

"Well, Henry?" said Alexandra again.

"Well," he said, "I can tell you, Alexandra, but I wouldn't tell anyone else," and he sniffed and blew his nose again. "It's a problem with going freelance. I'm not having a very good start. I've only sold one story so far." A tear rolled down his cheek.

"Now," Alexandra was sharp, "I know you, Henry Babage, stop that immediately!"

"Stop what?" he said, and sniffed.

"Stop crying, you stupid bugger, I know you, you can turn the water works on at the drop of a hat and I'm not impressed, do you hear?"

He sniffed.

"And stop bloody sniffing will you, I've no sympathy."

He pursed his lips.

"Not even a little bit?" He pulled a smile.

"No, none. You're not short of money, I bet your mother keeps you afloat, and you've only sold one story because you haven't got off your fat arse and found any others – got it?"

"Yes, miss!"

"Don't you dare call me 'miss' or I'll pour this beer all over you."

"You wouldn't."

"No, I actually wouldn't, but I will drink it and hit

you with the mug," and with that they both burst out laughing as Pete came up.

"Another drink?" he said to Henry.

"Yes please," Alexandra piped up. "Another pint, you're a good chap, Pete." She clapped him on the back.

"Henry?" said Pete.

"Thank you," and Henry pushed his pint mug along the bar.

"Who's been to see *The Birds*?" asked Alexandra. "It's brilliant."

"We went the other night," said Sally.

"So did we," said David. "Didn't we, John?"

"Yup, it was great," said John. "Have you been, Pete?"

Pete shook his head as Louise looked at her watch. "Time to go," she said as she looked in her bag for her keys.

"Do you want a lift, Pete?" She looked enquiringly at him.

"I wouldn't take him, Louise, you don't know where he's been," shouted John.

"And he stinks of pigs," David joined in.

Pete looked at Louise, drank the last of his brown ale and nodded and everyone jeered as the pair left.

"Have you seen *The Birds*, Louise?" Pete asked, as she drove down Castle Road.

"No, shall we go?"

231

"Yes, but I can't get to Luton very easily, it's a long way to bike."

"I'll pick you up."

With that arrangement made she dropped him off at Meadow View.

Chapter Nineteen

A Dummy Run

Ten days later, at ten-fifteen on the Saturday night, the big Zodiac was in the car park of The Honey Pot dance hall. Sunny was in the driving seat with Lionel next to him and Doug and Marco in the back.

"Marco, fag," said Lionel, and Marco took a packet from his pocket, took a cigarette out, put it in his mouth to light then passed it to Lionel.

"'ow long 'ave we got to wait?" complained Doug.

"Don't be so bloody impatient. It won't be long now. They close the bar at ten-thirty and all the ticket money's in, so it's any minute I reckon."

"'ow do yer know about it, Lionel, with it being all the way up 'ere?"

"I know the drummer in the band, 'e lives round the corner. 'e comes every week."

They sat in silence and watched the back door of the building. Doug's chin drifted to his chest, his eyes closed and soon he was asleep. The back door of the hall opened and people started to walk out.

"Who's that then, they don't look like dancers, they're a lot of old grannies by the look of 'em?" said Sunny.

"No, they're from the bingo 'all, they share the same entrance," explained Lionel.

They sat and watched as the crowd left the building and went to their cars. A couple, Helmit and Rose, walked towards the car next to them. Helmit unlocked his door, got in and leaned across to open the passenger door. As he went to close his door, he saw the front tyre on the Zodiac was nearly flat so he got out and knocked on the window. Lionel wound it down an inch or two and squinted at the stranger.

"Yous got a flat tyre, mate," Helmit said, in his thick German accent.

"What?"

"Yous got a flat tyre."

"What's he say?" Doug asked, waking abruptly.

"I can't understand him, I think he said we've got a flat tyre."

"I'll look," said Sunny, and he got out and walked round to where Helmit stood.

"Flat tyre," Helmit said again and pointed.

"Well?" shouted Lionel, glaring at Sunny now he had fully wound his window down.

"Flat tyre," Sunny answered. "Well, it's not quite flat, but it needs changing."

"Bloody 'ell, that's all we need, well get on with it, boy, get the jack out." Lionel smiled at Helmit. "Thanks for that, mate." Then he turned his attention to Sunny, showing his frustration. "Well, boy, get the jack then."

234

"We ain't got a jack."

"What?" Lionel shouted "We ain't got a jack? Why ain't we got no jack?"

"It's under Marco's car."

"Why is it under Marco's car?"

"He's got a flat tyre and he ain't got no jack."

"What are we gonna do then, you stupid oaf?"

"You can borrow mine if you like, if you're not too long," said Helmit.

"Thanks, mate, you've saved the day," said Lionel, and he opened his door and lifted his bad leg out then carefully got out and shook Helmit's hand.

"You Irish then?" Lionel asked.

"Do I zound Irish?"

"No, but there are a lot of Irish people in Luton, ain't there?"

"Yes, but we are not in Luton, this is Dunstable, didn't you know that?"

"Oh yes, I forgot." Lionel looked a bit taken aback.

"So if you're not Irish..?"

"I'm German," said Helmit. "Now, let's get on, we can't stand here all night," and he looked at his watch.

He pulled his car forward to make it easier to change the wheel, and Doug and Marco got out to help as Lionel sat back in the passenger seat.

"What are four chaps doing sitting in ze car park in Dunstable at ten-thirty at night?"

Lionel was initially lost for words as the others jacked the car up and undid the wheel nuts, but then came up with, "We were just waiting for someone."

"Oh yes, he must be important then?"

"'e is. 'e's the drummer in the band, yes, 'e's the drummer in the band."

"The band?" said Helmit.

"The band at The Honey Pot."

"We go there sometimes," said Rose, who had got back out of the car to see what was going on as she puffed on her cigarette, "It's quite good, ain't it, Helmit?" Helmit nodded as he moved closer to Rose and away from the others. "There's something fishy going on here, don't you think?" she whispered and he nodded again.

The wheel was soon changed, the jack returned and Helmit and Rose drove off. All the bingo players had now left and the gang got back into the car to wait. About ten minutes later, two men came out of the back door and one was carrying a butcher's basket stacked with linen bank bags.

"Look, 'ere they come," whispered Lionel, as the men got into a car.

"Shall I follow them?" Sunny asked.

"Yes, but keep well back."

He started the engine, and slowly followed them out of the car park. As he did so, two more men came out of the back door carrying bank bags and went to a van on the side of which was written Dunstable Bingo Hall. The first car drove to Barclays Bank in the High Street and the two men got out with the basket. The gang pulled into a car park opposite, waited in the Zodiac, and watched as the bank bags were put into the night safe.

"Piece of cake," Lionel said. "Piece of cake. Now we've got to make our getaway."

Meanwhile, Rose and Helmit had arrived back in Toddington and decided to go and have a coffee at the motorway café before going home so they made their way down the accommodation road.

Back in the Zodiac, Sunny put his foot on the accelerator and revved the engine.

"Straight up the M1 then?" he asked.

"Yes, let's go."

"Which way then?"

"Go on, left out of the car park."

Sunny revved again, let the clutch out and spun the wheels on the gravel as he raced off. He passed out of the car park and turned right.

"Where are yer going, you silly bugger, I said left." Lionel banged the dashboard. "I don't know why we 'ave you as the driver, yer don't even know yer left from yer right."

Sunny pulled the handbrake and spun the car round to face the opposite direction.

"This way!" he said, as they raced off.

"Who's going to report us then when we do the job?" Doug asked.

"Could be anyone, there'll be people about and the

two chaps from the dance hall might."

"Why don't we bang 'em on the 'ead then?"

"No violence," said Lionel.

"We could tie 'em up?"

"It'd take too long. No, if we do as I say, no one will trace us once we've swapped cars."

Ten minutes later they arrived in the car park of the motorway café.

"'ow long did that take?" Lionel looked at his watch, wrote a note in a small diary and put it back in his pocket.

"Good. Look, we're 'ere, can we get some grub? I'm 'ungry," said Doug.

"So am I," said Sunny. "We could 'ave a Full House again, what d'you say, Doug?"

"Sounds great, what about you, Marco?"

"No, it's too late for me, but I'll have an espresso. Come on, Lionel."

Lionel got out of the car and using his two sticks slowly made his way to the door of the café and the others followed. When they went in there was a group of CND supporters at one table and Rose and Helmit at another, having coffee.

"Look, Lionel, it's them people who lent us the jack, what're they doin' 'ere?" said Doug.

"It looks as though they're 'aving a coffee to me, it's a free world, ain't it?"

Rose looked up and then nudged Helmit. "It's them blokes again, the boss one's a cripple. What are they doing here?"

"I don't know," said Helmit. "Looks as though zey're going to have somezing to eat. No law against that."

"They're up to no good, I'm sure of it."

She took a cigarette from the packet on the table in front of her and lit it. Rita stood by the jukebox listening, as another group of CND supporters came in and sat with the first lot. She went over to where Rose was sitting.

"Mum, can you wait a bit and take me 'ome, I'll only be quarter of an hour and then Sheila takes over?"

Rose looked at her watch and then at Helmit.

"I'll get you another coffee for free?"

"Go on," said Helmit. "We can vait."

Three more CND supporters came in, all carrying placards. The gang sat down and Lionel took out his diary and flicked to the page where he had written the timings.

"Now, if it took fourteen minutes to get here from The Honey Pot, it will take twenty minutes to get back from 'ere as we'll 'ave to go up to the Toddington junction, round it and then back."

"What other car are we gonna use?" asked Marco.

"Yours, of course."

"Mine? I don't like that idea."

"Why not?" said Doug. "I like your car, it's got leather seats and it's got a sun roof and it's clean."

"That's cos I clean it every week."

239

"You're outvoted, Marco," said Sunny.

"Well, if we do use it, I'm gonna drive it."

"Okay," said Lionel.

"And if we are gonna use it, I ain't leaving it in a motorway café car park – it ain't safe."

"What you mean, it ain't safe?"

"Someone might steal it."

"You're insured, aren't you?"

"Nah. I don't bovver wiv that."

"What are we going to do then? If you won't leave it in the car park."

They were all silent.

"I know," said Marco. "I can stay here wiv the car, while you go and do the snatch. It will be easy enough with the three of you, and then I can be ready an' waiting."

"What's gonna 'appen to the Zodiac, Lionel?" asked Sunny.

"We leave it 'ere. It din't cost us nothing 'cos we stole it. Remember?"

Rita came over, stood and put the carbon paper into her order pad. "What you want then?" she demanded, as she chewed her gum and blew a small bubble, which burst and she gobbled the gum back into her mouth.

"Full House," said Doug.

"Same," said Sunny.

"An espresso for me," said Marco.

"And a cup of tea for me, miss," added Lionel.

Rita wrote the order, tore off the chit and stomped over to the counter and put it on the spike. She then went and stood with Rose and Helmit and looked at her watch.

"Five minutes," she said, as she looked at Rose.

"Rita, them men over there, we saw them at the bingo, didn't we, Helmit?"

"Yes, I'm sure it's them."

"They've been in 'ere before, more than once, up to no good I would say."

"Yes. That's what we thought," said Rose.

Chapter Twenty

Costumes are Fitted

The hall at the secondary school echoed as Crispin clapped his hands. "Attention, attention!" he shouted and looked around at those on the stage and others sitting on chairs in the auditorium.

"Everyone, that was so much better than last time. A very determined effort has brought you up to a rather poor standard. Now, we are two weeks away from the performance and the dress rehearsal is on the Friday, so we need to talk costumes and makeup. Trisha, that's you," he said, and bowed to her as she got up.

"We're getting on quite well, but the difficult ones are Lois and the hostesses as they are a range of sizes."

"You can say that again," said John.

"John, please don't say things like that," said Trisha.

"Why not, it's true."

"What's he wearing, Trisha?" asked Alexandra.

Trisha consulted her list. "Oh, he's a policeman, so have you got a uniform, John?"

"No, I'm going to be dressed in jockstrap and gaiters." Everyone laughed. "Actually, Robert has got a uniform from his dad who's a Special PC and he's borrowed one from his mate for me."

"Right, so we can tick you off."

"And the robbers, David and Tony, are getting their own, and there's a waiter – that's you, Pete, and you've got a DJ so you're fixed and we're nearly there. Oh yes and Louise says she will do the makeup and her granny will help her and so will Rose, Rita's mum."

"Trisha, my landlady, Joyce, says she'll help with the costumes too."

"Thanks, Pete, I suggest we start the next rehearsal early and everyone brings their costume, even if it's not finished and we can get them sorted out."

On the appointed day, the men were quickly dealt with as one at a time they tried on their costumes, and when all had been approved, they went to the pub, while the girls were fitted. The changing room was cold and Crispin sat in the hall, waiting for each one to parade.

"Have those damn boys gone, Crispin?" Trisha asked.

"Yes, they're all in the pub."

"Thank God for that, now, let's get on."

"Where can we change?" asked Alexandra.

"Well, this is the changing room, but you can go round the corner where it's a bit more private or you can go in the toilet, but I don't think that would work with your dress."

"Come on," said Joyce, "I'll give you a hand," and she marched Alexandra away.

"Who got the costumes?" Louise asked.

"Crispin did, from a place in London he knows.

That is he got the four hostesses and Lois's dress. Look, it's here," said Judy, pointing to the red silk dress hanging on a peg on the wall.

"Do you think I will get into that?" said Rita, as she held it against herself. "It's the right length, look." She pressed it against her legs.

Alexandra came from round the corner in her dress and did a pirouette in front of everyone.

"Look! It fits, or it more or less does," and she spun round again.

"Careful, careful," said Joyce. "Come here, you're not quite done up at the back." She grabbed Alexandra's shoulders, turned her round and tried to do up the buttons down the back. "Breathe in, girl," she said, as she pulled the back of the dress together. "No, it's not quite meeting, but I can move these buttons, it's easy. Now let's have the next hostess. Let's get them all done before we do Lois."

Rita held the dress to her body again and spun round.

"I hope you can get into that, Rita. It'll be a tight squeeze."

Rita grimaced and sat down to wait her turn for fitting. When all the hostesses had been done, they paraded together and everyone clapped.

"Now it's your turn, Rita. Do you want to come round the corner?" said Trisha.

"No, I ain't bothered, let's do it 'ere," and she sat down on a chair and took her shoes and socks off.

"That's a point, are there any shoes?"

"Yes, don't worry they're over there, size six and they match the dress."

Judy fetched them. Rita then stood up and undid the waistband of her skirt and took it off. Joyce stood in front of her and took the skirt, as the others sat on the chairs around the wall. Rita then removed her jumper and passed it to Joyce then undid the buttons of her blouse.

"How much else is she going to take off?" Judy whispered to Alexandra.

There was now complete silence as they watched Rita. Joyce took her blouse and Rita was left in a white bra and pants. She put her hands round her back, undid her bra and took it off, putting it on the pile of clothes that Joyce held. Trisha put her hand over her open mouth and blinked.

"Where's my bag?" asked Rita as she looked then pointed to it on a chair.

Judy picked it up and handed it to her, and she rummaged through the contents and pulled out what at first glance looked like a hanky. She gave the bag back to Judy, who sat back with the others who all appeared aghast at what was happening. Rita put the scrap of material on the pile of clothes and then took her pants off, adding them to the pile and exchanging them for the mysterious object. She then held it up so everyone could see it had strings on it, and she kept turning it around. She then glanced across at the others, who looked shell-shocked.

"What you lot looking like that for? Ain't you ever seen anyone wiv nuffin' on?" She kept organising the hanky with the strings. "This is a thong, which I'm now gonna put on."

She looked at Joyce, who was giggling, as she stepped into the thong and pulled it up, wiggling her bottom. Trisha was bright red with embarrassment and looked at the ceiling and then back at Rita. Joyce put Rita's clothes on a chair and picked up the dress, carefully undoing the inbuilt bra and zip, and held it for Rita to step into. Once she had both feet in, she pulled the dress up. The bodice fell forwards as Rita wriggled and Joyce pulled to get it over her bottom. It was very tight.

"This is why I wear a thong," and she pointed at her bottom. "I won't have any knicker elastic lines showing on my bum, that's right, ain't it, Joyce?"

"That's right, Rita."

The others started whispering.

"Where on earth do you buy such a thing?" Alexandra asked.

"Sex shop in Luton," muttered Gill.

"Well, I never," said Alexandra, as Rita held the bodice to her bust and Joyce slowly pulled the zip up. She reached in and did up the hooks on the bra and then pulled the zip to the top.

"Shoes! Where are the bloody shoes?" Rita shouted.

Judy brought them and knelt on the floor and Rita put her hand on her shoulder as she helped the high heels on. The bodice had no shoulder straps and Rita pulled it up over her large bosom then tottered forwards and took a bow. Everyone clapped and Joyce gave her a peck on the cheek.

"You look fantastic, Rita, you really do. Come on everyone, let's go and show Crispin."

They all paraded onto the stage, and Crispin put his paper down and applauded their arrival.

Chapter Twenty-One

A Trip to the Cinema

"Pete," said Steve, who stood in the mixing shed, trying to tie up a bag of meal. "I can't tie this bag, you've filled it too full. I'll never tie it up."

He stood up as straight as he could and took the piece of string that he was going to tie the sack with out of his mouth.

"Then untie a couple of the others and move some across." Pete sounded rattled.

"You'll 'ave to help then, I can't 'old the sack and scoop out at the same time."

Pete fetched a scoop and returned to where Steve held the top of the sack open. He faced Pete, but his eyes were looking to the left.

"You're doing it again, Steve," and he closed the bag up and burst out laughing. "Why do you do it? It makes you look so stupid." Steve looked at Pete again and went cross-eyed. "That's even worse."

"You could do it," Steve challenged Pete.

"I wouldn't even try, come on, open the bag and I'll move a bit across to the other sacks."

The operation was quickly completed and Steve returned the scoop, while Pete tied up the bags.

"Pete, Grafton says 'e can't undo your knots

and 'e 'as to cut them an' it's a waste of string."

"They don't come undone like your knots, but they will undo if you know how. Get the sack barrow and we'll load up."

Pete backed the trailer in and with Steve's help put the running board in place, which allowed them to wheel the sacks up onto the trailer.

"You stack, Steve, I'll wheel them up," he said, and quite quickly they had the two tonnes loaded.

When they got to the pigs, they unloaded one tonne at the fattening house and took the other tonne to the meal store for the dry sows and boars. Each time Steve pulled the sacks from the front to the back of the trailer and Pete carried them into the store.

"Pete, I'm 'earing you've got a young lady and she's got a car, is that right?"

"Well, what of it?"

"I'm told you before, boy, wimin will draw you further than gunpowder will blow you."

Pete said nothing.

"Did you hear me, boy?"

"Yes, I heard you."

"Well?"

"Well, what?"

And no more was said.

"Pete?"

"What now?"

"Is your young lady in that play you're doin'?"

"No, she's not in it, and she's not my young lady."

"Rita's in it, ain't she, Pete?"

"Yes, she's the star, but you're not coming so you won't see her."

"She's a bit of alright, don't you think, Pete? You could do worse; you could do worse."

Silence fell for a few moments.

"Pete, is your landlady in the play?"

"No."

"But I heard she was at the rehearsal and so was your young lady."

"She was, because she's helping with the costumes and Louise is the prompter."

"Oh."

"What part are you in the play?"

"I'm a waiter."

"Oh."

"They tell me it's the dress rehearsal on Friday, is that right?"

"Yes, and then the performance on Saturday."

"Pete?"

"Yes, Steve."

"Your young lady wears glasses, don't she?"

"Yes."

"She'll need them if she's the prompter, Pete."

"Yes, Steve."

"If it's the dress rehearsal on Friday, are you sure you know all the words, it don't seem long since you started rehearsals?"

"We've got one more on Wednesday, so we'll see."

Soon the trailer was empty and they put all the empty bags in a heap at the front and got ready to head back to the yard.

"Pete!" shouted Grafton. "Wait!" And he came up holding the slap marker which was used for tattooing the pigs when they went for slaughter so the carcass could be identified. "Pete, can you take this to Robert and tell him we've lost a letter. The 'T' is gone and we're going to need it on Thursday." Grafton handed the marker over to Pete. "I think the screw that holds the numbers in has fallen out, so tell him to get Helmit to have a look."

Pete took the marker and handed it to Steve to hold on to as he'd be travelling on the pile of bags.

"Grafton, you don't happen to have the number of the chap that Zeppelin came from, the one with the funny name?"

"No, sorry, Pete, you'll have to ask Mary for that. Why do you need it?"

"I know!" shouted Steve.

Grafton turned and took a few steps back.

"I know," Steve said again as he puckered his pop hole mouth.

"Why then, Steve?"

Steve grinned at Grafton. "Ain't there a daughter there?"

"Aha, you're right, Steve, she came round didn't she? Name of…? Now, let me think. Louise! Nice girl, did you see her, Steve?"

"I did and what do I always say about wimin? Come on, Pete, let's get goin', you've got to go an' see Mary and I want to go home. Scout is comin' round." Steve clambered onto the back of the trailer and made himself a nest in the empty bags. "Don't drive too fast, Pete, I'm back 'ere, don't forget."

Back at the farm Pete parked the tractor and trailer and went to the office to find Mary.

"Hello, Pete, we don't see you in here very often."

"No, I was just wondering if I could have a phone number?"

"Oh, and whose phone number might that be then?" She raised her eyebrows.

"Um... I don't suppose you have one for Colonel Dawingditmus?"

"What do you want to speak to him for?" she laughed. "You don't actually want to speak to him at all, do you? It's the daughter, what was her name? Let me think. Yes, I've got it. It was Louise," and she thumbed through the phone book on her desk. "What's it worth then?"

Pete blushed. "Go on, Mary, just write it down for me. Crucial won't know and it will save me going to Directory Enquiries."

"Okay, here we go, but you owe me one, understand?"

"Yes," said Pete, as she handed him the number on the back of an old envelope.

Pete cycled back to Meadow View, got some change and went up to the phone box. He phoned Louise and arranged that she would pick him up at seven pm.

"You going out then, Pete?" Joyce asked. "You don't want to see *Coronation Street*?"

"No, we're going to the pictures."

"You and who then?"

"Just a friend."

"What's her name then, come on tell me. Is she pretty?"

"Well, her name's Louise and she's got glasses."

"And?" Joyce said, "And I know her, don't I? She was at the rehearsal the other night. She's the prompter and she's going to help with the makeup. Now I remember. You went down the motorway café with her the other day."

Pete looked at Joyce and coloured slightly.

"You're going up in the world then, Pete, her dad's a colonel something or other, ain't he?"

"Something like that."

"All you public school types stick together, don't you?"

Pete didn't answer.

"She's got brains though, Pete, you can see that and she'll be there on Wednesday. I'm coming, you know, so's Rose. It's good fun. If I'm going to help, I want to know all about it; it's the last one before the dress rehearsal, we won't be any trouble. Promise."

Joyce took his pudding plate and put it in the sink. "What film are you seeing then?"

"*The Birds*, it's Alfred Hitchcock."

"I bet you don't see much of the film." There was a toot of a car horn. "There she is, Pete, you better go, can't keep her waiting."

Pete took his jacket from the back of the chair and left.

They were soon on the motorway and Louise put her foot flat on the floor as they sped towards Luton.

"Do you always drive this fast?"

"Always, well on the motorway I do, but it won't do ninety. Look, eighty-eight is as fast as it will go."

"But it's getting hot, look at that," and he pointed to the temperature gauge. "Look, it's in the red."

"Oh, that doesn't matter," she said.

"It does, you'll seize it up if you're not careful."

"What do I do?"

"Slow down and I'll check the water in the radiator when we get there, and tomorrow you can bring it over and we can blow the radiator out at the farm, they have a compressor."

"Oh damn, that reminds me. I'm going to have to come over tomorrow anyway. Father asked me to bring something for you and I left it on the sideboard."

"What's that then?"

"A tattoo something or other, Robert rang and Father had one, whatever it is."

The next day at five o'clock, Louise drove up to the door of the workshop where Pete was waiting.

"You found us then?"

"Of course, I've been here before," Louise said, as she got out of her car.

Steve, who stood holding his bicycle, raised his cap, smiled at Louise then went cross-eyed.

"This is Steve. You only saw him in passing last time," said Pete, "Steve, meet Louise."

Steve raised his cap again. "Pleased to meet you, miss," he said as he put his foot on the pedal of the bike and started slowly scooting down the yard.

"Here it is, Pete, I remembered today." She handed him the tattoo, which was a square of metal about half the size of a matchbox with sharp nails embedded in it in the shape of a 'T'. "What's it for?"

"It goes in the slap marker, come and look," he said, and they went into the workshop where Helmit was brushing the floor.

"Here we go, Helmit." Pete handed him the letter.

"Aha, this von't take long," and he picked up the slap marker, which looked like a hatchet with a square lump of metal on the end. He put the letter into the head of the marker and screwed it up. "There ve are, miss," and he showed it to Louise.

"'*TM23*'," she read. "What's it for, Pete?"

"It's to mark the pigs when they go for slaughter; you press the nails into an ink pad then you bang it on the pig's leg and that tattoos the *TM23* so they can identify the carcass."

"Oh, that doesn't sound very nice."

"It doesn't hurt them," said Pete defensively.

"How do you know? Have you ever asked a pig? You said castrating them doesn't hurt, but I bet it does."

Pete didn't answer, but grabbed the air line instead and pulled it towards the door.

"Can you release the bonnet, Louise, then I can blow out the radiator?"

"How do I do that then?"

"There must be a catch somewhere, have a look, it will be in the grille at the front."

"I vill do it," said Helmit, and there was a click and the bonnet released. Pete held it up by the prop.

Helmit unscrewed the radiator and looked inside. "It's a bit low," he said, and then pulled out the engine dipstick and looked. "That's low as vell and the oil is black as black."

"What do I have to do?"

"Ve can put some vater in the radiator and then you can go to a garage and buy some oil."

"Where does that go in?"

Helmit pointed to the oil cap on the top of the engine.

"And look, the radiator is full of muck. Get Pete to blow it out and it vill go much better. Pete, make sure you put the light out vhen you go."

"Okay, Helmit."

"Oh, and I forgot to tell you, Rose is coming to your rehearsal tomorrow, she is really enjoying helping."

"So is Joyce, my landlady. She told me Rose was coming."

"And so's my granny," said Louise. "I'm going to be bringing her, so let's get the car sorted."

Helmit left and Pete pulled the air line to the car and then went into the workshop and switched the compressor on. Clouds of dust appeared when he blew the radiator and Louise went into the workshop to avoid them. When he had finished, Pete coiled up the airline, put it back where it belonged and switched the compressor off. Louise held the slap marker and looked at the pins that made the tattoo.

"Granny's got a tattoo, you know, Pete?" she said, as she looked thoughtfully at the marker.

"I know."

"Bloody hell. I'd forgotten you must have seen it when you got her out of the bath. That's so embarrassing, I don't want to talk about it."

"Well don't then."

"No, but anyway, she has a tattoo, I saw it once, but she doesn't talk about it."

"I understand."

"She's Jewish, well I suppose I am part Jewish."

"Yes, I know, Henry told me."

"Why is Henry Babage going about spreading gossip? He's got nothing to talk about, you know that, Pete, he was expelled from Bedford before he even got to A Level. I really don't like him, do you?"

"I don't know, he's a bit different to most but at least he says hello when I meet him."

Chapter Twenty-Two

Robbers in the Pub

"Pete! Are you ready?" Joyce shouted up the stairs.

"Can't I come, Mummy?" said Patsy, who stood next to her mother.

"No, dear, you stop here, Daddy will put you to bed. Freddie, call Patsy," Joyce called and Freddie came out and took Patsy into the sitting room.

There was a knock at the back door, then it opened and Rose stepped in.

"I've let myself in, Joyce, I hope that's alright?"

"Yes, come on in, we're just waiting for Pete. Pete!" Joyce shouted again and there was a slam of the door and a clattering as he rushed down the stairs.

"Has Tony gone?" he asked.

"Yes, he went ages ago."

"So has Rita," said Rose. "She wouldn't wait and walk with her mother."

"Right, bye," Joyce called back into the house as they stepped out into the twilight of a spring evening.

"Pete, did you put your DJ out for me to press?"

"Yes, I hung it on the airing cupboard door."

"I've got Rita's in the dining room. She looks fantastic once she's got it on, don't you think Rose?"

"Yes, she does, it was all a bit embarrassing

watching her try it on, however we can't talk about that with Pete here, can we?"

"No fear, but it was a laugh."

When they got to the school hall, most of the cast were already there and Crispin sat on a chair in the middle of the stage, holding a copy of the script and checking off the actors from a list in the front. He looked up and scanned the room, "John. Where's John?" At the moment he finished speaking the door flung open and John rushed into the hall. His cheeks were flushed and he breathed heavily.

"Sorry I had to run to get here on time."

"I admire your effort, John. Well done." John smiled but then paused and patted his chest, his smile fading.

"Bugger, I'm left my jacket behind."

"Not that ghastly donkey jacket?"

"Yeah, it's special that is, it's from Wimpy."

"The only disaster here is that you will be reunited with it as soon as you're back home."

"No, no. I'm left it at the pub."

"At the pub?"

"Yeah, I 'ad a quick one on the way." Crispin raised his hands.

"And there was me thinking you were putting the play first."

"I'll go and get it."

"Get it later, we're starting now." Crispin clapped his hands to get everyone's attention.

"But someone might nick it," John pleaded.

"They'll be doing you a favour if they do, darling." Crispin turned away to gather the rest of the cast.

Louise came in with Geraldine, who went and sat in the front row with Joyce and Rose.

"You're Louise's granny, aren't you?" Joyce introduced herself.

"Yes, she's the prompt and I've offered to help with the makeup, so I've come tonight to see it for the first time."

"Pleased to meet you, I'm Joyce, Pete's landlady, and this is Rose, Rita's mother. Rita's the leading lady in the play."

Crispin clapped his hands. "Okay, okay, let's get started. Act one, scene one! Come on now, all on the stage and I'm going to sit in the audience tonight." And he came daintily down the four steps clutching his fur coat, which was draped over his shoulders. "Now, John, get up there. I don't want any cheek from you tonight, do you understand?"

"Yes, miss," John retorted.

"You are a pain, John, has anyone ever told you that? And you're not funny. Now, ladies, I'm going to sit with you." Crispin blew each one a little kiss. "You'll be safe with me," he said as he gave a forced smile, sat and pulled his fur coat over his knees. "Got to keep warm, you know," he whispered to Rose, who looked awkward as he opened the script. "Now, who's going to do the curtain? We need someone for the curtains. Trisha, who can do it?"

"It's alright. Harold will, he's not got a part and he's always here."

Harold walked onto the stage, took a bow, then fumbled his way behind the curtains and found the draw ropes.

"Close them," Crispin shouted, as Harold pulled on a rope, which opened them fully.

"The other way."

"You could 'ave said," they heard Harold mumble, as the curtains closed.

"Right, one minute, everyone take your places. Are you ready, curtain man, what's your name?"

"'Arold," a voice said.

"Right! Five, four, three, two, one – GO!"

In the pub, Desperate closed the curtains as the only customer, Henry Babage, sat at the bar.

"Are you going to the play on Saturday?" he asked, as he came back and wiped the bar top.

"I think I will have to, I should be able to send a report to the *Luton News*."

"You're scraping the barrel a bit, if you're selling to them. They won't pay much, will they?"

"No, afraid not, but beggars can't be choosers, can they?"

"I suppose not, but you're not a beggar are you, Henry?"

"No, but I'm not getting many commissions, so anything is welcome."

He drank his pint and stood.

"I'll see you at the weekend, Desperate. I'll need a drink to get through the play," and he left.

Ten minutes later, the big Zodiac drew up outside the door of the pub.

"Good, I could do with a pint," said Doug. "Whose round is it?"

"Now wait," said Lionel. "'as everyone got everything so far? This is the last time we're goin' to be 'ere before Saturday?"

"We've still got to bring Marco's car up an' park it at the motorway café, when are we goin' to do that?" Sunny asked.

"We'll do that on the day we come up. We'll get to the café, drop off the car an' Marco, then 'ead on to The Honey Pot. Then we'll do the circuit again, like we are now."

"Let's 'ave a pint then?"

"No, no, not till everyone's got it."

"I've got it," said Doug.

"So 'ave I," said Sunny.

"Marco?" said Lionel. "Marco?" he said again, and looked round to where Marco had his chin on his chest and was gently snoring.

Doug nudged him and he woke up and snorted.

"Pint, Marco?" said Doug.

"Yes, yes," he said and opened the door.

"No, no!" said Lionel again. "D'you know all the arrangements, Marco? D'you understand what we're goin' to do?"

"Yeah, we're goin' to 'ave a pint."

"You stupid sod! D'you understand 'ow we're goin' to get away?"

"Yes, course I do, it's a piece of cake that's what you said, Lionel. You're the brains, that's what you said, din't he, Doug?"

Doug looked at Marco, but didn't answer the question. Instead, he said, "I 'ope they've got some crisps in the pub, I'm hungry."

"You never stop goin' on about food, don't you 'ave anythin' to eat at 'ome?"

Doug looked at Lionel, but had no answer for him. They all got out of the car and followed Lionel slowly into the pub. He went to the bar, hung his sticks on it, and got his wallet out.

"Who wants what, then?"

"Pint," the other three said in unison.

"And a packet of crisps," Doug chirped up.

"And I'll 'ave a large scotch and a pint," said Lionel, as he looked at a poster on the wall.

"*The Queen of Hearts,*" he said, reading the words out loud. "Saturday. Hmm… I'm sure I've seen that one before."

"Yes, the Young Farmers are doing it," said Desperate, as he put the pints on the bar.

Lionel took ten shillings from his wallet and paid.

"You're not from around here?" Desperate said, as he handed Lionel the change.

"London," said Doug, as he took his pint "'Ave you got them crisps?"

Desperate opened the square tin box on the floor and handed a packet to Doug.

"What brings you up here then?"

Lionel looked at the others and thought for a moment. "Just 'ad a bit of business to do, yer know 'ow it is?"

"Oh," said Desperate, "And what sort of business are you in then?"

He looked keenly at Lionel, who hesitated. "A bit of this an' that, yer know."

"Oh yes," answered Desperate, as Lionel looked at the poster once more.

"Yes, I'm sure I've seen that play. It has a big part for the leading lady, if I remember."

"I think they're rehearsing tonight, so the cast will be in later."

Back in the school hall, Act One was just finishing.

"Curtains," shouted Crispin. "Curtains."

"Harold!" everyone shouted in unison and the curtains twitched but didn't move. Then suddenly they began to close.

"Sorry. I got the wrong rope," could be heard from Harold.

265

The audience of three ladies applauded as the curtains closed and Crispin got up and clapped his hands.

"Five minutes, everyone, and no one is to go down the pub. That means you, John, I'm watching you."

"Yes, miss," said John.

"Isn't Rita good?" said Rose. "Don't you think so, Joyce?"

"Yes, she's brilliant, must take after her mother."

"Not me," said Rose. "I couldn't act to save my life."

"She is very talented and she must have got it from somewhere," said Geraldine. "Your husband maybe?"

There was silence and Joyce looked at Rose and then at Geraldine.

"Go on, tell her, Joyce, everyone else knows."

"Knows what?" said Geraldine.

"Rita's father is not Rose's husband."

"Oh, I'm sorry. I didn't mean…" Geraldine stopped.

"Don't worry, Rita's father was a Yank, or rather he was an Italian Yank. He could sing and dance with the best of them. Operatic, you could call him. He could charm the pants off anyone, so to speak, and I'm sure I wasn't the only one it happened to. Then he went home and that was that. Then Helmit came along and I married him and he's a really good man, even though he's German."

"German?" said Geraldine, with an apprehensive edge to her voice.

"Yes, he was in a U-boat, then got captured and was

266

a prisoner of war. After the war he couldn't go home, as the Russians had invaded where he lived, so he stopped here."

"And you, Geraldine? Were you in the war? Your accent is not English," Rose asked.

Geraldine looked from one to the other and then Crispin clapped his hands.

"Act two, scene one. Everybody on stage," and the cast started rushing about.

"I'll tell you later," said Geraldine to Rose and Joyce, and they took their seats again.

"Curtains," shouted Crispin, and the curtains twitched twice, before gradually opening.

The gang took their pints and went to sit on a table in the corner of the bar, while Desperate got a bucket of coal and made up the fire.

"When we've done the snatch an' got all this money, 'ow are we goin' to divide it up?" asked Doug.

Lionel cleared his throat. "Well, it's my idea an' my car; so I'll have half and you lot can 'ave the other 'alf."

The three others looked up.

"You what? That ain't fair," said Marco. "I'm providin' a car as well as you."

"And I'm the driver."

"You ain't got a licence, Sunny, an'... an' you still don't know yer left from yer right, so you ain't much of a driver."

"And I'm the muscle so I don't agree," said Doug.

"Nor do I, we should 'ave a quarter each," said Marco.

Doug and Sunny nodded in agreement.

"But I don't think—"

"No 'buts', Lionel, we want it divided equally or we don't come," said Doug, and the other two nodded.

Lionel grimaced and took a swig of his pint.

"A quarter each, Lionel, or we don't come, that's only fair."

"Okay, okay, a quarter each then, but keep yer voices down, we don't want anyone to 'ear."

"There's no one in 'ere."

"There's 'im," and Lionel nodded at Desperate.

When Desperate had made the fire up, he took the brass scuttle and put it on the bar then went through the hatchway, took a bag from a cupboard and put it by the scuttle.

"Marco, it's your turn to get the drinks," said Lionel, and he pushed his empty glass across the table, as did the others.

Marco picked up the glasses and put them on the bar.

"Four pints, landlord," and he rattled the change in his pockets. "That bag full of money then?" He nodded at the bag propped against the scuttle.

"Sorry?" said Desperate.

"The bag, it says *Barclays Bank* on it."

"Oh no," and Desperate smiled. "It's got my brass cleaning kit in it. We've collected a few of them bags over the years to keep the change from the till in."

"Marco," Lionel shouted, "Don't forget the whisky."

"What did he call you?" asked Desperate, as he handed over the beer.

"Marco."

"How did you get that name, it ain't English, is it?" said Desperate.

"What, Marco? My dad was in the Spanish Civil War and when it finished 'e 'ad to leave Spain, so 'e came to London and met my mum."

"Well, I never," said Desperate.

At the hall, the curtain closed for the last time and the actors came out to meet the small audience. Crispin clapped his hands once more.

"We are getting there, folks. We are getting there. See you all on Friday for the dress rehearsal. All here at six," and he threaded his arms into his fur coat. "The pub calls, eh?" Judy followed him out.

"Are you coming, Louise?" Pete asked.

"No, I've got to take Granny home. But I'm coming to the farm tomorrow, my last visit."

"I'll see you then."

Chapter Twenty-Three

The Dress Rehearsal

David opened his sandwich box and took one out then lifted the corner of the slice of bread to see what was in it.

"What you got then?" asked Pete.

"Cheese. You?"

"Pickle."

"Swap?"

"Just one," and they exchanged one sandwich.

Steve sat opposite, where he could look out of the door of the workshop where they sat. He had taken his false teeth out as usual and was sucking and munching his sandwich, and every now and then he took a swig of cold tea from an old orange squash bottle, his mouth collapsing to a little pop hole. All of a sudden, he sat up as he noticed something outside.

"Pete?"

"Yes, Steve."

"Your young lady's just driv up. Yeah, it's 'er, she's goin' in the office, 'spect she's gone to see Crucial or maybe Robert." Steve continued munching and then he sat up again. "Gor, it's Mary, she's late on parade."

The click of Mary's high heels could be heard, as she walked across the concrete to the offices.

"Helmit?" Steve looked across to where Helmit sat.

"Yes, Steve."

"Are you going to bingo at the weekend?"

"No, we're going to the play, are you going?"

Steve chuckled and looked sideways at Pete and David.

"No, I ain't goin', I see enough of these two all day, let alone seein' 'em on stage. Any road, it's after my bedtime."

Viv came in and looked round to see who was about. He had his notebook in his hand.

"Right. Simon and Sean, you're going fencing, ready for the cattle to go out. Winston, the mixing shed. Helmit, Crucial wants you to look at the gate at the top of Manor Drive. David, you help Helmit. Tony, where's Tony?"

"Gone to the dentist," said Pete.

"Well, he can help Simon and Sean when he gets back. Pete and Steve, go down the pigs to help weighing, and, Steve, you can turn all the bags and heap them."

"How we goin' to get down there? 'Ave I got to go on the old grid iron?"

"Yes, have you got your bike, Pete? It would make it easier and then Robert can bring Louise down. All sorted. Okay, any questions?"

"Yeah," said Simon. "Why do I always 'ave to go fencing? Can't David do that and I'll go with Helmit?"

"No, just shut up, Simon. You always grumble,

whatever job I give you. Oh, I nearly forgot, Pete, make sure you take the slap marker with you. It is mended, isn't it, Helmit?"

Helmit nodded.

"Come on then, Steve, let's get going, fetch the old grid iron," said Pete.

As they cycled the sun came out, and once they got to the end of the drive, it was all downhill to the piggery.

"Pete, your young lady's coming down the pigs, that's what Viv said, din't 'e?"

"Yes."

Steve chuckled as he got off his bike and leaned it against the wall of the office. Grafton came out as they arrived.

"Good job you've come, Pete, Wally hasn't turned up this morning. Just cycle down and see what's up with him then we'll know what to do."

Wally lived in a flat in the stable block of The Manor, and Pete cycled through the arch into the wide yard and knocked on his door. His wife came to the door with her dressing gown on and smoking a fag.

"Is Wally coming? Grafton wants to know."

"No 'e ain't, 'e's got sciatica."

"Okay, I'll tell Grafton."

Pete turned and could see Rose on the other side, hanging out her washing.

"What's up with him?" she asked, as Pete drew near.

"Sciatica, whatever that is."

"He'll get the sack before long if he doesn't watch out," she said, as she hung up some linen bank bags with *Barclays* written on them.

"Dress rehearsal on Friday, Pete, are you ready?"

"Just about, Joyce is going to press my DJ."

"I think it's really good fun to be involved and so does Joyce and the other lady, she's ever so nice, ain't she, Pete?"

"Yes, you mean Geraldine?"

"That's her."

Pete cycled the two hundred yards back to the piggery, where Robert had arrived with Louise.

"He's not coming, Grafton."

"He needs the sack. Robert, you tell Crucial when you get back, he needs the sack." Robert grinned.

"I can help," said Louise, and she stood next to Steve who lifted his cap to her.

"Mornin', miss," he said, and went cross-eyed. Louise burst out laughing.

"You stupid bugger, Steve," said Grafton. "Excuse my French, Louise. Now let's get on, the lorry is coming at eleven and we have a lot to do. Pete, bring them down the passage. Steve, you open the doors and, Louise, you work the door on the weigher and I will tell you which way to send them. I will slap the ones that are going. You did bring it, Pete?"

Pete pointed to where he had put the slapper with the pins in the ink pad. Grafton picked it up.

"Let's put a bit more ink on. Louise, you pour it out

of the bottle and I will spread it with this bit of stick."

The ink came out slowly and was very sticky.

"Don't get any on your hands, miss, you'll never get it off," said Steve.

They started as Pete brought the first pen down and one at a time the pigs went into the weighing machine. The ones that were ready to go to slaughter, Grafton put a red mark on with a thick wax crayon and then slapped them on each rump with the marker.

"Why do you have to do each side?" Louise asked.

"So that when the carcass is split in half both sides are marked."

"It's like sending people to the concentration camp."

"I don't know about that," said Grafton.

"Well, they are being tattooed and the transport is coming and then they are sent to slaughter. I suppose they are not gassed though, are they?"

"Not at the minute, but they will be, with carbon dioxide, our place will change over to that soon. So, I suppose it is a bit like it."

Soon all the pens had been done and fifteen pigs were waiting for the cattle truck to come.

"Pete, Louise says it's like sending people to the concentration camps. What do you think?"

The phone rang in the office across the yard and Grafton went to answer it.

"What do you think, Pete?" Louise asked again.

"I don't know, there are similarities, but it was war time."

"But the tattooing?"

"What about it?"

"Granny's got a tattoo."

"Yes," said Pete.

"She doesn't talk about it."

"I know. Where was your mother at that time?"

"She was stuck here at boarding school. They'd sent her to learn English and she never went back to Poland, where my grandfather was born. In the war she joined the Women's Royal Air Force and translated for the Polish pilots and then met Daddy who was in the army."

"Quite a story," said Pete, as Grafton returned.

"There's a turn-up. I'm going from no labour to too much; they are sending Tony down here instead of him going fencing but there's still plenty for everyone to do."

In the distance they could see a car coming down the drive to The Manor and it turned and travelled up the short distance to the piggery. It drew level with Grafton and the driver wound the window down. Grafton lifted his cap.

"Morning, Mrs Howells."

"Morning. I've brought this malingerer," and she smiled at Tony. "I had to take him to the dentist, it's the only way to get him there." She leaned further forward and half whispered to Grafton, "He doesn't like me bringing him in the Jag, you know, says it's embarrassing, don't you, Tony?" and she smiled at him as he got out the car and went over to where Louise and Pete stood.

"Boots," she shouted. "Got a brain like a sieve."

Tony walked back and took his boots from the boot of the car.

"Louise," Audrey called out. "Come and have a word." Louise walked over. "How are you, darling? I can't believe you're here again. I don't know how you can stand the smell."

"You get used to it," Louise replied, as Audrey looked over to Pete.

"Oh, and look, there's what's his name." She waved at Pete, who looked embarrassed as Steve wandered up. "Are you ready for the play?" she shouted at Pete. "I'm coming, and so is Mr Howells, that will embarrass Tony here, won't it, boy?"

"Yes, Mother," said Tony, as Steve sidled closer to the car.

Audrey smiled at him unconvincingly, Steve raised his cap and mumbled as she looked to Grafton.

"Are you going to the play?" she enquired.

"Wouldn't miss it for the world," said Grafton.

"Well, I must go, don't want to hold up the good work." She looked round to see if there was anything behind.

"You got a flat tyre," Steve said quietly.

Audrey looked at him, "What did you say?"

"You got a flat tyre."

"I thought that's what you said."

"It's alright though," said Steve.

"Alright?" Audrey looked askance.

"Yeah, it's only flat at the bottom."

Steve turned and looked cross-eyed at Louise and Pete. Audrey got out of the car and looked at the back wheel, as the others burst out laughing.

"I don't know what you're laughing at, come on, give a hand here, Tony."

The two boys changed the wheel, while Audrey looked on and chatted to Grafton who was still holding the slap marker.

"What's that nasty weapon?" she asked.

"That's what we mark the pigs with when they go to slaughter. It's a tattoo, which identifies them as ours."

"Sounds a bit like a concentration camp procedure."

Louise raised her eyebrows as Grafton lit his pipe.

"I'll see you at the play then," said Grafton.

"Yes, but I'm not sure if I'm looking forward to it. A lot of farmers cavorting about on stage is not my idea of fun."

"Now, Audrey, don't be such a spoilsport, just because it's the Young Farmers," said Louise.

"Don't worry, dear, I didn't mean it, I expect it won't be as bad as all that."

The day of the dress rehearsal arrived and everyone was there well before the appointed time. Trisha stood talking to Crispin, as the girls went one way to their dressing room and the boys went the other.

"Are we going to put makeup on the boys?" she asked.

"Oh yes, especially the robbers, they want to look sinister."

"We'll have to be careful with the policemen, they're wearing real uniforms and we can't afford to have them cleaned."

In the girls' changing room, Rose and Joyce stood in front of Rita.

"Now, look here, young lady, we don't want another exhibition from you this time. Have you got your underwear sorted?" Rose looked at her fiercely.

"'Ave I got my thong on you mean? Yes, I 'ave."

"Let's get the dress on and then we can do the makeup. I can't see any other way, can you, Joyce? We will muck it all up if we do the makeup first."

"You're right, Rose. Let's get Rita dressed then and she can be made up while we get the hostesses dressed."

It was much quicker this time and Rita was in her chair with Louise and Geraldine starting on the makeup while Joyce and Rose dressed the hostesses. There was a knock on the door and a shout from Crispin.

"I'm coming in," and he pushed the door open and sashayed in.

"You can't come in here," said Trisha.

"Yes, I can, I'm the director."

"Shut the bloody door," shouted Rita. "There's an awful draught."

As her makeup was finished, the towels were removed and she stood and spun round. The flounce on the bottom of the dress bobbed up and down and her bosom wobbled.

"My dear, how sexy." Crispin walked around her eyeing her up and down. "You look absolutely wonderful, darling." Rita blew a bubble with her gum. "Don't do that, you silly bugger, you'll ruin the lipstick and it's so common. Now let's have a look at a hostess."

He faced Alexandra who was now ready and turned her face this way and so as to admire her. "Fabulous, darling, fabulous."

Alexandra bent forward a little and in a gravelly voice said, "Come up and see me some time."

Everyone laughed and clapped and Crispin offered his cheek to hers without touching.

"Who said that?" he asked.

"Mae West," said Geraldine. "Or she was supposed to have said it."

"Now hurry up, folks, and can we have some makeup on the boys?"

Everyone was now dressed and Rose went to the male dressing room, banged on the door and walked in, to find them all sitting on the benches around the walls.

"Who's first then? We can do two at a time," she

said, and gradually they were all made up.

"Now it's Harold's turn," said John, and Harold, who sat in the corner, looked up.

"Me? I don't need makeup to do the curtains."

"Yes, you do, we've all agreed, haven't we?" said John.

Everyone shouted, "Yes!"

"Come on then, Harold, here's the chair. It won't hurt, will it, Joyce?"

"I ain't," said Harold.

"Right," said John. "There's only one way." And four of them picked him up and sat him in the chair. Harold smiled weakly, but had to give in to being made up.

"He needs lipstick as well," said John, as Crispin came in.

"What on earth is going on, who's this character?"

"He pulls the curtains."

"So, why's he made up? It's you, John, I know this is your doing. Whoever heard of stage hands being made up?"

"There's a first time for everything, don't you agree, Harold?"

Harold got out of the chair and grinned at everyone, as he rubbed his nose with his fist and smeared his lipstick onto his cheeks.

"I have never in my whole life worked with such an unruly mob, that's what you are – a mob! It's you boys, look at you." Crispin pointed at John. "You're a policeman, aren't you?"

"Suppose so."

"Well, get your bloody costume on, we start in five minutes."

Crispin went from the changing room to the stage and shouted, "Five minutes everyone," and people started to assemble in the wings.

"Now, we want some hush," Crispin whispered, putting his finger to his mouth.

He pulled the curtain aside a fraction and looked at the audience where Joyce, Geraldine and Rose sat. Louise, having found herself a chair, sat next to Harold who was hanging on to the pull rope for the curtains.

"Don't pull that yet, Harold," said Louise, as she arranged the script on her lap.

"I know, don't worry," he said. "I'm got to pull them when the hall clock gets to seven o' clock."

"Can you see it then?"

"Just, if I look through 'ere," and he pointed to a small spy hole.

Crispin went and sat with the three women in the audience. "I don't know why I'm doing this. All's going well and then they go and play up. You know what they've done, don't you? They've made up the curtain man. Young bloody Farmers. I should have had nothing to do with them, a lot of animals, at least, the boys are."

"Come on, Crispin, it's going well," said Geraldine, as she patted his hand.

"I'm glad you think so, my dear," and he took a silk hanky from his jacket pocket and mopped his brow.

"What's the time?" he said as he looked at his watch and then turned and looked at the hall clock.

"Are you going to shout to start them off?" Joyce asked.

"No, I am not," he replied emphatically. "They're on their own now." At that moment the curtain twitched, the hall light went down and the curtains opened.

All went well enough and the interval arrived after an hour and five minutes.

"That was quite good," said Rose, turning to Crispin. "You'd better go and tell them."

"Do you think I should?"

"Yes, of course! You have to encourage them."

Crispin made his way to the girls' changing room, banging on the door before going in. He was greeted by Trisha.

"I do wish you wouldn't come in here, it's not right for men to come into the girls' room."

"I told you before, I'm the director, I can come in, anyway, everyone is dressed."

He clapped his hands.

"That was quite good, quite good, but a bit flat. It will be different tomorrow, with an audience. I'm going to see the boys now."

"You'll be lucky," said Rita.

"What do you mean by that?"

"I mean the boys ain't there, they've gone down the pub."

"Gone down the pub?"

"Yup, they all decided there was time for a pint."

Crispin put his hand on his forehead and stamped his foot.

At the pub, Henry Babage pushed his pint glass across the bar as he pulled an envelope from his pocket. "Another one please, Desperate," he said, as he pulled an official looking document from the envelope. At the bottom of the document was a disc with perforations round it and he proceeded to tear around the perforations to extract the disc.

"What you got there then?" Desperate enquired, as he pushed the pint across the bar.

"Tax disc for my new car."

"That car ain't new."

"I know, it's Mother's old one, but it's new to me and I've just taxed it."

"You'd better get that in the car, old PC Bell has had four or five in the last month, all parked around the green. It's a hefty fine for not displaying it, let alone if you ain't got one."

"I know, I know, don't tell me, you sound like PC 49 yourself."

At that moment the door latch clicked and Pete came in dressed as a waiter in his DJ, followed by John and Robert dressed as policemen.

"Eh, Henry, police," Desperate whispered and Henry looked round.

"Bloody hell. Can I get out of your back door?" He grabbed the envelope and tax disc from the bar and went out of the door to the toilets, as the gents was across the yard. Pete came up to the bar.

"Pint, Desperate, and be quick, we've only got ten minutes."

He got Pete his pint and then looked at the other two.

"Officers, what can I do for you?" he said cautiously.

"Pint each," said Robert and he took his helmet off.

Desperate's face lit up. "You bloody sods, it's you, ain't it?"

"I know it's me."

"Well, I never, you fooled me, you did, good and proper," he said, and he pulled the pints as David and the others came in.

"We've just seen Henry outside putting his tax disc in his car, he says there's a police raid going on in here," said David, and they all burst out laughing.

"Come on, Desperate, be quick about it, how long have we got, Pete?" John said, as he jangled the change in his pocket.

"About seven minutes," Pete replied, as they saw Henry's face at the window peering in as he held his hand to his face to see in.

"You buggers," he said as he came in the door. "You

gave me a fright. I thought you were the police."

"So did Desperate," said Pete, and he drank down the last of his pint.

"I've got to sit through this damn play. What's it called?"

"*The Queen of Hearts,*" they all shouted together.

"I'm sure it's going to be awful if you lot are performing; I might as well write the review now."

"You might be surprised, Mr High and Mighty Henry Babage, what a lot of old Young Farmers can do," said John, draining his pint then following all the others as they hurried out of the pub. He turned back at the door, "Say, Desperate. Any sign of my jacket? It wasn't where I left it when I came back for it the other night."

"Sorry, no. You can consider that gone, I think."

Back at the Hall, Crispin stood with Louise and the three makeup ladies waiting for the second half to start.

"You know where those damn boys have gone? Down the pub. I ask you. They'll all be drunk; I know they will."

"Don't worry, Crispin," said Joyce. "They'll be here and they won't be drunk, you'll see."

Rose turned to Geraldine. "You didn't finish telling me about the war."

Geraldine looked thoughtful. "No, I didn't. I don't talk about it much."

"So, you are Polish?" Rose asked.

"I'm a Polish Jew."

285

"And your husband?"

"He was Polish and he fought with the partisans, but he wasn't Jewish, he didn't survive the war."

"I'm sorry, and what happened to you?"

"I was in a concentration camp. But I spoke English, so I survived doing translation and when the Russians came, we marched as fast as we could to the American lines and that's about it."

"How awful," said Rose, and at that point noise could be heard behind the curtains.

Chapter Twenty-Four

Curtain Call

Trisha stood behind a table in the foyer of the school hall. Sitting at the table were Mr and Mrs Cotton, Gill's parents. Gill was one of the hostesses in the play. Her parents had volunteered to sell tickets and collect the ones that had already been sold.

"Trisha, we're so excited, we're sure it's going to be fabulous, aren't we, George?"

"Yes, dear, it's got to be better than when they rehearsed in our front room."

"That was so kind of you to lend us the room, and it has come along since then."

"We've spent our lives involved with the theatre, we can't leave it alone, can we, George?"

"No, dear."

People began to arrive and Trisha went into the hall to show them to their seats. Julia Dawingditmus came up to the table and presented her tickets. Thelma checked them.

"Ah, you must be Mrs Dawingditmus, and your daughter is Louise."

"Yes," said Julia, with an edge of suspicion to her voice.

"Well," said Thelma, "George and I are hosting a

little drinks party after the show and we were wondering if you'd like to come along?"

"You think we will need a drink after sitting through it?" Thelma smiled as did Julia who then continued, "Yes, we'd love to come, dear, wouldn't we, Trevor, most kind of you, most kind of you indeed, Mrs…"

"Cotton."

"Yes, Mrs Cotton. Oh, look who's here." She dangled her hand at Audrey, who had just arrived. "Darling, how lovely to see you. I didn't know you were coming."

"Wouldn't miss it for the world, dear." Julia pulled Audrey closer and they touched cheeks. Audrey had three tickets in her hand which she gave to Thelma, who then asked if they would like to come for drinks after the performance. "What a lovely idea, we'll need a drink after it, I'm sure, but we do have a guest, you know, the Chief Constable's wife."

"Bring her along."

"We will do, thank you."

The hall gradually filled and the chatter got louder and louder. Rose and Joyce joined Freddie and Helmit in the back row after they had finished the makeup, and Geraldine went to sit with Julia.

"You'll never guess?" said Rose to Helmit.

"No, I'll never guess, zo tell me."

"We've been invited for drinks after the show, ain't we, Joyce?"

"Yes," said Joyce, "and you and Freddie have been invited as well."

"Who by?"

"Mr and Mrs Cotton or rather George and Thelma, they live in Mander Close."

"I think we vill need a drink after it, don't you, Freddie?" said Helmit and they chuckled.

Most of the seats were now filled. Crispin stood at the entrance from the foyer with his fur coat over his shoulders as Henry barged through the outer door.

"Ticket please," said Thelma, as she looked Henry up and down.

"I don't need a ticket; I'm press, you know."

"I don't know about that, do you, George? How do we know you're press, you might just be saying that." Crispin heard what was going on and came back to the table.

"Crispin, is this man the press?" Thelma asked.

"I'm afraid he is."

"So shall I let him in, what do you think?"

"From what I hear, he probably can't afford a ticket. Not getting much work is what I heard, now he's gone freelance. What about the robbers coming up from London, I thought that was your speciality, Henry Babage? You've come down in the world, if you are doing reviews of a Young Farmers play."

Henry looked embarrassed, "What am I to do?"

"Oh, let him in, Thelma, and we want a good review, mind, Henry, none of this hoity-toity stuff you usually write."

"I don't know why I bother," Henry said, as he barged past Crispin into the hall. "And now there's no bloody seats left." The hall lights dimmed and the audience went quiet. "Where am I going to sit then?" Henry complained to Crispin.

"Down there look, there's a seat in the middle," and Henry went down the middle aisle and side-stepped in front of the first four people.

"Sit down," someone shouted, as Henry found his seat.

"Oh, it's you," whispered Geraldine, as Henry took his seat next to her as the curtains opened.

After an hour or so, the first half came to the end. Everyone clapped enthusiastically and the lights in the hall came up. Crispin went backstage where everyone was milling around. He clapped once and then again. "Well done, well done, everyone, that was excellent. Now, you boys, no going to the pub and no tricks, John."

In the hall many of the audience stood up.

"I'm dying for a G and T," said Julia.

"We can go to the pub, it's just over the road," said the Colonel. "What about you, Audrey?"

"I'm ready, I'm ready. Quick march, eh? Oh I'm sorry, Maxine, is the wife of the Chief Constable allowed in a pub?"

"My dear Mrs Howells, what makes you think I'm not allowed in pubs, quick march you said," she replied, and off they went.

Rose, Joyce and Geraldine went to patch up the makeup of the actors and Grafton came to have a word with Helmit and Freddie.

"You're missing bingo then, Helmit?"

"I'd rather be here, it's good don't you think?"

"I think it's brilliant. I never expected them to do so well," said Grafton.

Backstage, Alexandra was doing some organising.

"What about a party? These plays always have a last night party."

"But, it's the first night," said John.

"We will just have to have a first night party then, you cretin."

"I'm not a cretin."

"Yes, you are," everyone shouted.

"We can go to the pub," said David.

"We'll have to be quick, it closes at ten-thirty."

"We could go to the M1 café?" said Pete.

"We can go to both, we've enough cars between us, haven't we?" Louise said.

"Yes."

"Robert?"

"Yes."

"David?"

"A van."

"That's enough then. Rita, Judy, Gill can come with me and the others will fit into the other vehicles."

"Five minutes," shouted Crispin. "What are you lot plotting?"

"Tell you later," said Alexandra, winking at Crispin.

"I'm going out front now, it's all up to you folks," and Crispin left.

In the hall people were returning to their seats. Julia threw her cigarette down and trod on it as she came into the foyer.

"What a lovely night out there," Audrey said to her. "The moon is full and there's not a breath of wind. You can hear the M1, which must be over a mile away."

The lights in the hall dimmed as they took their seats and the audience fell silent. The curtains opened and the second half started.

In the car park of the motorway café Lionel, Sunny and Doug waited.

"Where's the bugger got to?" Sunny demanded. "'ere we are but where's Marco?"

"We're early," said Lionel.

"Why did we 'ave to come all the way up 'ere anyway, we've only got to go back down again straight away?"

"We've come up here to make sure he's here and waiting."

"I still can't see 'im," said Sunny.

There was a toot and they looked to the right to see

Marco grinning at them from a black Ford Popular parked next to the Zodiac.

"That ain't 'is car," said Lionel, as he wound the window down. "That ain't your car?" he demanded of Marco.

"Yes, it is."

"Where's the leather seats, sunshine roof and chrome spoiler?"

"Back at 'ome. I'm got two cars see, so I brought this one."

"But that's only got three gears and won't do sixty, 'ow can we get away in that?"

"You said you used your brain, so I've used mine. Who's going to expect we'd be in a Ford Pop, you said we 'ad to put them off the trail, so who's the clever one now?"

Lionel grunted and said nothing. Sunny looked at Doug.

"'e's right, you know," said Lionel quietly. "I'm afraid to say 'e's right. I 'ate to admit it. Well done, Marco, so get in 'ere and you can come with us."

"No, I ain't. I said I've got to stay 'ere and look after the car an' be ready an' that's what I'll do."

"That old banger's worthless."

"No, it ain't, it's vintage. I ain't goin' to 'ave it stole, or vandalised, so there. It's precious."

There was silence again as Lionel looked at his watch, which he held to the window and read in the bright light of the full moon.

"Can we go and 'ave somefing to eat while we're waiting, Lionel, I'm 'ungry, ain't you, Sunny?" said Doug.

"No, you can't. We will go in five minutes."

"We'll be too early."

"No, we won't, they close the bar at ten-thirty, then all the money is counted and they'll be out ten minutes later so we'll be back 'ere by about eleven. Did you 'ear that, Marco?"

"'ear what?"

"We'll be back 'ere by eleven."

"Yeah, that's what you said. Eleven o'clock. I'll be waiting. It's a good plan, ain't it, Lionel?"

"Yes, very good."

At ten o'clock Sunny pressed the starting button and the Zodiac's engine powered up as he pushed the accelerator up and down.

Back at the hall the play was coming to an end and Rita, playing the central character, Lois, collapsed to the floor in the centre of the stage and the curtains closed. The audience all clapped enthusiastically as the actors lined up for a bow and the curtains opened again. There was more cheering and clapping as the actors took their bows individually, the applause reaching a crescendo for Rita. Then Crispin came on, handing his fur coat to a stage hand as he minced his way to centre stage. He patted the air with both hands in a downward motion to indicate he wanted silence and it gradually went quiet.

"Well, well, who would have expected that from a group of Young Farmers, eh? Weren't they good?" and he turned and clapped the cast, and the audience joined in.

After a few more words, it was all over, the curtain closed and the audience got up to leave.

"Are we going to change?" asked Judy.

"Not likely," replied Alexandra. "We might as well make the most of it. Let's go like this, it's a lovely night. Agreed?"

"Agreed," they all shouted back.

From the front of the hall, the audience spilled out.

"Now, Mr Howells, do you know where we are going for this drink?" asked Audrey.

"No, I'm going to follow the Colonel. Apparently, Geraldine knows where the house is."

"Come on, Mother, get in, you're always so slow," said Julia, as Geraldine stood talking to Joyce.

"You're coming to the Cottons, aren't you, Joyce?"

"Yes, we've been invited."

"We can give you a lift, can't we, Julia?"

"Yes, yes that will be fine."

Audrey called out, "Shall we take the others? Whatshername's parents?"

"Rose and Helmit?"

"Yes, them," and Audrey directed Rose and Helmit to get into the Jag.

In the pub all the cast had arrived, plus Harold and Louise.

"Come on, Desperate, get a move on. We want to get another pint in before you close."

Desperate looked harassed as he pushed the pints across the bar. Henry sat on the stool with a pint and a whisky chaser.

"What did you think then?" John asked him. "Bloody good, weren't we?" He turned to Judy, who nodded in agreement.

"Well," said Henry, looking thoughtful.

"Well?" Crispin retorted. "Well. Is that all you've got to say? I don't know."

"Well…" Henry started again. "I actually thought it was quite good."

"Quite good?" said Rita, who in her high heels towered over Henry sitting on the stool. "Quite good?" she repeated and she took his half full pint of beer and held it over his head, threatening to pour it.

"No – *very* good. I mean it. I will give a good review. Now give me my beer back, there's a good girl," and he rescued his pint.

In the car park of The Honey Pot, the Zodiac came to a halt about thirty yards from the back door of the dance hall.

"What's the time, Lionel?" Doug asked.

"Ten twenty-seven to be precise," he said, as he looked by the light of the moon. "I don't know if I like this moonlight, you can see everything. I can read all the number plates without any trouble."

"We can't change that, can we?" said Sunny.

"No. Now, Doug, 'ave you got the suitcase?"

"Yeah, but there's not goin' to be that much money, is there? A couple of bags or maybe three don't you think?"

"We don't know, do we? You just got to be patient and keep your voice down. Someone might 'ear."

At ten-thirty the door opened and people from the bingo hall came out as before and got into their cars.

"When's the dance 'all shut?" Sunny asked.

"Another hour at least," said Lionel. "But they close the bar at ten thirty," and he looked at his watch again.

"Time?" said Doug.

"Ten thirty-nine. Any minute now."

Two minutes later the door pushed open and two men came out, carrying bags.

"'ere we go," said Lionel. "Look, they've got no end of bags, look at that."

"They ain't the same blokes as last time," said Sunny.

"They look like bank bags though, don't they?"

"Go on, you two," said Lionel, and Doug and Sunny got quietly out of the car and went over to the two men, who were about to get into the van.

It was over in seconds. The bank bags they carried were snatched and the two robbers ran back to the

Zodiac. The doors slammed, Sunny pressed the starter and the wheels spun as he revved the engine and let the clutch out.

"Piece of cake," said Lionel, as they sped towards the exit of the car park. "Piece of cake."

"Look," said Doug. "That' one's writin' our number down. I can see 'im doin' it. Look, he can see the number in the moonlight."

"Which way?" Sunny asked.

"Left."

Sunny swung the car to go right out of the car park.

"No, you stupid bugger – that way!" and Lionel pointed.

"Up the M1, it will be ages before they phone the police."

At the pub, Desperate rang the bell hanging from a beam.

"Come on, drink up, you lot, and get home. I'll get in trouble if the policeman comes."

"Okay, so we're going down the café now, are we?" said Alexandra.

"Yes, everyone's coming. We've got enough cars," said Pete. "Are you coming, Henry?"

"No way, I'm going to the Cottons. I can get another drink there. Come on, you can give me a lift."

They dropped Henry at the top of Park Road and he walked two hundred yards down and then turned left into Mander Close. As he did so, a black Ford Popular sped past; its engine spluttered and it momentarily slowed before it suddenly picked up again and raced on.

When he got to the Cottons' house, Henry let himself in and went into the packed sitting room, where people were smoking and drinking.

"Here you are once again," a voice beside him said and he turned, to see it was Geraldine who was standing with Rose.

"Where do I get a drink?" he enquired and looked around.

"They'll come round, don't be so impatient. Patience is a virtue they say," and she looked whimsically at him.

"I don't have many virtues."

"You said it, Henry."

"Hmm," said Henry, who went to look for a drink.

"I thought they all did very well," said Audrey. "Even Tony got his words right and what about whatshername, quite a star."

"Rita, Audrey. Her name's Rita. I don't know how she didn't fall out of that dress though. The Colonel's eyes nearly popped out."

"Come on, you're jealous, Julia, just plain jealous!"

"I don't know Audrey, she's a bit common, don't you think?" Julia whispered.

"They are all a bit that way, if you know what I mean," Audrey whispered back and then looked around the room. "They've got a nice place here though, don't you think?"

"Yes, very smart and they've got some nice things."

"I can see that, but they are all bought you know."

"Yes, dear."

At the motorway café Alexandra's big Vauxhall Velox arrived and she banged the bumper on the curb as she braked hard. "Oh dear, I always seem to do that, hit the bumper I mean. But I suppose that's what bumpers are for, aren't they?"

The three girls got out and went into the café. As they did so they passed a chap with jet black hair standing by the door and smoking a cigarette. He was tall and had a donkey jacket on with *Wimpy* written across the back. The jacket was too small for him and his arms stuck a long way out of his sleeves.

A minute later Lionel's Zodiac drove up and parked next to the Velox.

"'ave you put all the bags in the suitcase, Doug?"

"All done, boss, there's seven of them. All got *Barclays Bank* on them. There must be a lot of cash in 'em 'cos they're all full and one's got a label on but I can't read it."

"Shut up, where's that stupid bugger Marco, and where's his car? It's not where it was."

Marco made his way over to where they were parked and knocked on Lionel's window. He wound the window down.

"There you are, Marco, where 'ave you moved the car to?"

"Well…," Marco hesitated, then blurted out, "I ain't moved it nowhere."

"What d'you mean? Where's your car?"

"It ain't 'ere."

"What you mean, it ain't here?"

"It were stole."

"What did you say?"

"I went in for a pee and when I come out there were two sods in it and they stole it. I saw 'em drive off."

"'ad you taken the key out?"

"Yes, but they lifted the bonnet an' jumped the starter."

"Bloody 'ell, what we gonna do now?"

"It's alright, Lionel, help's on the way cos I've rung the police, I did. 999."

"You did what?"

"I've rung the police. They stole my car, din't they? Well, it stands to reason – I 'ad to ring the police, it ain't insured so I need to get it back."

Lionel put his hand to his forehead. "I can't believe it. You rang the police?"

"Yes, well..." and Marco stopped and looked around.

Just then David's Thames van pulled up across the car park from where the Zodiac was. John and Robert got out, still in their police uniforms, put on their helmets and made for the door of the café.

"Lionel!" said Sunny. "Can you see what I see?"

"Yes, the bloody police."

"What they doing in a van then?" asked Doug.

"Putting us off the scent, like Lionel said," said Marco.

"Shut up, you idiot, what're we gonna do now? We can go in this one, but they must have our number by now. I can't see any other choice now Marco's 'as been stolen though."

"They won't get far," said Marco.

"Why won't they get far?"

"It ain't got no petrol in."

"What? So how were we gonna get away?"

"I 'ad a can in the boot, but they won't know that, will they?"

"Bloody 'ell. What are we gonna do?" Lionel was fuming.

"Steal another one," said Doug. "Come on, look at that one, it's not locked, she didn't lock it. I see 'em get out. We can jump the starter."

"Come on then," said Lionel. "You've got the case, Doug. Sunny, lift the bonnet. Who's got a screwdriver?"

"I've got a shut knife," said Sunny, as he located the starter.

There was a flash and the engine fired up. At that moment, Louise drove in with Judy, Rita and Gill, and parked near David's van.

"Look, Louise, those blokes are stealing

Alexandra's car. Come on, let's go and find her and get David and the others, they must be here," and they rushed into the café.

"Quick, quick, someone's stealing your car, Alex!"

Everyone leapt up and rushed out as the bonnet of the Velox was slammed shut and four men got in and drove off.

"It's them blokes, we've seen them before. Look, that's their car," and David ran over to the Zodiac and pulled the door open.

"Come on, let's chase them. Open the bonnet, Robert, we can soon get it started. Who's got a screwdriver?"

"I've got a comb, it's metal, that'll do," said Sally. "Let's get in. Alexandra, come on, you drive," and the four girls got in.

"Can you see Robert?" asked David, as all of a sudden the engine turned over and Alexandra put her foot down.

"Go on, get going, we'll follow in my van."

There was a dreadful grating noise as Alexandra tried to find reverse, which she eventually did, and as the car jumped backwards everyone inside was thrown forward. She turned the car round and sped off with David, Robert and John following.

In front, Sunny put the brakes on as they drove into Toddington. There was a short queue of traffic going past a police car. The two policemen were waving the cars past as they looked at the number plates. Lionel shrank down in his seat as they passed.

"Bloody 'ell, that was lucky," he said, as Sunny accelerated away. "Now, Sunny, turn right at the next junction. Right! That way!" and he pointed.

They drove down Park Road and past the drive down to The Manor and the piggery and went up the hill and past the drive to the farm. In front of them they could see the Ford Popular stopped on the side of the road and PC Bell, with his bike, peering in the windows with a torch.

"That's my car," whispered Marco.

"Back up, Sunny, turn in that drive, the police are everywhere."

He backed a few yards then turned around, travelling back the way they had come. They soon reached the drive to The Manor.

"Go down 'ere," Lionel demanded. "We've been 'ere before."

They turned left past Grafton's house at the lodge. Sunny switched the lights off and let the car freewheel down the drive. The Manor could be seen in the distance and on the left was the roadway to the piggery.

"Go down 'ere, Sunny, we can 'ide the car and wait till it all calms down."

The full moon was now high in the sky and lit up everything. The piggery was a mixture of buildings, from barns to the long fattening shed and a shorter barn for the farrowing house while the boars had pens with runs at the back.

"Drive round the back of that one." Lionel pointed at the bale shed and after a bit of shunting the big Velox was hidden from view.

"Bring the suitcase, Doug, let's go and find somewhere to hide where we can see anyone coming."

They crept slowly between the buildings and Lionel pointed to the fattening house with his stick, the door of which faced down the drive. They opened it and went into the meal shed where the bags of food were stacked and the feed barrow waited, full of meal for the morning feed and with a bucket on top. Sunny opened the door to the feeding passage.

"Come in here, it's lovely and warm," he said, and walked in followed by the others.

The door swung shut behind them. It was nearly pitch black, the only light coming through the pop holes into the dunging passage. As their eyes grew accustomed to the dark they gradually picked out hundreds of pink dots staring at them.

"What's that then?" asked Doug.

"I'll go back and open the door to let some light in," said Marco.

He pushed the door open and as he did, he knocked the bucket off the feed trolley. Behind him, in the fattening house, there was a loud, "Woof."

"What the bloody 'ell was that?" said Lionel, as Marco tripped over the feed bucket again.

The sound of movement surrounded them as the pigs got to their feet and the bucket clattered as Marco fell over it once more. One pig started to squeak and in seconds two hundred and fifty took up the cry. The noise was totally deafening. Marco propped the door open and the others ran for the exit and out into the moonlight.

"What the bloody 'ell is that? I ain't never 'eard anything like it," shouted Lionel, looking at the others in amazement.

"What are we gonna do then, you're gonna hear that row for miles?" Doug asked, looking at Lionel for instructions.

The big Zodiac came up to where the police were parked and an officer stood in the road with his hand up. Alexandra pulled up and opened the window.

"What's the number again?" Sergeant Read shouted to his colleague PC Toon, who handed him a piece of paper. "We've got 'em, we've got 'em!" he said after checking and went round to the driver's door. "We 'av reason to believe that this 'ere car 'as been involved in a robbery and you are under arrest."

Alexandra got out of the car flicking the skirt of her hostess costume. She stood in front of him and said, "Do I look like a robber, and look at her?" She pointed at Rita, who tottered in her high heels as she wiggled up to Sergeant Read. "Does she look like a robber? Someone stole my car, so we stole theirs. That's why we're in this one. Did a big Velox go this way?" Read looked at Toon, who nodded. "There we go then, *they* are the robbers."

At that moment, David drove up behind the Zodiac in the Thames van. Robert and John got out and went over to where everyone stood.

"We got some support then, look – they're Specials, ain't they? Good job you've arrived. Come on then, this lot's under arrest."

"What for?" Robert asked.

"Robbery, that's what, come on, you get in our car. We're off to the station."

In the distance a sound pierced the night.

"Listen!" said Robert. "That's the pigs. There's something going on."

"What do you mean?"

"It must be the robbers down there. Come on, do you want to catch them?" Alexandra put her hands on her hips and glared at Sergeant Read, who looked perplexed.

"We'll go and look on our way to the station, so get in there all of you," and he pointed to the back of the police car. "And you lot follow us," he said to Robert.

As all the girls got in the back of the car, the suspension lowered and the alarm bell went off.

"Shut that bloody thing up," Read shouted.

In Mander Close, the drinks party was breaking up. Goodbyes were said, as people milled round before leaving.

"What's that noise?" said Julia, "Listen everyone," and she put her finger to her mouth.

"It's the pigs," said Helmit. "There's something up, we must go. Come on, Rose."

"We'll take you," said Julia, "jump in."

Henry looked round to find a lift home as Audrey came out.

"Ah, Mrs Howells, can you give me a lift to The Manor, there's something up down there, can you hear the pigs?" She put her hand to her ear and in the still of the moonlit night the squealing of the pigs could be heard clearly. "Come on, Mrs Howells, let's get down there."

At the piggery, Lionel confronted the others.

"Where's the suitcase?"

They looked round at each other and shrugged again.

"It's in there, ain't it?" Doug indicated to the shed they had just exited.

Lionel pointed. "Well go and get it!"

"I ain't goin' in there, not for all the tea in China I ain't, so there."

"You go then, Sunny."

"No, you go, Lionel, it was all your idea, so you go," and Lionel turned and made to go back into the fattening shed.

"'ow the bloody 'ell am I going to carry a suitcase." He stood leaning on his two sticks.

"Lionel, there's someone coming, I can see lights."

Sure enough, the heavily laden police car was making its way down the drive, followed by the Thames van. The figure of Grafton walking quickly towards them was picked up in the lights of the police car, and Louise's car could be seen bringing up the rear. Lionel looked at the cars and picked out the bell on top of the police car.

"We've got to 'ide – come on, in 'ere," and he opened the door of the outside run of one of the boar pens and they made their way into the kennel part.

The police car arrived and turned round to point back in the direction it had come. Everyone got out, including the four girls, as Grafton arrived, out of breath, and went into the fattening house and put the lights on. All the doors were open and the bucket was on the floor. Robert and David came in, followed by Sergeant Read.

"Robert, feed them. That'll shut them up," Grafton ordered, yelling over the noise.

Read looked at Robert and shouted, "You're not a Special then?"

"No, I'm dressed up for a play."

"You're impersonating a police officer, that's an offence, you know."

"Come on, let me shut this lot up," and Robert grabbed the bucket and started the feeding with David's help.

Pete and Louise pulled up to where the four girls were standing.

"What are you doing here?" Louise asked.

"We're under arrest," said Alexandra.

"What a laugh, look at us," said Rita, as Sergeant Read walked over.

"Where's this car then?" he demanded of Alexandra. "What did you say it was?"

"A Velox," she snapped back at him.

"There are tracks over there, look," Pete pointed. "I'll go and have a look."

Two more cars arrived. Helmit got out quickly, followed by Rose, and he went up to Grafton.

"Good, Helmit, give me a hand, we're going to have to feed the sows and boars as well or they will be out. Follow me."

Julia also got out of the car, just as the Howells pulled up in the Jag and Audrey got out.

"What's happening, darling? And what's all the noise?"

"My dear, I simply have no idea. All these people, what are they doing?" said Julia, who lit a cigarette.

"I've found your car, Alexandra. It's round the back," said Pete.

"There, I told you," Alexandra said, pointing at Sergeant Read.

"Told him what?" asked Henry, breathing alcohol over Alexandra.

"Someone just stole my car and they say there's been a robbery."

"Didn't I say? Just what I predicted. They came out of London up the M1, just what I said would happen, eh, sergeant?" Henry looked at Sergeant Read and blinked.

"Who are you then?"

"I'm Henry Babage, freelance reporter," and he burped.

"Freelance prat more like," said the sergeant. "Where's this car then?"

"I'll show you," said Pete, and the sergeant followed him up the side of the building. When he came back, he stood in front of Alexandra and opened his notebook.

"So this car is yours?"

"If it's a Velox, yes."

"And you say it were stole from the M1 café?"

"Yes."

"And you then stole the Zodiac?"

"Yes."

"Hmm," the sergeant pulled his chin, "So the robbers must be here somewhere."

"Well done, sergeant," said Henry.

"Shut up, prat," the sergeant snapped at Henry.

As Robert and David finished feeding the fattening house, the squealing stopped abruptly.

"Thank God for that," said Julia, as she puffed her cigarette and Henry walked away.

"Where are you off to?" David asked, as Henry walked purposefully up the yard.

"Just going to turn the old bike round, it's all the beer you know," he said as he walked faster, looking for somewhere more private. He passed a row of pens and looked round to see he was not observed then slid the bolt of a pen and went in.

Further down, Lionel's head slowly appeared above the wall of the pen he was in.

"What can you see?" Doug whispered.

"There's no end of them. I can count one, two, three, four policemen and no end of others."

"What we gonna do then?" Sunny whispered.

"Sit tight," said Lionel.

There was a scream further up the yard as Henry shot out of the pen, with Zeppelin in pursuit. Zeppelin caught up with and butted Henry to the ground, and as he landed on the concrete Zeppelin put his snout under him and rolled him over, his tusk ripping Henry's trousers. Henry leapt up and ran as hard as he could to the railing fence, jumping over into the muddy wallow in the sow field and landing with a splash and a yelp.

Back at the fattening shed Robert shouted, "Look what we found," and he held the suitcase up.

"Where was that then?" asked Pete.

"In the middle of the feed passage," and he put the suitcase on a pile of sacks and was about to open it, when there was a shout from Grafton.

"Zeppelin's out! Robert, David, Pete, come and help." And they all dashed to the sow pens, where Zeppelin was running up and down trying to get in. "Come on, get some boards, don't go near him without one." Everyone watched as they gradually moved Zeppelin away from the sow pens and down the wall of the farrowing house. "There's an empty pen down there," Grafton pointed. "Louise, can you open it?"

Louise dashed to the pen that Lionel and the gang were in and opened the door. Little by little Zeppelin came down the wall and with Grafton and Robert each side and David behind, they got him into the pen and shut the door.

"Get him some food, Robert," said Grafton, who wiped his brow, but suddenly Zeppelin woofed and there was a scream as he attacked the gang. One after the other they dashed from the kennel, Sunny, Mario and Doug bundling Lionel over the wall then jumping after him.

"Sunny," said Lionel. "That police car, let's 'ave it, okay?"

"Yes, boss, I'm ready."

The four ran towards the car, with Mario and Doug supporting Lionel, and Sunny running ahead to check the key was still in it. Sunny switched it on, pressed the starter and away they went, passing PC Bell who had just arrived on his bike and saluted as they passed. Sergeant Read threw his helmet to the floor as Rita opened the suitcase and picked out a bank bag with a label on it which read:

Dear Rose,
Here are about two thousand cards. When you have rubbed out all the pencil marks, bring them back and I will pay you the usual rate.

"What a laugh," cried Rita. "You know what's in the bank bags?"

"No," said the sergeant.

"Bingo cards, Mum rubs them down and they use them again."

The police car sped off along The Manor's drive; its bell ringing. Its lights could be seen as it went up the hill, out of the gates and turned right. When it got to Marco's Ford Popular the occupants switched cars, filled up from the can in the boot and drove off, leaving the police car far behind, its bell still ringing.

The End

A Note from the Author

The timing of *Feeding the Pigs* is from September 1962 to September 1963 encompassing the unprecedented cold winter starting on Boxing Day 1962 and lasting until early March. Eleven weeks of severe and unremitting frost with huge amounts of snow, ice and freezing rain. In this era of global warming it is difficult to get over how unprecedented the conditions were that were faced in that year and for the length of time it went on. In the 80 years I have lived, only 1976 compares in the extremes of weather in 1963.

As a condition of the course I was to attend at Wye College, London University and like most other agricultural institutions, I had to spend a year on a farm before starting. My father organised for me to go to Toddington Manor Research Farm, where he knew the manager, John Cowper. The farm had a vast range of livestock and tested out their rations, on a 'feed them and weigh them' basis, to find the economical way to produce meat. Beef, sheep, pigs, turkeys, laying hens and a hatchery were all to be found on the farm, along with a large arable sector.

I lodged with one other student with an old lady, Mrs Johnson, in the village and paid £5 per week for breakfast, lunch and high-tea for five and a half days a week. We then moved to a three-bedroom house where we lodged with a couple and their young daughter for £3.75 for the same terms. The house had one bathroom and toilet and only an open fire in the lounge to heat the property. Keeping warm through the cold period was extremely difficult for all concerned.

I joined the local Young Farmers Club, and the friendships made then have been life-long and the experiences gained invaluable. The Club having a County Organiser had a structure from above, but was essentially run by local young people, most of whom had a farming connection of some sort or other. It was supported by a dedicated group of older generation farmers who kept it as best they could on the straight and narrow. The Young Farmers movement is an extremely valuable part of the farming structure and is just as important today as it was then.

The book is fiction, but illustrates some of the issues of the day, one being the numbers of displaced people who were welcomed to Britain after the Second World War and ended up in the agricultural industry. The motorway cafés were few and far between but offered a 24-hour service, which was unique in those days and provided a setting for some of the action in the book. The village pub was also an essential part of rural society in those days and an essential meeting place for the community. Every large village had its own policeman, who was left to control law and order in their area from the police house and office. The inclusion of a group of hapless villains in the plot is an echo of the much more famous robbery which happened quite close in the same year.

Acknowledgements

The author of a book is only one person in the production process, and I am immensely grateful to many others who have gone toward the production of *Feeding the Pigs*. Firstly Henri Merriam, who once again typed my handwritten script, correcting the spelling and adding the commas. The readable version was then passed to various friends for their comments, criticism and suggestions, which has been very helpful in coming up with the final version. Those were Mo Brown, Jane Sinnot, Jane Lambert, Richard Wilding, Jill Wilding, Mike Muncaster, Roger Pierce, Jo Burton, Robert Cowper, Roger Fox and Antonia Phinnmore.

Thanks also to Julia Gibbs who did the proof reading and to Simon Emery who laid out the cover. Thanks to Robert Cowper who provided the photograph which inspired the cover drawing.

Mary Matthews has been once again pivotal in the production of this book and it is fair to say that none of my books would have got into print if it had not been for her. This time she has done much of the editing as well as preparing the book for publication, at the same time as writing and publishing her own works. Her attention to detail is second to none and her advice and guidance always extremely sound.

Finally, I would like to extend a special thank you to Richard Wilding who has taken it upon himself to introduce my books to a wider audience, organising interviews on local radio and articles in local magazines